# BORDERLANDERS

GILLIAN POLACK

Published by Odyssey Books in 2020
www.odysseybooks.com.au

ISBN: 978-1922311184 (paperback)
ISBN: 978-1922311191 (ebook)

*To Christina Ryan, Rayna Lamb and Virgina Lee for reminding me that some stories are worth the struggle to write.*

# THE BEGINNING OF THE GREAT RETREAT

# ONE

Bettina had been dreaming of cold bodies in a dead Russian forest. As she woke up gently, the chill air of pre-dawn helped her count the bodies into wakefulness. Her anti-sheep.

It wasn't a dream: it was a memory. Something her mother had done during the Cold War. Something Bettina could not possibly know anything about.

This morning, it was her mind's reminder that she was about to ride into the unknown. Breakfast would be a cold bowl of cereal in this dreary motel room in country Victoria. In an hour she would follow the instructions from her mother's will and finally scatter the ashes. In a few more hours, she'd be at a retreat in the home of the Great Potato. Her mother would not influence her art. Not this time. This was the day she made her art her own.

One in three of her dreams was accurate. She hoped that this one was one of those that was simply a dream; she didn't want to meet the eight bodies from her mother's past.

The drive was entirely uneventful until lunchtime. Lunch was a cheese and tomato toastie at a Laminex-lined bakery in a random small town. Bettina didn't want to notice names. As long as her GPS found the destination, she'd be fine. For her mother, life had been adventure. Her mother had set her up for adventure one last time, and it was adventure Bettina didn't want. Still, she found herself chatting with the café owner, a woman her own age who had somehow kept her waist under control despite the cakes that surrounded her.

"On your way somewhere interesting?" asked the bakery owner, whose name was, unaccountably, Sheila.

"Robertson, eventually," Bettina explained. "I'm going to scatter my mother's ashes on the way. Before my art retreat."

Of course, Sheila wanted to chat about the unspeakable. "You're going all that way to scatter ashes? That's nice of you."

"Not as much as it sounds. I've been putting it off. I combined it with meeting a friend and going to Robertson. That's how I managed to make myself do this thing."

"I don't get it."

The damn walls holding her emotions in broke and Bettina found herself drowning in a torrent of truths. "The whole family wanted a burial, but Mum wanted me to scatter her ashes. And collect something. My mother lived in her own mystic reality. I'm not cynical so much as relieved that the process of losing her is nearly over. And I don't usually tell strangers everything. I feel as if I've stepped out of time."

"We do that, sometimes, don't we? I'm in that mood, too," said Sheila, putting two mugs of coffee onto the table. "My mother left me her pet hamster," she volunteered, and slid into the seat opposite.

"A hamster? Really?"

"Mum died in a road accident. She never meant to outlive that hamster."

"Your mother sounds like quite a character."

Sheila nodded. "I'd rather have a road trip."

"I'd rather have a hamster. We could swap." Bettina breathed a moment of hope.

"Can't. It died. Hamsters don't live very long. Why a road trip, do you know?"

"I don't know precisely." Bettina looked for words very carefully. Her dream was specific, after all. And so were the instructions. "But she always said to me that she was in the wrong story. She said it was important to know what story you're in and to live the right life for the right story."

"When I was a teenager, I knew what story I was in," Sheila admitted. "I was going to marry a lawyer and move to the city and have a flash car and no mortgage. Mills and Boon romance."

"Did any of that happen?"

"I got pregnant to the lawyer, married the boy next door, divorced the boy next door, and got stuck here bringing up four kids."

"Do you regret it?"

"Some. My dream wasn't quite right, though. I should've wanted to be the lawyer, not marry him."

"Mum was right, then. You were in the wrong story."

"Maybe. I like the bakery. My kids are growing up okay, except for the layabout."

"Is he a charming layabout?"

"How did you guess he was a boy?"

"There's a teenager who looks a bit like you who's been making faces in the window for the last five minutes."

Sheila excused herself and chased her son back off to school, and by the time she had finished, Bettina was ready to move on.

"Have a great road trip," said Sheila. "If you come this way on the way back, tell me about it."

"Tell you the story of my story." Bettina found this amusing.

"Damn right." And Bettina could see from Sheila's face that, exactly like Bettina, something had gone wrong and somewhere there was a different type of story waiting for Sheila. She didn't know if she should tell her or if it would hurt too much. Bettina decided it was safest to get into the car and drive away. So she did. *My story has safe choices,* she told herself. *Like Melissa's when we were kids. She never did anything daring.* She drove as far as Eden, dreaming of her childhood.

Bettina's mother's instructions contained notes about looking for a place where two rivers joined but said that Eden would do. Bettina drove until she found a likely spot. There was parking, and the lake was a mere patch of grass away.

Bettina sat in her car and thought, "I don't want to do this." She should do it graciously, with measure and thought, for it was her mother's ashes, but every time she planned words to say, her mind rebelled. "I don't want to do this." After sitting far too long in argument with herself, she clambered out of the car, walked across to the lake, scattered the ashes, and said to herself, "I can move on now."

Except she couldn't. She still had to traipse into an office in Eden and collect the thing. Whatever the thing was.

The office turned out to be the hotel. The bar, in fact. Bettina was terribly polite to the staff member who handed her the parcel, but decided she didn't need to lunch alone in a pub. Pubs and she shared bad memories. The chippie was close, so she bought a souvlaki and took it back to the car and drove on. If she hurried, she wouldn't keep Zelda waiting.

---

"Today I am going to talk about liminality," Zelda said brightly. If she didn't say it brightly she would lose her temper. She was teaching one of the best subjects in any universe, and her students patently didn't want to be there. They wanted to be on summer holidays, or out earning money to pay for next year's fees, or getting drunk.

Zelda's thoughts were savage. Since the supposed love of her life had dumped her—trophy younger girlfriend, Zelda thought viciously—her natural sweetness had been unnaturally soured.

*But my students are innocent,* she thought, *of this, anyway,* so she scanned the class and developed an intentionally long pause. If they were nodding over their books, she was going to make them think she had said something totally crucial, like, "One last essay due that I forgot to tell you about." And indeed the pause was effective.

She stopped thinking wild and angry thoughts and stepped up her brightness a notch. "I see that I might have to explain liminality."

Dutiful laugh. At least a laugh meant that some of them were paying attention, which meant she was bound by the Rules of Teaching to give the class her full brain again.

"It is a very important part of understanding the Celtic world." Ah, Celtic meant the Wiccan student looked up. Words acted as triggers—different words for different people. She wondered if she could find the right trigger to persuade the supposed love of her life that the best place for him was over a cliff.

"It is all about borders." And finally, her mind settled. "Woods and forests and bodies of water. Dusk and dawn and midnight. Eclipses and full moons. Places and times when the boundaries between worlds are thin. Beings from other worlds can cross to this world there and then. Only there, and only then. In the medieval tales, this is when the beautiful woman appears, beckoning the hero to join her. It is also when fears descend, because those people who are drawn into these Celtic otherworlds don't return."

"Not ever?" said her Wiccan student.

Zelda took a moment and thought it through properly. "Not often," was her final reply. "The only figure I can think of who is really celebrated for returning is Thomas of Ercildounc." Not a scrap of comprehension from the faces. "Ellen Kushner," she prompted. "Thomas the Rhymer, Tam Lin." And the class took off.

She took that memory to her moon-viewing that night. Some people watched the new moon, but for Zelda, the full moon reminded her that she was a woman and a dreamer and a scholar, all neatly bound into a single, trim body. That body was bound for the outback in the morning, to meet a friend and to write. To do so very much writing. The moon tonight, however, was hers.

---

"It'd be worse if I needed a wheelchair," Melissa offered.

Hal laughed but kept his eyes on the road. "I wish this place were closer."

"So do I," admitted his wife. "I've got triplicates of all my medicines and I know one of the other retreatees. Retreaters? Anyhow, it's in a town. And they have a phone number for you to ring if you're worried. I'll be okay. You know this for sure because I didn't make a single joke in explaining it to you. Not one. Be proud of me."

"I know." Hal's voice wasn't that deep, but when he was affectionate it rumbled. A cat's voice. "And you're capable enough. It's just …"

"I know," Melissa whispered. Their lives were full of crises. Too many crises, too recently. She was better because of them. Because her new doctor had taken everything on board and finally given her some sort of diagnosis, with the promise of a better one, eventually. Because things were finally under control enough to live again. "I still worry," she admitted.

"I'm going to quote you as you," Hal said evenly, not letting any aspect of the pressure he felt show in his voice. Melissa could see that pressure sing painfully throughout his body. He needed time out as much as she did. "I got lost. I found my way back because you were my guiding light. I need to take up this offer to consolidate, and to do the world's best photo exhibition and dedicate it to you. And it has to include a joke for every year of our marriage, for we are the funniest couple in the universe."

"That was not what I was expecting you to quote at me," Melissa observed. "Not even close."

"Too bad," said Hal. "I like this one."

"I should stop giving you compliments."

"You should, but you mucked up that time and these compliments are mine. All very much mine."

"Yeah," said Melissa. "No one else's."

They were silent and comfortable together in the car. Emotionally comfortable, not physically. *Not my cleverest idea,* Melissa thought. The doctor was right about walking. She would hurt if she did, but hurt more if she didn't.

Moss Vale was the last place she would have to stretch everything before Robertson, so they planned to stay a bit longer there. Maybe as much as two hours.

"I'd rather say my best goodbye somewhere pleasant," admitted Hal. "And it'll shake off the car blues. Turn them into pinks and greens."

"It'll shake them off so damn hard I'll be able to walk again tomorrow." Melissa was determined. Her tone brooked no unwillingness from nature to oblige.

Moss Vale had a park in the centre of town. There was a small clock tower in the middle of the main road, with a clock that not only didn't work, but that had unreadable messages posted to its four faces. On one side of the road was the pub, and on the other, the park.

"Park then pub then park, I hope," said Hal.

"Sounds good to me. We've got the time. I'm not expected much before dinner."

The old rotunda in the park held a couple in drifting clothes; they looked like exiles from Bellingen. This appallingly slender and floating male and female emerged from time to time to collect rubbish. Hal and Melissa only developed three theories about why they were bringing rubbish to the rotunda.

"There should be a quartet inside, not dead bottles," said Melissa.

"Bach," Hal said dreamily. "Then we can say we came back to Bach on our way home."

"Not with all that bird noise. Something fizzier. Sherbet."

"Not even classical," half-mocked her husband, and they held hands as they took their third loop around the park. With each loop, Melissa lost pain and walked with more vigour, until now, when her hips betrayed the exhaustion. Hal had learned he could tell just as much from holding her hand and looking aslant at her as he could by asking, and he turned them off the path when it came close to the road. "Lunch for me. I need a beer."

"With Duncan. That's who you need your beer with. Me, I need coffee," Melissa said wistfully. "And a steak. Can I have a steak?"

"If you ask nicely."

The Moss Vale pub was a classic. Both a pub and a bistro. Polished wood and much glass and mirror and canopies advertising drinks visible through every window. The couple walked through the pub section. Most of the tables were full.

"I can see one right at the end," Melissa said, "next to the fireplace."

"Good vision." Hal approved and they veered left, still holding hands. They went left until the pub changed to a bistro and until the bistro ran out of space. Then they snagged that end table. It was too large for a couple and it was all theirs. Polished wood with no cloth.

"We walked through so much brown," Melissa marvelled.

"And now we're sitting in it. We need to find you a book about this pub."

"One without covers?" Melissa said, laughing.

“Of course,” Hal said with dignity. Melissa shook her head. “What’s wrong?”

“Not wrong. I think my eyes are playing tricks. Look out to your right, at the main street. Can you see two women?”

“Hard to make out. Crossing the road to the park? Yes, I can see them.”

“I think they’re going to the station.”

“What about them?”

“One of them looks like Bettina. You know, the old friend who told me about the fellowship. She might be going. But that’s not the odd bit. What’s odd,” commented Melissa, “is that it looks like she’s with Zelda, which can’t be right. We were a trio in primary school and stayed together until we were fifteen. We’re not going to magically appear in Moss Vale at the same time. We don’t even live in the same cities. It could be Bettina. If she got that fellowship. An important one, she said. Same place as me. More important fellowship, but same place. I told you about it, so don’t look so blank.”

“How long since you’ve seen them?”

“About twenty years since we’ve all three been in the same place. But Bettina and I talk on social media. She’s very serious. High-minded and full of sobriety.”

“Well, then,” Hal said pragmatically. “They’ve changed.”

“Probably just me remembering times when. And expecting to see Bettina at the retreat.”

“Times when what?”

“I’m not sure,” Melissa confessed. “I was going to say ‘times when I did things’, but that would be a lie. I still do things. Just with more pain and greater distraction. It’s really something I did that was quite particular and hasn’t happened since. It’s times when I had that two-friends thing that some women get into. I never needed it from the moment I met you.”

“You dumped them?” Hal was puzzled. His tone and whole body said, *This is not my girl.*

"Not ever. I'm not the dumping kind. I dump rubbish, not people." She frowned at her joke. It hadn't quite worked. "They went every way they could to go to uni or get work or whatever. All over Australia. We meant to stay in touch and life got in the way."

"Whatever." Hal laughed.

Melissa was relieved. She never talked about that part of her youth. Not even to Hal. Maybe she should volunteer a bit more. "We were best friends in primary school and all the way to the second year of high."

"You said that. You've got problems with your memory from old age. Can't be only twenty years ago," Hal teased.

"Okay, so it's longer. I'm a venerable bitch."

"That's my girl." Hal smiled intimately across at her.

WHAT LED TO THESE MOMENTS IN TIME?

# TWO

Hal's mother was finally moving to a nursing home. That was going to happen. Not merely had to happen, but everything was in place. A nursing home that she liked would take her, and she was less reluctant than she had been and …

"This is when it should've got easier," said Melissa.

"Why would my mother allow such a thing?"

"I still don't understand why she agreed to everything, signed everything, and is now distressed that you're going to sell the house. We talked about it with her."

"Extensively," agreed her husband. "I must say, you handled her temper 'specially well."

"It's not the first time she's blamed my health for things she doesn't want to face. And it won't be the last. And … what's wrong?" she asked. Hal's face had a look. Guarded. Troubled. Very worrying.

"I can sell things. I can tidy things. Hell, I can even dump half my childhood at the rubbish tip, but …" He paused.

"Yes?"

"I can't deal with her emotions," he said bluntly.

"And we have to."

"I love that we—but I can't. It hurts in ways I didn't know I could hurt."

"It's because she's your mother. And she's fragile."

"I can't even walk out," said Hal. "There are other family members, but I'm the only one who can do this."

"I bet you being silenced is worse than not being able to walk out," Melissa said thoughtfully.

"You're right." Hal was gloomy. "And it's not once. It's every day. If I make the conversations difficult or if I look emotional, we'll never get her into the home."

"She's losing her whole world." Hal looked shaken at this, so Melissa kept explaining, reasoning, talking until her help reached him. "It's safe for her to shout at you. You need a way of dealing with all the emotions that these conversations roil up. And I think I know just what will work." Melissa suggested that Hal go onto social media and tweet his way out of trouble. "Punning is popular on Twitter, I believe," she said wistfully. "And tweeting your way out of trouble is so very 'you'."

"I have an idea." Hal had a glint in his eye. "You tell me so often about mansplaining, yet I've never endured it."

"Yes?" Melissa said cautiously.

"I want to use your name and speak as if I were you. I want to make political comments and say the things neither of us say in public."

"Just as long as it includes puns."

"Whenever I can, my dear. And you'll see it all."

"I bet there's no mansplaining at all," Melissa said gloomily. "I bet you find it tedious and dump it after two weeks."

Melissa was wrong on both counts. Hal took great delight in printing out the first time he was mansplained, and the second. By the third, he had targets for his temper. Anyone who thought they were "helping" his wife, he considered fair game.

So many people had "helped" his wife, starting from high school. Hal was angry at the way, one by one, their forces had merged to destroy her life. He found safe outlets for his anger, and this was one. Hal measured his day by how much anger he diverted, just as Melissa measured hers by pain. "Spoons," she called it, intending to imply a lack of strength or energy, but it was pain all the way. Anyone who made that pain worse, or who carried attitudes that might indirectly make that pain worse—these people were fair game.

---

Time passed as time does. Embedded in that time were those events that reminded Bettina of who she was and kept her secured safely within a chronology. More than clocks or watches, they were her measurements.

Her favourite was usually Sunday lunch with her honorary children. It anchored her whole fortnight. They were interested in her work, and she was interested in them and theirs, and they made a trio of contentment.

Some parts of her life were hidden from them. She'd never told them about her dreamstuff. When they entered her life, they were too young and then ... there was no real opportunity. They might have believed it, they might have laughed, they might have derided—she never knew, for she'd never explained it. It wasn't a happy secret, but it was a secret.

It wasn't an unhappy secret either, she thought, unlike the other one. The other one was the opposite of sordid. It was odd.

Their father and she had never had a romantic relationship. They'd never even slept together. Dov was gay, but he had only come out to Bettina in a whirlwind of despair when his wife walked out.

He didn't want to be open. He couldn't be open. The vast extended family that surrounded him and gave so much love, that family was profoundly homophobic. He had married in a denial of who he was.

Bettina was his soulmate, he claimed, without being his bedmate. She was happy to continue believing that, despite everything.

She had just walked out on a relationship where the physical side was sporadic but was all she needed, but the bedmate was no soulmate. He had been a little child, in need of care. She was his mother and his housekeeper and the sponge that absorbed all his problems and left him emotionally stable and able to face the world and have a brilliant career. She found that she rather wanted to paint, and he had taken a knife to a painting when her exhibition was getting in the way of his career. That's how he described it. "Getting in the way of his career."

She'd dreamed it. That's when the dreaming had ceased to be a series of bets with the world. Would this come true? Would that? Would the other? This time she'd taken action, in case; she'd prepared for it. She put a failure of a piece up, as if it were the critical work for the exhibition. When he slashed her painting, he didn't ruin anything except their relationship.

That Sunday, Bettina was not looking forward to lunch at all. Dreaming hurt again. She wished she didn't have this … thing. This superpower. This special ability. This unavoidable skill at hurting herself. Her dream last night had shown her a house littered with loss. A plate filled with favourite food, a toy from an early Christmas, a school report—all of these were strewn over the floor and a giant broom came and rid the house of her life-experience. All she had was emptiness and forlorn love.

She had to tell them, the dream said, that their father and she had never had a physical relationship. She hated this. It poisoned her whole morning.

Over lunch, she explained to her beloved honorary children. The explanation was riddled with a throat full of tears and a stomach that was about to turn nauseous. She couldn't tell them about their father's sexuality. It was so odd that he couldn't tell his own children the truth. All she could say was, "Best of friends. But we never lived together." Then she tongue-bit, severely.

The three of them created a triangle of silence at the table. Then the elder reached for more bread. This was his old trick. It gave him time to think.

"You always were our adopted mother," the younger said cheerfully.

"Yeah, but …" said the older, and texted his father furiously. The texts were so furious that their father rang back almost immediately. Ten minutes later, he was there.

"What damn lies have you been telling the kids?" he asked, in his gentle and understanding way. He took her to the garden and read her the riot act. He wouldn't listen to a word until he'd finished his tirade.

Bettina was so very drained. The whole emotional roller-coaster was no longer her thing.

When she was given a moment to explain and he found out that she'd been entirely honest without revealing his secret, he eased up on her. He then let her into a new secret. He was in love. Not just dating. It was serious. He would talk to his mother about it next week.

"In that case," she said tartly, "it's just as well the kids know we were … not the way we looked."

"I guess," he said. "I'm worried about the whole …"

"I know," she said sympathetically. "I'll be with you every inch of the way, you know that."

"I do. But what do I tell Mum about us?"

"Tell her the truth," she suggested.

"I'd better bring Ted round to meet you."

"If you want," she said hesitantly. "We can all three talk about it."

"He thinks you're my ex."

"Is he unhappy about it?"

"Yes. How did you know?"

"I guessed," said Bettina, for her dreams were something he'd never tolerated. "That means it's better we talk. Maybe he'll understand us as having been in an asexual relationship and keeping things from your family that way. Except ... does he know about your family?"

"Oh god, yes. I've decided that if they can't take him, I'll still want him. No matter what the family says, I will stay with Ted."

"How long?"

"Since we've been dating? Six months. We're getting married."

"It would've been nice to know earlier."

Dov was silent and the silence showed all the emotional insecurities. No wonder he'd been furious about the talk she'd had with the children. He was putting off an even bigger one. Or had he? She thought back to the look the eldest had given her when she had explained the relationship. She smiled at Dov.

"Still, I'm glad. I love it that you've found someone and that you've got this courage."

"You can be a witness," he offered. "He's not Jewish, so it'll be basic. If I could marry under a chuppah, I'd make you a bridesmaid."

"Your family? Will they be okay?"

"They'll never be okay."

"I wish they could just accept you're gay."

"That's not why I had the children, you know. Why I took up with someone I couldn't stand, but who'd be a good parent, I thought."

"You were wrong." Bettina was wry.

"I should never have done it. But that was the year the oldsters finally told me about their childhoods. They said that the only thing they were living for was grandchildren."

"Inheritance?"

"More like revenge against Hitler."

"I kinda knew that. I try to not think about what their parents went through."

"I hate it. I hate what it did to me, to all of us. Not telling you meant I could stay a little sane, and staying a little sane meant I could share the kids with you, and that I could eventually emerge."

"Into love." Bettina's voice was soft with her happiness for him.

"Exactly," Dov said, and the two went back inside. Bettina made a big pot of coffee and they all talked all afternoon. By the time her visitors left, she was exhausted, for she was the emotional north for them all, and her youngest had needed her.

The child wasn't at all worried about her father being gay. She was very worried that he'd kept it, as she said, "A big honking secret."

"Well, you're in on the secret," he said, his businesslike self returning, now that all the impossibilities—so many of them—were finally out in the open. "And I can deal with whatever the family does as long as I have you three at my wedding. Will you? Be there? Support me?"

"I want to decorate the wedding cake," said the older. "Since I'm great at those things and besides, I know about being gay."

"How do you know about being gay?" his father said very quickly and somewhat suspiciously.

"Guess."

And a whole new round of conversation began.

Eventually, Bettina was alone. Father and son were going to have a man-to-man about family secrets and there were many hugs and declarations of love and …

"I'm exhausted," Bettina said as she shut the door behind her family. "Wiped out." And then, "I can't tell Zelda any of this. What the fuck do I talk to her about?"

Bettina laughed her incapacity to stop talking after such an afternoon, but didn't laugh at the problem of chatting with

Zelda. For Zelda had said to ring her that night. "Just to catch up."

Bettina needed to calm down, pretty promptly. She grabbed a cheese and biscuit packet and sat down at the computer to check her email.

It wasn't at all calming to check her email, but it certainly gave her something she could tell Zelda. There was a happy congratulatory message from a guy named Adam, telling her she'd won the fellowship she'd applied for months ago. He asked her to ring. She was relieved he didn't call to tell her the news. He gave a mobile number, and in her experience people who used mobiles had a tendency to ring anyone anytime. She imagined the call coming in the middle of lunch. Or halfway through the afternoon. Late afternoon was better. She rang Adam and managed to sound delighted and to write notes about a lot of things that he said needed to be done. *I'll be pleased with it after dinner,* she thought, *when I've had time to recuperate from family. And when I'm less in shock about the amount of paperwork.*

Bettina waited until evening before ringing Zelda. It was all official, and she was allowed to break the silence. And it was a nice thing to hide behind. Bettina's life was full of hiding, and she didn't mind at all. She toyed with the idea of writing her life down and maybe turning it into a book one day, but she preferred her words to disappear when they were finished. Coffee or phone, but not notebook. While she was thinking that, she dialled Zelda.

"Hi, it's Bettina."

---

Zelda was beyond busy. Talking to Bettina had cost her precious time. It would be a late night, but she would finish this paper, and the marking. That was a given.

The paper worried her. It was pulling her in a new direction.

How prophets were embedded into the Celtic identity had fascinated her when the call for papers came out, and now it scraped her skin and made her restless.

"I need to get away from the pressure to produce papers and short pieces." Why? Zelda took out a marker and drew possible reasons on her home whiteboard. It didn't take long.

The book was a pressure: it had to be finished. Until then, the only friends she would talk to were on social media and occasionally on the phone. Zelda cleaned her whiteboard, made coffee, and got back to work. Her brain rattled with notes and one of them said, "Can I pair my social life with work to benefit both?"

She didn't like these thoughts. Academia was impossible for the ambitious without them. And Zelda was ambitious.

# THREE

Melissa's private notebook

This is it. As of right now. I bet it will be full of ripped and torn pages. Not because I'm an emotional person, but because I keep forgetting my shopping list.

Why do I have to write this thing, anyhow? I'll explain that later. First, storytime. I'm going to leave out most of the screams and quite a lot of the throwing up.

I don't want to remember this story, so it's got to go down on paper. I hate how this happened. I've calmed it down a lot, but there's still trigger pain and this memory is definitely that. So, the story …

This is just one. The one that got me onto a new track, why I'm writing, why I'm angry, and why the world and I do not talk.

Sometimes days start the same. As if they're ordinary. As if, when someone asks, I'll be able to answer "Not really a special day" without lying. Except I would be lying because that kind of day is special just for existing.

I woke and thought I was the kind of person who leapt out of bed shouting, "Places to go! People to see!" I got out placidly.

Without pain. And I said, "Ordinary day." That was my high point.

A piece of paper had drifted. Not from my marbling toolbox, for that was safely away because of the cats. It was there. On the floor. Where it shouldn't be. I could slip on it and that would not be a good thing.

In a moment of extreme virtue, I picked it up. Sometimes I sweep things up the wall a bit, to make it easier, but today, I bent. It was only a little bend and I only felt a little twinge and I was getting a massage that day. A massage! On bad days massages bring me back from the edge. I was dreaming of that massage from the moment I got up, because a massage on a good day can get rid of that toxicity that floods my system. I can take steps forward with such massages on such days. And twinges were just twinges on days like this.

I drove. I know I'm not supposed to, but I did. And I was fine. Well, not fine, but not so bad. And the massage was everything a massage should be and I felt almost good. As if my life could be like this every day.

I could deal with twinges. I felt so damn confident that I bent down to put on my shoes. Stupid, stupid, stupid idiot that I am. I don't have that kind of flexibility most days. I don't wear shoes that require bending down. I fell into old patterns because my body felt possible … alive … almost normal.

It hurt. I didn't ask for help, even though the kind massage person was there. I felt so damn normal that when it stopped hurting because I stood up straight again, I stopped worrying about it.

Got back into the car. It hit. Worst damn pain ever. Throw-up kinda pain. I didn't, but I wanted to. I wanted it to go. To never have come. I couldn't think. I was sitting there in the car and had to do something. I couldn't. I couldn't do a damn thing.

My brain melted. All I could think of was "go to hospital". Which would've been fine if I'd used my damn phone. I didn't. I drove myself there. I don't know how often I nearly rammed into other cars or they nearly rammed into me. The whole trip was me in my body, screaming for help.

I got to Emergency. Yay me.

I couldn't get out of the car. (This is why I no longer drive. Taxis. Always.)

Finally, I opened the door and pushed the seat so far back it was almost flat and I half-tumbled out. I don't know how I stayed upright. I don't know how I got into the hospital. I don't remember shutting my car door. I was in the hospital saying, "Help!" and they told me to sit down. I couldn't. I said so. Hurt so much. So damn much. I sent a message to Hal and he must've closed the door to the car, because I don't remember doing it. I stood for thirty minutes before anyone saw me. In the end, they saw me because another patient said, "I think you need to see that lady before me. She's in real pain." Then I was triaged.

Thirty minutes wasn't long for the hospital, but it was long for me. Other people measure pain by spoons, but that was the day I started measuring pain by how long time felt. By a minute turning into an hour and an hour turning into a week. I didn't put it in words then, but I could feel time pulling apart, elongated by pain. It was ten weeks of pain.

The doctor made me walk up and down and then gave me an injection and threw me out. Didn't tell me what was wrong. They don't unless I ask and when I hurt that much, I can't ask. Hal was ready for me and took me home. Or tried to. There were delays when I threw up.

I should've gone back to the hospital.

Some decisions are too difficult to make. They look so easy from outside pain, but everyone asks and asks, "What do you want to do?" "What would be best?" and all you can think about is the pain eating up your life and stretching time. That's right, I remember, the shot was wearing off by the time I got home. Time was stretching again.

When we got home, Hal said, "I'm going to take you to the other hospital."

I couldn't face waiting there. All I wanted to do was go to bed and hope that sleep would subdue the pain. Sleep can do this, if I'm lucky. It did, for a bit.

It was midnight. I remember that. I thought it was an unlucky hour. All the pain was back, and none of the things I do to deal with pain were working. So many pain tricks I have. Sometimes it's walking, and sometimes breathing, and sometimes … so many pain tricks I have. Tablets aren't as useful as everyone says. I need the pain tricks. But they didn't work that night.

Hal called the home doctor. We didn't know about the home doctor until then, but he was worried and researched to find an alternative to hospital. At 2 am the doctor came. The doctor said I needed to go to hospital. Then I waited an hour (a big hour, a bloated hour) for triage to be done and I was told to wait because someone would see me. Soon. Their soon.

Their "soon" was four hours. I found this out afterward. Such pain. I can't compare it to other pain because it was all its own and I hated it. Every long second. Throwing up didn't help, but I threw up often.

I don't know what the hospital staff thought. All I know is that they didn't give me any help until five hours after I'd arrived. I don't know what they thought of me screaming with pain, because they didn't talk to me about it. I was a sick person in a hospital and the hospital didn't want me there. That was what I felt.

When the doctor finally came, he asked about my history and about medication. He gave me two Endone tablets and told me they would make me sleep. An hour later they hadn't and he was very surprised, but he sent me home anyway. I wasn't in as much pain, so I could leave. Simple.

I'd stopped screaming.

My new doctor is the one who sent me to the physio who gave me a diagnosis. I should've been in hospital for three days, the physio said. My pelvis had slipped. My new doctor listened to the physio and did an examination. The first examination.

I said, "What can I do?"

She said, "Write everything down. Some of this is for you, and some of this is for me to help diagnose, but some of this is so that if anything like this ever happens again, you'll have notes."

I said to her, "I wouldn't've been able to write that night."

"Dictate. Or write when you can. Do as much as you can when you can."

She's helped. I haven't had anything as severe as that since. I started living my life again. Not in the same way everyone else does, because I was sick before my pelvis slipped and I am still sick. But my life is back. I can do things. And I will.

Now I don't need to remember that day, because it's all written here.

# FOUR

Bettina woke up with a twinge of memory. Not a dream. She smiled to herself.

Then she remembered. When her mother died, she'd left Bettina a box. That box was with the public trustee person and had to be opened today. This was in addition to the thing she had to collect after she scattered her mother's ashes. Her mother liked making life complicated.

The public trustee person had told her on the phone how much he was looking forward to it. "So unusual," he'd gushed.

Bettina wasn't looking forward to it at all. She would drive all the way to Melbourne to collect the box from its miserable storage and then she'd open it and then she'd know (maybe) why her mother had talked so much about a special legacy and said nothing about what that special legacy was. When she was a child, Bettina had dreamed of a Fabergé egg from a century ago, or a book of spells. Now she was an adult, Bettina had stopped dreaming about what was in the box. Real dreams were quite sufficient.

She was meeting Zelda for lunch, but she didn't have to leave for two hours. There was time to do her regular sketch. It was a little thing, her sketch, but it was building. The same window at the same time of day and as many days a week as possible. Merely a sketch. Nothing more than a sketch. Sometimes a magpie peered at her. Once a little boy did.

Every Sunday she'd work through those sketches and turn them into portals. The window in the final art would show somewhere different. The magpie might glow green, or the sun might shade the window with purple and dream-gold. All the differences were in the paint. Bettina and her watercolours transformed nearly identical sketches into something special.

Sunday was watercolour day. Today was sketch day. Out the window the drab rain turned the world green. She wished she were painting it, but she wasn't. She switched her eyes to the right setting, the way she switched her brain to its everyday setting when she woke after one of those dreams.

She was almost ready for another project. As she packed her stack of sketches away and got ready for the car trip, she wondered whether this was the project she'd use to bring her dreams into her art.

Bettina had a dream about her dreams. She wanted to use them to show the world its own magic. "The stuff we don't see unless we're taught how to look," she explained to Zelda, two hours later. "I think that's what I'll use to apply for the fellowship. It's for a retreat at a place that calls itself 'magic' and 'full of portals', so they should like a project that lets everyone see portals on paper. I'll make it a book, and create a visual story about using an old house to explain the reality of dreams."

"That sounds interesting," Zelda said, her voice non-committal.

"No it doesn't," said Bettina. "Not yet. Now it's only a vague idea. It will be fascinating when you see it, but I don't have words for it."

"You need words for an application."

"I know." Bettina sighed.

"I can help, if you want," suggested Zelda.

Bettina looked across the table at her, evaluating. "I bet you'll apply too." It wouldn't be the first time.

"While you explained, I was thinking about it," Zelda admitted. "Would you mind?"

"We'd better have damned different applications."

"I'm sure we can do that." Zelda smiled. "I have a question for you. You don't have to answer it."

"A question I don't have to answer? I'll try it."

"It's about Dov," said Zelda.

"Okay," Bettina said cautiously.

"I don't understand how he has a boyfriend," Zelda began. "He's not bi. I know it."

"You're right, he's not bi. He's gay."

"But you and he ..."

"It's complicated. You know he's Jewish?"

"Yes?"

"His family is very religious and don't accept him being gay. Or haven't, until now. He tried to make them all happy."

"How does hiding something like that make anyone happy?"

"Oh, God. I can't explain. He needed children. The old-fashioned way. He had a wife. His wife was Jewish. She wanted him to not be gay and she walked out on him."

"His family is that old-fashioned?"

"More than that. His family is very traditional and they were nearly wiped out by Hitler. He cares as much as his parents that there be a new generation."

"But he didn't have to marry," Zelda said.

"He's not Orthodox anymore, but he was. His parents are still. His Judaism descends through the mother. He needed children from a good Jewish girl and if he was going to do that, he was going to marry her and make it all proper. I read up on it and he didn't have to marry her according to Jewish law, but old-fashioned Australian Jews marry to have children, so he did."

"They had this horrible break-up. You told me about it."

"Yeah. And he recruited me to be his pretend-girl, because he wasn't coping. It suited me just then. The truth is that we're old-fashioned best friends."

"With benefits?"

"Irrelevant," Bettina dismissed. "I'm happy he's come out and has a boyfriend and can be himself. He's taken his boyfriend to synagogue to introduce him to Judaism. That was the big thing. He fell in love with a non-Jew and came out, all at once. His family ought to be devastated."

"But?"

"They came to talk to me about it. Every single one of them. And they're okay as long as I'm there."

"But you're not Jewish. How can his mother even talk to you?"

"You do know that most Jews are not destroying things? That the group at your university tell you a shitload of lies?" Zelda didn't reply, so Bettina pressed on. "The family decided they liked me years ago, even when they knew it wasn't quite a normal relationship. I go to the family on Friday nights and for New Year, and the children are partly my children. I can't be Jewish for them, but I can be the mother who won't walk away. You've known all this for years. I don't know why it's even a question you can ask."

"Because I didn't understand it."

"Yes?"

"His mother thinks that I kept him from suicide when things got too bad. You were in the US then, so we didn't talk about it. She thought he was gay and she was too nervous to ask. She whipped herself to shreds over it. I think she still whips herself. She'll accept almost anything that makes him happy."

"Okay," Zelda said dubiously.

"Don't tell anyone about any of it," said Bettina. "I'm only telling you 'cause of who you are."

"Sure," said Zelda, more confident.

Bettina went to the lawyer's almost light-hearted. She hated secrets and she hated applications. Her portfolio was awesome and her words were … not. Zelda's words might get her the fellowship.

She needed it for more than the time it gave her to create. Being an artist in the modern world required a continual updating of self before the public. More items on her CV would open her life to more opportunities and make the fight to get income almost-not-impossible. Bettina hated that aspect. She hated the applications and the self on show, and talking about herself rather than doing her work, and having to be frighteningly literate when she was an artist, not a wordsmith.

Zelda would help. Zelda would make sure she looked her best on paper and she'd turn Bettina's words into English and … it'd be okay. And now that she knew Zelda knew the reality of her relationship with Dov, there would be much less pussyfooting on their Sunday-night chats.

Her life was much less complicated now that Dov was open about being gay. And he was so much more the person she'd always seen him as. That was one reason he'd stayed with her, even though things were … not normal. She saw him as himself, not what he'd been stuck being because of the vagaries of history.

Now that she didn't have to carry Dov's secret, the major issue remaining was the problem her mother had left her. Bettina sighed. Dov's mother was everything her mother had never been. Dov and she had a running joke about "family by choice" and it wasn't that funny.

The public trustee person wasn't that helpful. He smiled and had her sign a paper and gave her something in exchange for that signature.

It was a locked box. A very tiny box. Covered with curlicues. Locked. Cheap modern Chinese pretending to be something special. Locked. Locked tight.

The public trustee person said, "I don't have a key."

"What am I supposed to do?" Bettina's voice took on that I-am-lost tone that always, always gave her help. She didn't know why, and she only used it when she genuinely needed help. Like now.

"I have some notes," said the public trustee. "I always take notes when I talk through a will." He looked through his notes, and there was nothing on his computer that explained the box or a key, or even Bettina's mother.

"I didn't get any of Mum's papers," said Bettina, feeling helpless. "It's probably with them. They're in a museum somewhere and haven't been catalogued and she didn't give me access rights." Bettina still felt aggrieved about those access rights. She wanted to know about Russia, and about the Berlin Wall, and about … so many things.

The public trustee person looked surprised. "I forgot about the papers." He looked almost relieved. "I can ring about that." Why he hadn't rung the museum the moment he knew she was getting a locked box was beyond Bettina's capacity to understand. Why he kept all those notes and then forgot to check them for papers, even.

When things went wrong like this, she felt as if she were swimming beyond her depth when she had learned how to swim barely an hour ago. Not drowning, but helpless.

When Zelda had been around all the time, she'd stepped in to help. No one else had. All that non-help made Bettina feel grudgy and upset. Sometimes people would talk with much generosity in their own voices and it would come to … nothing. No help at all. She drove all the way home, carrying with her hours of feeling slightly lost.

She walked in the door, threw her handbag onto the couch and saw a message on her answering machine. Was it going to help? Would it make things worse?

Bettina pressed the button.

"Apparently you have the key already," the public trustee person said. "You were given it when you were a child. The decoration on the key matches the decoration on the box. If you've lost it since your childhood, I'm afraid I can't help. Maybe call a locksmith?"

The public trustee person had seen her necklace the first time she'd gone in. Commented on it, in fact. "So unusual to wear a key," he said. He'd taken a picture for his wife. It felt like a plot. Except it wasn't. It was rampant stupidity. Bettina did not tolerate stupidity.

Weariness overtook all the earlier emotions and she made herself coffee. The box could wait. The fact that her precious key belonged to a cheap Chinese box could wait, too. Everything could damn well wait.

Eventually, she was ready to deal with garbage from her mother. Her mother had been better than her father, she admitted, but … she just didn't need any more of it. When her life had been attacked by that rabid mess she'd called a husband, neither of them had done anything.

Gaslighting was not something anyone could handle. She knew this. But she still carried so much hate for anyone who judged her according to the set-up he'd made. The safe corner of her world was very small and she didn't allow people into it. Only her adopted family, Zelda, and maybe five other people. Even pictures of her next to her art made her uncomfortable. She was more freaked when her pendant showed because it was as if her private life was visible and now, now, it was that pendant that was the key. She hated those coincidences. If they were coincidences. Life would be much easier without magic.

Sometimes she admitted that the world wasn't rational. Mostly, she lived. She put the strange and wonderful into her paintings, but she told everyone that her dreams were simply dreams she painted. Inventions. It was easier to believe what she told people at exhibitions or who were interviewing her. So very much easier. And she was probably right to not believe. Especially today.

"I've got to sort this out," she said very loudly, to the whole world. "I've got to find out what my dreams do and I've got to find out how to tell what's coincidence and what's scary. And I've got to damn well deal with it." What she didn't say was that this meant she had to creep out of that corner and confront some of the world she'd lost.

She tried to unlock the box with the key she was wearing. Three times. The lock was fine, she thought. The box was so small she twisted it and dropped it and nearly broke the thing trying to unlock it with the key still hanging from her neck. *I'm scared,* Bettina admitted and stopped to drink a now-cold coffee.

This shook her brain back into place. Bettina took off the necklace, wrapped the chain around her hand to secure it (for it was a tiny key), held the box in her right hand, and unlocked the damn thing.

In it was a note. Nothing more.

This was not a bad "nothing more". The note was in her mother's handwriting and gave her instructions to collect a thing. Literally "a thing".

"It'll help," the note said. It didn't say what "it" would help with. Of course it didn't. Most importantly, the note finished with, "I believed you. I couldn't do anything to help you then. This will help you now. When you turned twenty-one, I told you that one day you'd have a magic quest. You laughed at me. This is that quest. I'm sorry it's almost too late. I wasn't brave enough to give all this to you when I was supposed to. When I was eighteen, I was given this box and used the key. When you were little, the key to the box made a wonderful present. When you were older, you were sick and I was tired and Dad was … not good to us."

"To us" echoed in Bettina's mind. The echo lasted until after her criticism of her mother's words. She always pulled her mother's words to pieces, as if under them she'd find a real person and not a hero who'd walked out on her daughter. It read as if there were two keys. Poor English. She wouldn't show Zelda—Zelda would mock it. Bettina pushed past this and into memories.

Dad had not been good to Mum. He spent more time with his mistress than with his wife. Divorce wasn't easy back then and Mum had to deal, somehow, without enough money and without a job and … it hadn't affected Bettina in the same way. She took her mother's side when she had to, but her feelings weren't engaged.

It was as if she saw through the farce the three of them played and decided to stay away from it. Maybe that was why Mum hadn't given her the box. Maybe Mum was revenging in her petty way for not being loved enough. Yet she was the one who had walked out next.

Bettina thought she loved her mother, but she refused to play the games that consumed her parents' generation's lives. Since she was quite young, it was easier to wrap herself in her own concerns. More than easier. Safer.

Anyhow, this was the family legacy. Or the start of it. Collecting something from somewhere would be the next step in understanding her dreams. The note said so.

This creeped Bettina out. She hadn't known her mother

knew about this thing she herself didn't quite believe in. Her right hand clenched and unclenched as she tried to keep her feelings under control. She'd never told her mother the truth about the dreams.

The first time she had dreamed, she didn't keep it a secret from either of her parents. She talked about it at breakfast and caught her mother staring at her father in fascinated horror. Her mother thought Bettina had seen something in real life and was calling it a dream to avoid blame. Her mother had sent Bettina to her bedroom and then Bettina had heard the shouts and thumps and ... she had never told either parent about a single one of her dreams, ever again. She did this with everything: protected her mother. Above all else in her life, her mother had to be protected. Until the day the family stopped existing for her.

*That was the morning I lost my parents,* she thought bitterly. *And it was the morning I learned to lie to keep the peace.*

Unless her mother meant spiritual dreams? Or career dreams? Bettina had only talked about one dream, once. How could she have known about the other dreams? Whichever it was, Bettina would have to deliver the note to the address and pick something up. On a given date. Any year, but only on that date.

Of course it was on a given date. Her mother had watched too much of a certain kind of film. She liked putting drama into everyday life. That was why it was a quest, of course. This was one of the reasons Bettina had been able to keep herself clear of arguments and calls for support. She saw the drama and it was TV drama and she didn't want a bar of it. She loved her mother beyond anyone. She never played those games.

Gifted children were supposed to play those games. *Someone else deserved the power of the dream,* she reflected. *I only use it in my painting, really, so it's wasted on me. If the world needs Cassandra and they have Bettina, then the world will collapse. I am no hero. Special. Not heroic.*

She wasn't heroic because of the reasons she had fled deep into herself. Because of her parents. Bettina grimaced. Missing her mother overtook her irritation with either parent.

She'd pick this *thing* up from this place on the right day. Months away, it was. Still. It'd be a day she could use to remember.

Time aside just for her mother. A better farewell than the public one at the memorial service. That afternoon, everyone had stared to see how she would show her emotions about her parents and about her own situation. She hated being the centre of all this melodrama. She'd stood by the grave with all her emotions hidden. She'd shaken hands and hugged and done everything necessary, but she'd showed nothing. Not even a single tear. This wasn't fair on her mother; Mum was not the best person in the world, but Bettina missed her.

*If I got that fellowship,* Bettina realised, *I could line everything up and do it all in one hit. Also, it would give me somewhere to go after picking up whatever from wherever.* She didn't want her mother's quest. She wanted her own life. Having something special to do immediately after completing the message would work. It was a question of logistics.

She looked up Eden on a map, then she looked up Robertson. Not precisely on the way. Not even close to on the way. But still.

Bettina stopped looking at maps and pulled out the fellowship application form and started working on it. She felt naked without her necklace, but the key was tainted. Maybe the taint would fade. Maybe she would go shopping tomorrow and get a replacement.

The next night, Zelda rang to discuss the fellowship a bit more. Bettina went through her notes with Zelda and improved her application a great deal. This saved Bettina from explaining what her mother had left for her.

Bettina's focus fascinated Zelda, and she expanded on her own earlier thought. They had done the same thing as children. Zelda tagged onto Bettina's ideas and they'd done things together. It felt comfortable.

Zelda told Bettina, "I want to see the moon in its perfect place, full and framed by branches tonight. It's part of my work on the mystical everyday. I finished with the mystical Everyman, by the way. It comes out next week."

"Do you need to leave now?" Bettina asked.

"No," Zelda said. "I've got plenty of time."

They talked about Zelda's work then, for Bettina wanted to ask how the moon framed by branches fitted in with historical research. This led to the inevitable. Thrice inevitable. Zelda always discussed matters three times and from three directions before actually doing anything.

"Bet I could get a fellowship, at that," Zelda said confidently into the phone. "I could use it to finish my book on Celtic deity and how we translate mystical into our everyday and create a sense of magic."

Twice. Then thrice. Bettina smiled at Zelda, even though Zelda couldn't see a thing. It sounded like the same kind of idea as her portal and dream one, but it really wasn't. That was how different the two women were and how long they'd known each other.

Zelda had no idea that the smile was hidden behind the phone. She continued talking. It was as if Bettina's thought had not taken place.

"It would be excellent for work, to be honest, now that my other project is done. We need things like the book and the fellowship to demonstrate we're doing our job. Academia sucks."

Bettina thought it through a bit more, aloud. She translated the dreams out of her explanation. "It won't get in my way, I don't think. There's more than one at a time and mine is about something different. I want to write nature poetry through pictures, turn them into magic. Gardens in the outback. An old house with a big garden in a country town in the middle of nowhere would be perfect," said Bettina. "Why don't we share each other's applications and help each other? Like you did with mine just now?"

"You're nervous?"

"About everything. Life isn't easy. My cousin tells me that one day it will all come together and make sense. My bad dreams, my art … everything. And so I'm nervous about everything." Bad dreams. That was what she called them. Even though most of them weren't bad and might not be dreams.

"Well, it's not easy, with your health." Zelda sounded supportive as only the oldest of friends can be.

"Let's do it," said Bettina, nodding to show herself she appreciated Zelda's support. "Let's both get fellowships and spend two weeks together instead of seeing each other when one of us happens to be in the other's town."

"Old times," said Zelda, who'd never moved. Bettina found it curious that Zelda never mentioned this out loud. She let everyone assume that she had gone on to bigger and brighter things away from home whenever she didn't want to do something. Like the upcoming school reunion. Zelda hated being tied down with Lilliputian rope.

"Old times."

---

Melissa's old times included her dream of singing. Not opera. Never opera. She loved lieder, but she also loved music that was rough and dark. The heavier, the more metal and the more disturbed, the more she loved it. She had a voice, too, back then.

Her teenage years had included a band and a choir and a great deal of Schubert.

Medicine had stolen her voice. It rubbed the volume and stripped the edge and made it hardly useful even for karaoke. The doctors said the medicine was more important. "Play an instrument," one said. But her instrument was her voice. She had a mediocre talent in all others. And mediocre was not something she would accept. Better to lose music than to lose herself.

Her health was critical, sure, but more critical than living her dream? Melissa wept quietly to herself and moved on.

She played with a great deal of art, but it was never music. Her eye was perfect, but her hands didn't behave. If she'd learned the skills before the illness set in, maybe they would have stuck, or maybe she would simply have lost a second dream.

This time it was easier to move on. This time she had Hal. Hal looked at her work and saw good in it and found alternatives. He was determined that she not lose what he called her "expressive side".

With his support, she had created hundreds of bookends and pictures by floating paints in water. She sold her work at markets, to collectors, and was able to fit it in between bad times. Even when she'd lost work for a time, she had her art.

Sometimes she started a conversation with Bettina about it, for it amused her that they were both creating. Bettina didn't share her amusement and explained rather than discussed. Bettina's art was all her own, and special. It was, in fact, art, whereas Melissa was a good solid craftsperson. Melissa took that message on board and found other things to talk about on the rarer and rarer occasions they met. Illness had been off the table for years, so art joined it.

It didn't worry her too much. A substitute for music that

made her almost as happy as music was a simple and great magic.

These were the years of happiness. She had Hal and the cats and her paper art. Marbling and its kin.

Melissa was about to add decorated edges for classic books to her repertoire. She'd bought many throwaway volumes and had worked on them and already had two showcase examples to prove she could create beauty in endpapers, edges, and almost any other part of a book.

Some of the throwaway volumes had been sold online. There were customers who shared her view of the oddness of life and the need to turn the oddness and the hurt into beauty. They were the ones who asked for specific volumes when she talked about her work in updates. She didn't need prizes or exhibitions. Melissa had Hal, and her art (or craft), and that dedicated audience who not only understood it, but had particular passion for her experiments. Everything else was secondary.

It was just as well everything else was secondary, for when she listed what had gone wrong with her health and friendships during that time, the psychologist had been shocked. Almost as shocked as he was impressed.

"You don't need me," he said. "To be where you are with what you've gone through means you're a survivor. You find your own solutions."

"Hal helps. And it gets harder and harder as my body becomes more fragile. That's what we need to work on here," was Melissa's response. "I need to keep finding my own solutions. And I need them to bring me into the wider community. Isolation sucks."

The reason she'd gone to a psychologist was because, thinking about Bettina's response to her art, she'd finally learned how to describe the dynamics in meetings with Zelda and Bettina.

All the conversations about illness had focused on how brave Bettina was, and almost everything about the lunch had focused on how to make it possible for Bettina to have a good day, too. It looked … nice. But it hurt Melissa (literally) and it didn't really help Bettina. Melissa thought it didn't, anyhow. Bettina enjoyed the focus on illness, so maybe she was wrong.

Melissa still loved her old friends, but Zelda had never asked a single question about Melissa's life. This is why she had stopped going to those lunches. The other two talked about her life when they met for two sentences, maybe, and it was gone, buried under other things. They asked if work was fine and how was her family, and then they moved on to more interesting subjects. Bettina had dismissed any discussion of Melissa's health as secondary to her own.

The reality was that comparing illness was a mug's game. They could have compared lives and solutions. Except that Bettina never talked about solutions. She enjoyed the fuss. And, of course, wouldn't talk about work in a way that shared that work.

They'd always been that way, Melissa realised. Zelda was the elder and the strong one and was going to change the world. Bettina was the fragile but brilliant one who needed cosseting. And Melissa was the cheer squad and provider of the words, "Yes, you're right."

The others hadn't changed those parts of themselves. They were fine people, but they were no longer *her* fine people. She wondered aloud to Hal why they were still in her mind.

"They've dumped you," said Hal. "Doing all the things and not telling you."

"They dumped me emotionally years ago."

Hal nodded. "What do you want to do?"

"Something stupid. Not related to old school friends in any way, shape, or form. Well, probably not related. Maybe not related? Anyhow, it's stupid."

"Stupid?"

"I overworked one of my trays and was going to clean it up and start again, then something happened. Not a stupid something. An odd something. Weird."

"Can I see?"

"If I can get it to repeat, I'll show you," she promised. Her mind half thought that she'd test it for six months in case and also half thought she should just do it, right away, and find out if she was imagining it. Except that she knew she wasn't.

"How does it replace your old friends?"

"It takes their place in my mind. If I'm right, it's the sort of something that has to be a secret. No one's going to believe it."

"Just you and me, then." Hal smiled intimately.

"Precisely. If it fails as an experiment, we have a private joke. And if it *is* real and the universe changes … we have a bloody big secret. I can fret about it, rather than about people I never see."

"Show me now!" Hal demanded.

"If it works."

"I trust you so much, you know."

"I love you so much, you know."

"I know. Can I add something?"

"What?"

"You need a public thing to hide this other whatever. So that you don't have to tell anyone if you don't want to." Hal had this way of taking what she did or said and turning it round. Most people turned things round in sad ways or bad ways, but Hal always turned it round in a good way. Melissa smiled whenever he did this. It was his special gift and she loved it. He could turn a few words inside out and make sense of what she was trying to say.

He asked for payment for this talent of his. He needed to be asked to explain it. Every time. This was not an unendurable payment.

"A public thing?" Melissa asked dutifully.

"Something that you can do on high pain days. Something that will get you through everything. Something that lets you be your full self, regardless."

"Sounds nice but impossible."

"Not at all," said Hal, half-hiding a smile. "I'll be right back."

Melissa sat back for a moment. She let the pain wash through, as was her wont when she'd held too much in. She shut her eyes and forced her muscles to relax. That was the other payment for Hal's ideas. She needed the energy to appreciate them. His ideas were always good and always worth appreciating, but two minutes focused on her body would reduce the physical price.

He brought back a cardboard box. Inside the box was a camera. Not a heavy one. Not even a fancy one. The fancy extras were in a second box: lenses and a tripod and a spare battery and charger and two huge memory cards.

"On a good day you can command it to do anything and you can use different lenses. On a bad day, you can point and click. And if anyone asks what you're doing, you can talk about your pictures."

"You are such a clever man," said Melissa, admiring.

"Are there rewards for cleverness? That's the question."

"It's cake today, because of pain. I took it out of the freezer this morning. And you'll have to put it on a plate yourself. I wish …"

"Don't say it." Hal was fierce. "I'd rather have you on a bad day than anyone else, ever."

"Best of husbands. Best of people," Melissa said, and they used the coffee and cake to toast her future in mysteries and in photography. Her first pictures were of Hal eating cake and then of the cake crumbles on a plate.

"New cameras are so odd," Melissa commented. "Even though my hands are shaky, the picture doesn't wobble."

“Am I clever?” Hal needled.

“You’re a genius.”

“Does that mean you’re going to try this experiment again so that I can find out?”

“Later. I want to hear the latest about that idiot at your work, first. I hate her, you know.”

“I know. And she never learns.” Hal made more coffee and they sat down to gossip.

# FIVE

I don't want to write this down. Not any of it. The doctor says I must.

I wrote the heading last time. Then I went to bed for three hours. Five minutes that turned into three hours.

The doctor says these notes rule my life until we find out more about what's wrong, she says. I say I need to live. She says fine, but write everything down. I say it hurts; she says fine, dictate it. Don't edit, just dictate. If it comes out funny, that's fine. I hate dictating. Only if it hurts—I'll only talk into my goddam computer when my fingers can't type or my body's so weary it doesn't give a damn about anything and even breathing's hard work. And I'll keep my notes and my doctor will add them to all these damnblastedidiot blood tests and maybe one day we'll find out what's wrong. Maybe. One day. I say the same thing every time I write because saying it will make it go away.

I don't write everything. Not all the incidents, just the ones I feel I have to write. Not all the pain, just the stuff that feels a bit different or makes me think of something. All the pain would be all day writing, every day. No, that's not true. I had an hour without pain last week. I wanted to throw a party. I was so happy. A full hour!

Sometimes I'll write (when I can) and sometimes I'll dictate and today I'm doing both and it's taken me a bloody hour to write this much. My life. Welcome to it. Everyone else's nightmare is my everyday.

Let me note something I dislike intensely. I dislike the repetition. Why does every entry so far feel as if I'm saying the same things? Why do I have to damnishly live through these same things, over and over? Maybe other lives include exciting pain. Different pain. I can't imagine a life with no pain.

# SIX

Zelda hated conversations about children. She was not someone who had a natural inclination to love children. She loved her own, of course. That almost went without saying. It was the conversations about other children that dulled her mind.

Her colleagues knew. They would save the special stories for Zelda. She knew they did, so she schooled her face to show only polite interest. No matter what story she was told, her face was polite and interested. It had become a competition in the department to find material that would push her face into emotion.

"Petunia was with her cousin yesterday," she was told, and she decided to keep her safe face by contemplating why on earth a modern child was named "Petunia".

Petunia had found a bicycle pump that her uncle hadn't bothered putting away. Why should he put it away? Who could get up to any kind of mischief using a bicycle pump? Zelda wished she were more imaginative. Wouldn't it be perfect if she thought of twenty uses for a pump while her colleague told her of one small game a six-year-old had played?

"You know that Petunia loves her science and adores cartoons?"

Zelda nodded. She had no idea, but she knew she was expected to know. Did the amazing amount of data parents kept affect their academic capacity at all? She suspected not, but it would be nice if it did. It would be nice if there were some advantage to not having a child. She had to take second choice of holidays, and had to justify emergencies in such detail, not having a child to rely on anymore. Bettina would say there were also things like Christmas, but Zelda celebrated those in her special way. No disadvantage in being different but special.

She didn't miss any of the story, because her colleague had to do the child-check on his phone. Zelda didn't let herself drift back into research thoughts, despite the temptation. She'd have to wait until tonight. Her whole body ached to finish the research for the current chapter. There was something about the question she was asking that brought forward results in spades. Not only exciting, but the stuff of dreams. The rest of the study wasn't the stuff of dreams. Some of it was the stuff of nightmares. For this chapter, however, she could take special notes so that when she wrote it, the writing would have a divine reflection of her argument. It would shine. Shine required focus, which meant she had to wait until she was home. Her feet were restless, and her brain was restless. It was with great effort that she kept her face straight.

She focused on the face opposite her. He had very sensitive eyes and a long jaw. Almost a Sherlock Holmes, with the eyes lost to drugs. Except they weren't. They were lost to his mobile. Finally, he finished typing, closed his phone, and turned back to her.

"Where was I up to?" he asked.

"Bicycle pump," Zelda prodded.

His daughter had tried a scientific experiment on her cousin, using the pump. She'd tried to blow his head up so it became a balloon—"exactly like characters in cartoons," the fond parent said with a voice that was mixed despair and pride.

"Was he hurt?"

"They're just coming out of hospital now," he said. Zelda felt a momentary stab of guilt and was glad about her straight face. "Minor damage only. Could've been worse."

"How worse could it have been?"

"He could have lost his hearing in one ear."

"I'm—" Zelda's comment was interrupted by her own phone.

It was Johnno. Her own dear sweet not-quite-yet-and-not-nearly-soon-enough ex-husband. He nagged her about not having given his new girl the engagement ring.

"From my family," she said. "It was my grandmother's ring. And I'm in a meeting."

She hung up and made the most expressive grimace she could.

"This bit is always tough," the father of the juvenile delinquent said supportively.

"Always unique, too, I bet," said Zelda. "I'd better get going. He rings ten times when he's got a beef. You shouldn't have to deal with it."

"Petunia'll be home, so I'd better pick up my wife and go be a dutiful parent. God, I'm glad that I didn't have to do the hospital run."

"Who did it?"

"My brother. It was his son."

"Buy them something nice."

"And takeaway dinner." He nodded. "That'll help a bit."

Zelda's phone buzzed angrily at her. That was the sound she used for her ex, a swarm of nasty bees. "I'd better go."

The calls lasted a good two hours. By the time they were finished, Zelda was also finished. She was home and had eaten dinner and had taken care of so many small things. It looked as if everything was under control, but it really wasn't. She needed a haven.

Step one in creating the haven was turning off her mobile and disconnecting her landline and switching off the Wi-Fi. Life could wait.

That was her doorway. It was the portal that Zelda was going to use to run away from the mess that was her recent private life into her safe place. Her argument about the prevalence of the Celtic in the medieval everyday, that the Normans and that the Anglo-Saxons had simply slipped into the Celtic world and accepted critical cultural elements from that world, was her personal battle against almost everyone.

She wasn't the first person to believe this, nor would she be the last, but it was her special subject. She was lonely without it right now, due to the university's publication demands. The advantage of promotion (if she got it) was that she'd have the new book published along with the one she was already so far past that it felt decades-old. Her new book would be edgy and marvellous and challenge assumptions of reality. It would translate into the present-day, which guaranteed a higher profile for it. And she wouldn't have to dedicate it to that damnfool.

It still hurt too much that she'd dedicated her big work to an idiot. Her dream subject should be hers, alone. Maybe she'd dedicate it to Petunia. She dreamed of that for a moment and then returned to her research.

She knew already the path her study would take and had paved some of its byways. She would demonstrate how the strong shouting of the ancient Celts led to documents and to art in the Middle Ages, which showed so much about what that shouting was about and this led to …

Magic. That was her new path. It linked to her Everyman work and to the present. It would bind realities together so neatly. To the Celts, other worlds existed. Arthur could take an otherworldly voyage on ships he didn't quite own and knights could challenge beings at a ford.

That latter was a bit biblical, perhaps, but she would talk about any latent Celtic thread in those romance fight scenes. Biblical was not magic, that was the thing. Religion and magic were close in the Middle Ages. She just had to follow that trail and show that magic wasn't alien, that the unexpected and the wonderful belonged in modern times. Sexy scholarship.

Zelda's intellectual life was governed by magic, and her research was led by the search for magic. Particular magic. Special magic. For her, sources contained and demonstrated the strong likelihood that other words existed and that the world she knew was on the brink of discovering them. She had looked a great deal at nineteenth-century stories of the medieval and otherworldly and Celtic kind, and now it was time to go back to the heart of it. Anything in translation would fill her pages and help her demonstrate what magic could be.

These thoughts led, of course, to notes on her computer. Notes were how she started her planning for a big project.

The first note she wrote was about the thoughts she'd had earlier. Writing style. This was going to be so damn good—style notes would help.

"Avoid passive voice," she wrote. "Don't get lyrical unless you're getting lyrical about some*thing*. Make the prose direct and compelling. Don't let anyone use the language as an excuse for not trusting your result." She copied and pasted the words into her "Teaching Thoughts" file. She'd promised herself an update of several handouts, and these ideas would be useful in two of them.

Then she walked through that portal into her safe place.

*Magic,* she thought. *Walking into places we do not know for reasons that are neither mystical nor scientific.*

"We can't see these things. We've lost critical cultural

components that permit us to take voyages of this kind. Where can we find the shadow of them in our culture?"

*Boundaries are the best place,* she decided. The moment she thought this, her research took on the three-dimensional feel of a castle. She knew where it would go and how to get there. All she needed was to write down the organising principles while her mind was castle-clear.

Zelda chose a simple path. If she kept it clear, then the book would be readable by the wider public. Academic and attractive to publishers. Perfect all round.

She typed madly for twenty minutes. Then she twittered at the keyboard and added and deleted and thought and changed and typed and untyped and moulded. When she finished, she had a list of all the types of boundaries starting from forests and ponds and ending with mystical sea voyages to Annwn. That led her naturally to all the places those boundaries reached, starting from Annwn and other worlds. She also began her dual list of sources.

*Things about the Celtic version (century and source) and modern equivalents to demonstrate what we've lost.*

*It'll be a sad study,* she resolved. *About how we could have had so much more and how we're left with shadows. From the thirteenth century, there were green men, foliate heads, and so much more. In the twenty-first, there are novels about them.*

She added the green men to her list and both Walter Map and Gerald of Wales to her sources. These sources weren't strictly Celtic, since they were writing in Latin and were with the English, but they had stories she could use and one of the two writers, she remembered, was snarky and snippy and very much her dream boy. Maybe she could find a translation on the web and start a computer collection of sources? Books were a passion, but most libraries shut her off from those Celtic borderlands she dreamed of.

Medieval carvings in Wales and Ireland and Brittany would

reflect what she was saying. Wooden explanations that brought borderlands into churches. She made a quick note of this, under the heading "Illustrations".

A bit of a joke, there, in the file for her new project. Just for her. Pretty pictures that would illustrate and illustrate and ... it wasn't quite so good when she spelled it out to herself. Zelda frowned very slightly. She wanted this project to be perfect.

"How the physical illustrates the verbal," she typed. Then she moved the word "Illustrations" so that it sat politely directly below that description. All was well.

Zelda smiled. She was going to have such a good year.

---

When Bettina was twelve, she had the dream for the first time. The Dream. The one that made all other dreams almost tolerable. It was her safe dream. The house was her safe house. She counted the times she'd had the dream, and it came to fifteen. There was no logic in the number. No meaning in it. But still, the dream was important.

When things were very bad, she remembered that dream and she always kept an eye out for the house, just in case it was real. For if it was real, then all kinds of things were possible. She wrote the dream down when she was seventeen and dreamed of being a children's writer. She wrote it down to protect it from what was happening around her at that time. She didn't want to remember herself at seventeen. But the dream came back to her, in the words she'd used when she was so very much younger, and she pulled to the side of the road to read her own writing on her travel computer. She didn't want to contemplate the bad stuff now, in her forties, on her way to another house, but she wanted to remember the first house. It had always been real to her. No, not real: hyperreal.

Every word she read aloud this time, singing the bear song and making that dream real. From hyperreal to merely real.

"We're *going* to the *Strange* House," chanted Kylie. "It's a very big house."

"What a beautiful day,' Sadie joined in. "*We're* not *scared*. Uh oh …"

The girls paused to think of the right words.

Sadie was first. "Walls. High brick walls."

Kylie nodded.

"We can't go over them. We can't go under them. Oh! No!" The girls made horror hands and horror shoulders at each other. "We've got to go *through*!"

They stopped. In front of them was a big wooden gate.

"Number 13," Sadie said very softly. "It's the most hidingest gate ever, I think. If there's anyone waiting, we can't see them."

"We could buzz." Kylie sounded dubious. She wasn't really a big brave bear-hunter. Besides, Maribelle wasn't there yet. Kylie never did anything without Maribelle.

A car pulled up beside them. Maribelle's mum stepped out onto the pavement, her red heels clicking with importance.

"Hi, kids," she said. She always said, "Hi kids." Soon Maribelle's mum was standing next to the gate. Her mouth made a straight line, as if she had eaten something bitter. "Mari's had an asthma attack. Can't come. Sorry." Her words were short and biting.

"Can I come back with you, Mrs Sharp?" Kylie sounded relieved.

Sadie wondered whether Mari's mum's gaze could cut holes in wood. It was reading Kylie's insides. "Are you sure you want to? You only get this one chance."

"I couldn't go without Mari," Kylie said. "It wouldn't be right. Besides, Mari needs me."

"She's pretty bored," Mrs Sharp admitted. "How about you, Sadie? D'you want a lift back into town?"

Not an offer to see sick Mari, Sadie noted.

"It would be rude if none of us went in," she said.

"By yourself?" Kylie's eyes boggled. "Into the Strange House?"

"It won't be strange when I'm in there," Sadie said. "And we've been invited."

Mrs Sharp's lips pressed thinner still. They were almost invisible. She pressed the buzzer. "The girls are here," she said into the box, her voice tit-tatting clearly, exactly like her red heels had sounded. "Only one's coming in."

"That's fine," a man's voice answered, slightly furry from the intercom. "We have two more children arriving tomorrow. She'll be right."

Sadie didn't like the thought of being alone even for one night in the House, but she bit her lip and told herself that there were no ogres or giants or beasts in the wood. This was no bear hunt. The Strange House was special, not dangerous.

The gate buzzed and opened. All Sadie said was, "Bye—see you the day after tomorrow," and she waved her hand as if she were cheerful and courageous.

*I'm going on a bear hunt,* Sadie thought. She put on her brave face. Sadie walked through the gate alone.

She had never seen the Strange House. It hid from the street behind a vast fence and a forest worth of trees. Those trees were always green, even when they should be frizzled with heat. Once, a boy from her class had caught a glimpse of them in winter, and every tree he could see had summer fruit. Apricots and peaches and plums and cherries. That's what he said, anyhow. Sadie hadn't believed him. Today, though, she could believe. The moment she stepped through that gate, it was as if the seasons had shifted. Outside it was mid-December, hot and placid. She had woken up with the sunlight so strong and hot that she had wished she could go to the pool before breakfast.

Now she was here, inside that heavy gate. The breeze blew

crisp across the gravel path. Sadie stood for a moment, convincing herself she didn't need her usual summer fun. It wasn't summer at all here, really. It was cool and beautiful and weird. The Strange House with the even stranger garden.

Sadie pulled herself out of her thoughts and walked up the path. She jumped, though, when a man's voice said, "Which one are you?"

Without the intercom turning everything to fuzz, his voice was very deep. Gravel-deep, with a hint of the rustle of autumn leaves. It fitted the garden, somehow. So did his looks, when he stepped out from between the trees. He was different shades of brown and red, from his skin to his shoes.

"I'm Sadie," she said, looking up so high her neck hurt. He was very tall and very, very thin. If he walked over a crack in the path, he would fall right in and never come out.

The man took a hurried step back, as if Sadie's thoughts scared him. Except she wasn't scary. Especially not when she wore her polite face. Even her timid cousin Dalia, age two, held Sadie's hand when Sadie wore her polite face.

The man's voice was more smudgy now as he stood under a tree. It was all a bit odd, but Sadie had said she was staying, so she put all the oddness at the back of her brain. She could explore it when she was home. Three days was a long time, but not impossible.

"Go straight in. Choose yourself a bedroom. There's food in the kitchen." He didn't give her a chance to say anything. "Tins in cupboards, packages in the fridge, ice cream in the freezer. No stove. No cooking. The teachers and parents insist." The man's voice rustled with the discontent of leaves about to fall. He didn't approve of teachers or parents.

"When you've chosen your room and eaten, you can explore whatever you like. Choose your room first. It's important. Take your time."

"Excuse me," Sadie put on her polite voice to go with her polite face, "who is in charge? Is it you?"

"The house is in charge." The man was amused.

"And if something goes wrong?" Sadie didn't want to ask.

"Just come outside and wait in the street—we'll send for your parents. I promise."

"Okay. Thank you." *My voice didn't wobble. Maybe.* Sadie wished the others were there. She finished walking down the path anyway.

In front of the House was a lawn. Plush and green and perfect. *Why do they have a lawn there? It must be to make people like me stand back and look.* She nodded her head wisely. She stood back and looked.

The Strange House wasn't strange at all. It was red brick and white paint and old and had more odd angles than anyone could take in at once. There was a twisty tower on the right, and a big window facing the lawn. The window bulged out a bit and she could just see a window seat. It reminded her a bit of her grandmother's house. Then it reminded her a bit of houses in books. Then she decided it was just itself, and perfectly lovely.

Sadie walked to the front door, put down her backpack, and lifted the knocker. She let it drop once, twice, three times. While it echoed, *thud-thud-thud,* she realised that the knocker was a goblin's head with a ring through its nose. *If this were a magic story, that goblin would wink at me.* Except it didn't. Sadie was safe.

No one answered. After a bit, Sadie put her backpack on again, turned the crystal handle, and pushed the door hard. It opened just enough. She went inside.

There was so much to see inside the Strange House. There were little rooms and big rooms and rooms with Christmas decorations and rooms with roaring fires and rooms all dressed in purple and rooms that shone with light. There were corridors round every corner, and stairways in odd places, including one with a Harry Potter room underneath.

*Later. I'll work it out later. Now I have to choose my bedroom.*

She felt a bit like Goldilocks. The first bedroom was too big. It was empty and it echoed. She didn't want to sleep there, but there was a rug in the middle of the floor, all creams and reds and flowers and flowing patterns. Sadie had to dance on that rug. After Sadie had finished her dance, she looked around again. Nup, still too big. She picked up her backpack and moved on.

The next room was boring. It was neat and tidy. It had a good bookshelf and the books on that bookshelf were her sort of books. But the room made her sleepy. Sadie moved out of there quickly.

After that, there was an icy room decorated in dark blue and silver. The bed had hangings and posts and there was a big glinting mirror. She really didn't like the look of that mirror. She shivered. Time to look for another.

The next room was just right. It was narrow and high-ceilinged and furnished in warm colours. There was the sweetest, neatest writing desk she had ever seen, tucked gently into a corner. Lots of places to sit and little bookshelves filled with good books. There were other things on shelves: trinkets and seashells and little dancing dolls. Two chests of wooden drawers lined the long wall.

On the top of one chest of drawers was a rosebud. She ran her fingers along it: perfectly flat. She examined the flower—it looked as if it would blossom any minute. Sadie peered very closely indeed, and saw that the bud was made out of different woods. If she stayed here long enough, she thought, maybe the bud would blossom.

There was a little pale blue door in the wall. Sadie could turn the door handle without stretching. She left that door for later.

The windows were all on one side, and they looked out over

the trees. Sadie opened one and peered out. The twisty tower was on her left and quite close. Sadie couldn't remember going upstairs. It didn't matter. She didn't need to find the kitchen yet. She had two types of sandwiches and a drink in her backpack. She could stay in her lovely, complicated little room until the new people came. All she needed was a bathroom.

She followed her ears and discovered a big, steamy bathroom with white fluffy towels just one door away. It beckoned her: Come, have a bath in my tub. The tub was made for the children of giants, and one side of it was lined with bottles. Bubble bath bottles and bottles of salts. Crimson and cerulean and deep purple. Sadie collected colours and she enjoyed naming those bottles. No sisters or brothers to share with. No hot water running out. And she could play in the bath as if she were still little, because no one was around to tell her off. Sadie sighed in perfect happiness.

She went back to her room to eat her sandwich.

Hiding the rosebud was a letter. The envelope said "Sadie".

Dear Sadie (the letter said),

Welcome to the house of your dreams. There is paper and there are notebooks and there are pens in this chest of drawers. Choose your favourites. You can take them with you when you go.

Write about your explorations. Write the stories you tell yourself. Learn this room—it will hold the stories you wish to tell. Explore the house: it will give you the courage to explore your own imagination when you leave.

Enjoy being alone. Being alone contains special stories.

Tomorrow afternoon you will share the house. Don't be scared, even if things change. Don't forget to keep writing.

Welcome to the House of Dreams.

Sadie nodded wisely to herself again. She investigated the

drawers and spread all the paper out and all the pens. She put the papers and books she didn't like back neatly. The rest she piled on a corner of her pretty desk. She tested all the pens and pencils, too. The ones she intended to keep she made a pattern with, right next to the rosebud.

After that, she ate the cheese sandwich.

The last thing she did before taking her bath was to choose a pen and a pink notebook, sit down at the desk, and start writing.

*I have the whole of today to explore the House. I don't know what I'll find. I can't start my exploration yet. First, I have to tell you how I came here, to the Strange House that calls itself the House of Dreams.*

Bettina was always Sadie in the dream, until today. When she was a teenager, Zelda and Melissa were the other two. Melissa was Maribelle, of course, "m" for missing things, was what they'd called her when she was a kid.

Today she thought, "That's wrong."

Zelda was Sadie. Things happened right for her. Life didn't get in the way. And she was the one who thought things and made lists and wrote everything and had a special pen. Mari was Melissa still. That went without saying. Which left Kylie.

Bettina trusted this kind of dream, because she'd tested it. For her to be Kylie, the colourless one who ran away … that was wrong.

Not wrong. When something like that happened in a dream, it could be challenged. Sometimes the challenge happened in her everyday, but this one was special. There would be something important, and it would include all three of them. If the dream was right, Zelda would find out everything as she did, and research, and write it all up in glorious prose. Challenging the dream might mean a change in their relationship.

Still, she couldn't challenge anything until they arrived together, outside the Strange House.

Last night in her dream, the Strange House had changed.

That was one of the reasons she'd read her story aloud. Instead of a wall and the street near home, the house was behind a big gate. You couldn't see past the trees, but there was a person looking out of the trees and that person cast a shadow far bigger than it should be.

That change gave Bettina hope that she wouldn't be the one to run away. That she would have her adventure. Bettina smiled. Even when she distrusted her art, she knew her dreams. She knew the ones that were her mind wandering at night, or that were emotional trails left by the day. She always knew which dreams reflected the world outside. Those were the dreams that needed deciphering, and she was on the way to deciphering this old dream. It had happened before. A dream changed when it was about to happen.

Bettina smiled in expectation.

---

Melissa was more than somewhat nervous. She didn't mind Hal watching her work usually. It reassured her. Made her feel safe and loved. This time, though, she wondered if the weird would work if he watched. Or if it had just been a fluke and they'd have to turn it into a joke.

Hal and she had bought a special table so that she could set up by herself. She pulled out her equipment from under the worktable. It was smooth and clever and made her feel independent. *I* am *independent,* she thought. *At least in my work. We worked to make my work work.* Melissa set it up for classic marbling slowly, with caution and care, making bad jokes in her mind the whole while. Nothing different to usual. Not yet.

"Pick the colours you want. Not too many," she said to her husband. "Also, I need to do a few sheets of the usual before we can move to the maybe-unexpected."

Hal chose two colours. Yellow and orange. Melissa created some mottled sunshine. She put the sheets aside to dry.

Then she moved to her pile of paperbacks. Those poor books were bereft and needed love. No covers on those paperbacks, just white paper. The ink in the tray had become a blurred, tangled web. It wasn't easy to use a whole book the way she treated a single piece of paper, but covering it with floating paint took seconds. Melissa laid the paperback to dry and the water and paint flowed off gently down the slopes.

Hal asked, "Should I flatten it?"

"It's really odd," Melissa said. "But this whateveritis doesn't work when the book's flattened. Besides, flattening is not good for the spine. But it's okay. We're watching paint dry."

"Ha, ha," said Hal.

They watched the paint dry.

One the way to becoming dribbles on the drying table, the paint changed colour and texture. The drips and drops gently formed a single picture on the cover and that single picture was …

"What's that book about?" Hal asked urgently. "Does the story match the cover?"

"Bingo!" Melissa said triumphantly. "Got it in one."

The book was *When Marnie was There* and the picture that had created itself from the yellow and orange was full of green and blue and delicate black lines. A faded child looked out over solitary sand to a house across a lake. It was impossible. Elegant and subtle and beautiful. But impossible.

"I want to say, 'Look, I'm magic'," confessed Melissa.

"Do you know how it happens?" Hal was handling it well, Melissa thought. Much better than she had the first time.

"I thought it was when I hurt. You know, high pain day creates magic. Present from somewhere crazy to make my world beautiful. But I can do it anytime. Only two books a day.

One tray. And I have to have the tray at the right level of swirl. Used, but not overused."

"Do another one," her husband pleaded. He was like a child with the biggest treat, just out of reach and only for him.

"Pick a book." Melissa indicated the big stack in the corner.

Hal almost bounded over to the books and riffled through them, choosing one, then another, then, finally, "*Half a Sixpence*!" he exclaimed, and handed his wife an old paperback.

"It calls itself *The History of Mr Polly*," she corrected him.

"It became a musical or a film. Both. A musical film. And it's HG Wells. Can't go far wrong with HG Wells." Melissa opened the book and, starting at one end, covered the front and the spine and the back cover with a slow, curved, dipping movement. It emerged yellow and orange and white, with swirls. She kept it open and laid it with the cover up, and they watched the scene develop. A man on a bicycle on a grey road, with grass all around and a blue, blue sky.

"How is this even possible?"

"It isn't," Melissa said bluntly. "Look at the first papers I did. You chose those colours."

"I did, too." Hal looked smug as he admired the beautiful golden patterns on the sheets of paper.

"I'm going to print poems on those papers, I think. If you don't mind offering up your poems for sacrifice again. You wrote a lovely one about sunshine last Sunday, which would match these so beautifully."

"Money into holiday fund?"

"Of course," Melissa said with dignity.

"You can't sell the books, though, can you?"

"Maybe. Maybe not. Probably not. I'm not the artist. Besides, I want to see if the pictures last. That pile of novels are ones I got for nothing because they didn't have covers, but I was told they were worth reading. All the good stories."

"So these can be ours," said Hal.

"That's what I was thinking. That way we can find out what it's all about before doing anything stupid. I can cover costs and make a regular income from the normal work. Not much, though."

"Why not much?"

"I don't have the control I did. I'm fine on good days, but less fine on bad. I'm going to create a big stash of pictures to carry me through in case of bad, so that there's always something for sale."

"Good idea," said Hal. One of the things she loved about him was his willingness to accept she needed to pull her weight. Pay for her own medicine, her own treats, and her share of the holidays. In her perfect world, she could do more, but even paying application fees was becoming difficult. She knew that at some stage those books might have to be sold, but … she didn't want that.

"We need a special bookshelf." Hal's mind went back to the exotic and impossible. Melissa loved how happy it made him. His happiness made her heart ring with joy.

"In our bedroom?" asked Melissa. "Where no one but us sees them?"

"I was thinking …" He became hesitant. "I was thinking the man cave. I have a bar I don't use."

"You use it! You've got drinks and glasses and you restock. I've seen you! And you've invited me to drink with you!"

"Yes." His agreement was intentionally drawn out. Ocker. *Yairs*. "But that's just the top. Where the glass and mirrors are. Everything hidden is empty."

"If you don't mind," said Melissa, "that would be safer. We use the bedroom for coats when we have a dinner party."

"I use the man cave then, too, but I'm the only one who goes behind the bar."

"You're as worried as me?"

"I'm worried because it's strange and wonderful. I'm going

to do some research and find out what it is, without giving you away. I don't want you to sell any of these until we're certain it's not dangerous."

"Dangerous?"

"Deals with the devil, maybe. Or more magic floods us. I don't even believe in magic." Hal said this confidently, as if the lack of magic was a buttress in his life, yet he had accepted those books instantly.

"I don't, either," she answered, smiling. "It may disappear as quickly as it came."

"Then we have the books, unless they fade."

"Then we still have the books, just they'll be boring again."

"The outside is boring. The inside is beautiful."

"That's it, isn't it? That's what the magic does. It shows the inside on the outside. I wonder how, though, and if it's my tray or my paints—"

"Or you," Hal finished quietly. "I'm going to lay odds it's you."

"Why?"

"Something my grandmother told me. I'll ask the family if I can share. Get back to you. We didn't sort out dinner ahead tonight, did we?"

"We did not. And today I can't cut or slice or wash dishes. I hate pain days."

Hal grinned. "I feel lazy. Let's get takeaway."

"The pain has only just kicked in. I wonder if the covers are linked to good days?"

Both gazes floated back to the drying books with their pictures. Watercolours. Despite the paint, not fine art. More … real. Not photographic. Watercolours showing the world.

"I had a thought," said Melissa.

"What?"

"If it's me and not my equipment or the paint, I might be able to do it with the camera. Or I might not. My camera has a watercolour setting, though, so I want to try. It's not real watercolours, but it's fun. I like fun."

"Now?"

"Not for a bit. I want to see more of what happens with the books. And I want to get some rest."

"I wasn't going to say you look pale." Hal sounded almost defensive. "I was going to ask you if I could make us some coffee."

"I wasn't accusing you. I was being surprised that I didn't notice the fatigue coming. This was so interesting that I overrode the pain."

"Which isn't good."

"Which is why I'll lie down now."

"Coffee?"

"Make it the slow way and I'll get up and join you."

"See you in a half-hour, then." He gave her a cuddle and let her lie down on the daybed. That was, after all, why she had one in the workroom.

Melissa wanted to pick up one of her books, but it was too much. She lay there and let waves of pain and ache and discomfort roll through.

# SEVEN

I'm not going to do this as a diary. I keep writing as if it's a diary, but I can't. Too much everything. I'm going to write down deep personal thingummies, when I can. Everyone says, "Get a counsellor." But all the counsellor can do is be there for me as a conduit. That's what happened last time, with the psychologist. This journal can do that, too. Too. As well. Equally. Maybe not equally. Maybe better.

One thing I hate about being ill is that no one believes it unless I share it all with them, and even then they don't act on it. My nice neighbour said he'd pick me up today so I didn't have to walk two miles with the bus strike when Hal was the other end of town. He picked me up and then he went to two different supermarkets and the petrol station. I wasn't quite as tired as I would've been if I had walked. My ankles weren't as protesting. I could walk slowly and I can write slowly. But I hurt.

And there was no medicine. If he had said, "I'll pick you up, but it'll be an hour before you get home," I would've packed a bottle of water and the right meds. No worries. One deals. But now I'm frazzled and I hurt at the edges and I have to lie down for two hours. If I don't, there will be a pain avalanche. I'm losing half a day because my neighbour was nice and picked me up.

That's why I'm writing instead of going to bed. I need to get this out of my system so that it doesn't cause another kind of avalanche. An emotional one. I hatehatehate being at the service of people who want to help. I hatehatehate the need to feel grateful for hurting and if I took this to bed, I'd pay for it bigtimebigtime.

Now I won't. I've been rude about my nice neighbour here, and I can sleep off the physical problems. And it will only be an afternoon lost, not three whole days. This is good, for I have plans for tomorrow.

# EIGHT

Dreams. That was what the conversation was all about. Bettina talked about her own dreams and how they reflected reality and sometimes predicted it. She gave her best example. Or rather, her clearest example.

"One time," Bettina said, feeling as if she was telling a fairy tale, "I dreamed that I had a big family that demanded everything from me. They invaded my whole life and turned into bees, swarming around me. I thought I was the queen bee and I tried to fly, but couldn't do anything. Then I thought, 'What if I feed them?' So I fed the bees. The table outside was full of cake and pastries and fruits and the bees buzzed around the table until they found chairs and then they became the family again. I sat at the head of the table."

"Yes?" asked Zelda.

"That was the dream. What happened was that I ended up calling the kids my children, and they started calling me Mum."

"Even though you've never even had a real relationship with their father. I'd wondered about that."

"The oldest left home and asked me if I could help with his washing. That was fine. Both kids started to visit regularly and ask things. That was fine, too. The bees buzzing around was when they started telling me all about their birth mother. That was not so fine. One day I made them a big afternoon tea, and the older said, 'We'd better stop upsetting you.' I asked, 'Why?' and he said, 'Because whenever we upset you, you use salt where there should be sugar.'

'How did we upset her?' his sister asked.

He turned to me and looked me straight in the eye and said, 'We tell her things that hurt her. Like the things we find out about our birth mother.' This was so true. I'd cry all night because of the things I was told."

"What things?" asked Zelda.

"Horrible things," said Bettina. "Those children are much better off without her, if even half what they tell me is true. I'm not sure it is, though. I don't know. I don't want to know. My kids thought I needed to know."

She brought Zelda back into her tale.

"At the table that afternoon, the youngest complained quite plaintively, 'But she needs to hear them.'

'Why?' he asked, and none of us had an answer.

I remembered the dream then, and I sat at the head of the table and said, 'When I sit here, I don't want you to talk about these things because they'll upset me. When I sit in the middle of the table, we're fine. Does that work?'

And it did, and the dream told me what would happen and solved everything."

Zelda was patient, but not understanding. Bettina tried to explain, "This is like your work on mythology and magic."

"You have Celtic dreams?" Zelda didn't like talking about her work with her old friend. It sounded to Bettina as if she was talking about it, but she simplified it and pretended it wasn't crazy-tangled and deep so that she wouldn't have to say anything at all. Several of the other staff didn't follow this simple rule and ended up teaching every day of their lives.

"Living 101" was Zelda's secret term for this polite obfuscation. She'd already told Bettina, many times, that she didn't carry her work with her all the time, that she needed breaks, so patience was all Bettina would get.

What Zelda saw as patience, Bettina saw as switching off. Zelda was good with listening to problems, but not good about this stuff. Normally, she wouldn't talk about it.

It was private. And it was special. And it showed a shape of the world most people didn't see. But Zelda had known about it when they were children. Their dares depended on Bettina's dreams, and when Bettina had a bad dream, the three friends would cancel plans.

Bettina had always thought that this is what had led Zelda into her career, but Zelda didn't remember that aspect of their childhood. She had a selective memory. Bettina tried one more time to explain.

"Not that. You write about the links between mythology and daily lives. How they influence each other and tell us who we are and what we can be. My dreams are like that, but come to life."

"I can't see it, I'm afraid," Zelda said, polite but dismissive. "You need to do your own project. Not piggyback on my research. It'll mean more to you."

"My project is how my dreams affect life. Not just my life."

"Then write that up. Put it in as art and story. That means you don't need to find an academic underpinning." Zelda had put on her model teacher voice, professorial garb dominating her voice. Bettina instantly gave up. If Zelda was instructional, then nothing would work.

"How about if I link to illness?"

"You've been ill enough," Zelda said thoughtfully. "Pain must seep into your subconscious and shape your dreams."

"Art and story …" Bettina thought out loud.

"You can't do my research at a retreat in any case," Zelda

pointed out. "For my fellowship," she was talking as if she already had one, "will depend on research I've already done. Writing it up in a simpatico environment."

"Why is this place so simpatico for you?"

"It's … people tell stories about it. They're to do with magic and culture and visiting other worlds."

"I don't get it."

Zelda tried again. "When these retreats come up, everyone talks about the work they did while they were away, and how transformational it was and how challenging it was and how it changes things." Her fascination shone through even as she lost her more sophisticated speech. No professorial garb—this was the Zelda that Bettina had always known. "And they don't talk about magic anymore. It's as if they've taken a vow of silence. Except they've all taken different vows. Some hate the place. Some protect it with their lives. Some don't want to believe anything and spread silence around it as a way of making sure it's not taken seriously. All the reactions are large, and quiet, and each is different and … it's a legend in the making, this house. I don't know how the family that owns it does this. I want to find out."

"So, your writing is just an excuse."

"Not in any way. I have to finish this book, and two weeks' focus will make a giant dent in it. I need published research for work and I have a publishing deadline and all the rest of it. The mystery is a bonus. A perk."

"A perk," repeated Bettina. She could see why Zelda wasn't interested in her dreams. The reality of magic was extra. A perk.

She sounded out the idea a bit further. "You don't mind me trying to prove that my dreams are special."

"My dear, they're special to you. They always have been. That's what you're exploring."

Bettina didn't know whether to rejoice at the support or be repelled at how little Zelda had taken in over all these years. She wondered about Melissa. Maybe it was Melissa who had believed. For someone had. One of the two must have listened and trusted, for otherwise why would anyone have acted on the dreams?

Those dreams had saved their lives three times.

It had been so very long since she'd seen Melissa. Her old friend hadn't moved, she didn't think. Still at the same place, with the same husband and surname. She popped a brochure about the house and its fellowships into the mail. No cover note. Bettina didn't want anyone saying, "Why did you send me this thing?" Not even Melissa.

Melissa would only have a couple of weeks to apply for this round and probably didn't have enough art as an adult. Her craft was interesting in its way, but would it be enough? Melissa didn't talk about that kind of thing when they spoke. She'd been the most artistic as a child, but that was different. *We're all different as adults,* Bettina told herself dreamily as Zelda and she went to the cash register to pay. *I would like it if we all went to the Strange House together this time.* That dream of the Strange House wasn't real. She knew it. It was a children's dream and not even the way she'd written it down was real or authentic or good in any way. Still, it made her think of this house near Robertson and it made her want the three of them as adults to revisit important things.

"Let me know next time you're in town." Zelda issued this as a command, as she always did.

"Of course," said Bettina, as she always did.

Bettina didn't precisely forget conversations with Zelda, but she moved past them quickly. She volunteered at a local charity shop, and this time she turned her attention to work the moment she hung up the phone. Bettina worked five hours a week there, and she would tell anyone who asked that it kept her grounded. The reality, however, was that it told her she was real.

She loved her art, but the art world required manoeuvres and contacts and arrangements. From time to time she looked at Melissa's Etsy shop with her charming (but not terribly difficult) work and thought, "This would be easier." She was determined to have a classic career, however.

Art didn't make her a full income, even though she had reached the stage where she could sell a fine work for a fine amount of money. The rest of her money she made through teaching in the evenings. Fifteen students at a time. Her mind was in a different space for that, too, and she wasn't sure that it was her natural space. It kept her going, however, as did private students.

It not only kept her going, it helped her explain why there was no husband or wife and why her children had fallen into her life unexpectedly. Gender neutrality was a great theory, but it wasn't what she had. She was female and simply not obsessed by sex.

This should've led to a more straightforward existence, but some people took advantage of it and so much of everyday was dependent on relationships and so many of those relationships depended on rather more than holding hands and smiling nicely that it left Bettina very lonely. Or very burdened by others.

When she was alone, these days, she was lonely. Bettina sometimes talked aloud to herself, to sort things out, and today was no exception. It was because the children weren't with her and she'd lost the capacity to be silent. Or maybe she never really had it.

"I'm adrift," she said. "All the boats are for people who have strong sexual proclivities." All the fighting was to get life for those who were gendered differently. She didn't complain about that. They needed to be safe and loved. Everyone needed that. Besides, she didn't actually suffer.

She felt it ought to be a lack. Something she was missing. But it wasn't. It really wasn't. Even the doctor, after ten years of sending her down rabbit holes and ten years of creating illness in her body where none existed just to give her a greater sex drive and a greater desire for normal life, even the doctor after ten years had admitted that it was part of her. "Try dating apps," the doctor suggested.

"Are there dating apps that don't assume physical relationships immediately?" asked Bettina.

"I have no idea," said the doctor. "But you don't need to be alone."

"I'm not alone. I've got my art." This was bravado. She'd had housemates at various times with various consequences. She really didn't want to be with anyone. Not unless it was a real relationship. That mythical thing she'd failed at four times.

"I'm adrift," she said to herself again, accusing her memories of cutting her loose from humanity. "Not well, but not dangerously ill, or even severely ill. My illness gets in the way, but it won't kill me. It's thrown me off a normal path."

She had no idea whether it had done this or not, honestly. She had no idea how she became the person she had become. No, that wasn't true. She'd been treated for her lack of sex-interest and it had triggered symptoms, but that was the only way those two things were linked.

"I'm adrift," she said to herself, meaning her soul, not her body. She really did know her body now. Just had to accept it.

Apart from her art, she hadn't the faintest idea what she should do with her life. The things she did—the volunteer work, the dinners with old school friends—all these were because she thought she ought to do them. They helped fit her into a place where her identity was less questioned. It was valuable, but it was not Bettina.

After all these years, Bettina wasn't certain she knew who she was. She'd tried all the usual things and they hadn't helped and right now she was lost.

Those aches and pains she had most days weren't her either. They were part of her physical self, but didn't impact on the internal self. She hoped that snark about people, where she put them down in all the verbal ways she could find, she hoped that wasn't here. But she didn't know about that. She kept in touch with Melissa and used a softer snark on her. Melissa was kept in her place. And Bettina felt a twinge of guilt about this. Melissa wasn't entirely well all the time, Bettina knew. And yet Bettina still had to reduce her to the right size.

That was stupid. Melissa would never be competition. Bettina didn't have to be petty about it. It was all kinds of wrong that an old friend should walk in her special place, but Melissa didn't know it was her special place when she had given up music. Or maybe she did. Maybe she walked on over because she knew someone who did art. Bettina.

It was always like this in Bettina's mind when Melissa appeared. Circles and turgidity and mild self-torment. It came down to Melissa not being quite aware enough and not giving her enough space.

If she had enough space, she'd feel her life was under control. That was it.

There had to be more to it than that, though. Bettina spent the afternoon and evening going through all her boxes of old trinkets and photographs, trying to get a bit more insight into who she was.

Zelda was in all of them, but not Melissa. Of course not. But Zelda was supportive and Melissa was … Melissa. Not actually wrong. Just not quite right. Bettina wanted to think "Not quite there"—that Melissa was the one who was adrift, but Melissa never looked adrift. She invented most of her illness, Bettina was sure.

With these thoughts foremost in her mind, Bettina found a picture of the three of them, just before the threesome broke up. Bettina herself was ashen. Pale blond and grey-eyed and skin that never tanned and never burned. Zelda was tall and robust and had a graceful figure and stared straight at the camera from blue eyes and had that slightly sexy smile she put on when looking at anyone other than Bettina. "I'm Zelda's safe place," Bettina realised, then looked at Melissa. Melissa looked like her ancestors. Curly dark hair, big golden-brown eyes. Greek or Italian.

She was Greek and she was Italian and she had a dab of Irish. Zelda was all British, and Bettina herself was mostly from the far north, but with a touch of Scottish. None of their names matched their looks, the trio had claimed at primary school, but it wasn't true. Melissa's name captured her ancestry and her sweetness. This was why she was still occasionally around. She had a quality that made everyone just a little happier to be with her.

*I'm fixated on an old school friend. That's not me. I'm turning my brain half-off again. I don't like that. It's not me, either.*

Bettina decided she should stop questioning herself and go back to the big dream. The one Zelda had persuaded her out of, five years before.

*I will get that PhD and I will find a way of turning my intellect on when I need it and especially for my art and I will make it work.*

In that moment, everything came to her and was clear. She would find a way of ordering the dreams that so disordered her existence. She would do that PhD and not become an academic. It was income for a few years and a learning tool. A good learning tool. She would solve the dreams before then and use the PhD to translate the concept of dreaming and art into a fine and beautiful reality.

Where she'd gone wrong when she applied without Zelda's support was putting in the Dreamtime. She'd taken someone else's culture to reinforce her own, and she didn't need to do that. One great-grandmother did not make Bettina Aboriginal, she thought, not for the first time. It was a moment of wistfulness that had put that reference in her project outline and that moment of wistfulness had lost her the funding. She knew this. There was something she hadn't known, however. For the first time, she realised that she never thought about that great-grandmother when she looked at her own ancestry. A token shoved into a project outline was not the same as knowledge.

*Another project. I can get sponsorship for that. Find out where my great-grandmother came from and talk to those people. Find out what I've lost in becoming what I am and who I am.*

Turning into an academic wouldn't solve anything. Looking at Zelda's workload and how her inner drive ate her whole life made Bettina shudder. But right now, Bettina only had the externals for life. A PhD would help give her those internals.

She reframed her earlier application to include the need to discover the Dreamtime she had lost. She quietly submitted it to the university she'd talked about it with, originally, the one that accepted applications at any time of the year. It wasn't as hard to do as she had expected. The writing for her application for the retreat had trained her. Two weeks to get the idea of translating dreams in train—and then three years to live it. That was what she wanted and needed. Her dreams would have a real place in her life. And she would be able to translate their meaning and to endure them—no, more than endure, to use them. She would no longer be at the mercy of either the dreams or the illness. And she'd know a bit more about how she fitted into Australia.

Bettina celebrated all of this with the end of a bottle of wine.

---

The room at the nursing home was a bit bleak. It looked homey, but still bleak. The objects her mother-in-law had chosen to keep were small, and passing. It was as if she felt she wouldn't have long there. Melissa could see it as a way of handling pain and illness, but there was the everything else. And the cost. It would take all Hal's mother's savings and the house to keep her in this place for more than a few months.

"I saved so much from my first job," said Hal. "Right place, right time."

"Personally, I want to avoid needing a nursing home. I shall swim to Antarctica instead."

"You're going to take the promotion, then?"

"I want to," Hal admitted. "But it means I can't be here for you as much."

"In a way you can," she pointed out. "A lot of things you did for your mum are now being done by the nursing home. You will visit her and ring her, but that's not as time-consuming or as energy-draining."

"That's true." Hal cheered up a little. "And we can still take her your cooking. She loves that. And your art."

"Sit down and do the maths. Put aside a little from the extra income so that I can take taxis or get a cleaner in when you can't be here."

"Leave it with me," said Hal. "I'll find a solution for all of us. Now is the time to make that decision, anyhow."

"'Cause?"

"Mum says I can. We can take what we want and the rest gets sold or given to other rellos, and the house gets sold."

After enough time had passed, Melissa broached the most difficult subject.

"Can I help?" she asked.

"What?" Hal's mind was entirely on the book he was reading.

"With your mother's stuff. With life."

It took a while and much discussion, but Melissa was allowed to help. Immediately, she helped sort through the boxes of books Hal had already brought home. She noted (but said nothing) that one was missing from the top box, and she smiled. Book after book went into the "must read" pile.

One left Melissa thoughtful. It was a volume given to Hal's mother when Hal was thirteen. "I bought this with my earnings," the inscription declared. "This means you must read it."

"Did your mother read science fiction before you did?"

"Not a bit," declared Hal. "I converted her. I gave her some Clarke."

"Look," said Melissa. "Clarke. From you."

"Oh my god," said Hal. He turned it over and over and reverently read a few lines. "I like it when life turns full circle," he said.

That evening, the couple took one more thing to his mother, because they decided that there was space for one more book in any new home. She herself was not in agreement. Also, she wasn't in a good way at all. She ripped the covers off the book and threw it out the window. What she had was "possible Alzheimer's", and on days like this, whatever was wrong inside her brain was not possible at all. *Strictly impossible* was how Melissa described it to herself. The actions hurt her because they'd hurt Hal.

"The inscription's still fine," Melissa said when she recovered the book. "I'm sorry it was such a bad night for your mum, though."

"She ripped up my childhood," Hal joked uncomfortably. He shucked off the pain and a thought lit his eyes with unholy glee. It didn't take much to persuade Melissa to put that novel through cover creation next.

# NINE

Tea saved me today. If I had someone who could've made me that cup earlier, I would've been saved earlier. Now I understand why some people aren't atheist. I shall have a break and return to this later.

Later:

Oh God. They're doing that damned RU OK thing. Today was a good day till I saw that. I'm dealing. Doing stuff. Not too much pain. And I'd put it all on the back-burner and got on with everyday until some damn idiot rang me to ask if I was okay. Now I'm not, thank you, for you just made me realise how difficult my everyday is.

You don't help me. You put the burden of mental illness on me. And I'm only mentally ill because I'm physically ill and no one around me really deals with it except my husband. I've got to handle the help they need because I let them know I'm ill. So no, I'm not okay. Today is officially a bad day.

I said, "I could do with a bit of help sometimes, but I'm not actually suicidal." And they told me all about their day. Didn't offer anything except information about themselves. Didn't really want to help. Wanted to feel good about themselves. This is a shame, because, actually, I need help.

I'd love the deep housework done. I really really want to live in a clean place. To not worry about the fact that I can't get anything electrical serviced until Hal discovers it hasn't been serviced for a decade. To have someone sweep the outside without me nagging. To be able to pay someone to do the things without being told with that grand sincerity that with only one of us working we needed to be careful about money. That would make me more okay than RU OK. Or it would if people didn't turn their effort to be virtuous into an emotional burden for me. "I'm doing this because I'm wonderful and you're an invalid. You shouldn't really exist but I'm making it possible because look, I'm washing your dishes while I tell you how to live." And it's not Hal's fault. He is much better than RU OK people. It's only sweeping and electricity, really.

I. AM. NOT. A. VICTIM. Just sick. Nothing more and nothing less.

The advantage of this being a better day than average is that I can get incandescent and it doesn't send me to bed. Being able to emote freely is a lovely luxury.

Today I hate Bettina, for she did this. On the telephone. Because she was thinking of me.

I'll get over it. Life's too complex to hate friends for being sodamnstupid. If she's not capable of asking what would help and what wouldn't and if she's so emotionally sensitive that all she can do is hurt when she means to help and my world is so small that I can't just move on by … that's another mark on the black side of the ledger that's due to me being sick.

Will chocolate hurt today? I think not. Time to put the book away.

# TEN

Melissa was tired. Not normal-tired, but so tired by the evening that thinking of anything pushed her beyond exhaustion. She sat very still and wished she hadn't got out of bed that day.

"You slept properly last night," Hal had nagged once.

"Fourteen hours," was what Melissa said. "And I was too tired to turn my head on the pillow. I have the fatigue back."

"How do you want us to handle it?"

"I'll sit here until I can photograph. Today can be a photography day."

"I'll make you lunch alongside mine, then, so that all you have to do is take it from the fridge. Don't beat yourself if you can't work."

"You know I will." Melissa's muscles grudgingly let her face pull forth a slight grin. Then the exhaustion overtook them and she sat there, silent, while Hal did the busywork.

Two hours before he returned, she finally took pictures. Not a lot, but enough so that she could claim she'd worked that day. It was a help. She wanted to thank God fasting for Hal's gift of the camera.

Hal came home and they talked. Melissa admitted she couldn't do the moving house stuff.

"I thought I could. I helped with the books, but I was pushing myself the whole way."

"You hate this?" Hal asked.

"Of course I hate this," Melissa snapped. "I hate being helpless so very much. I hate bad days with such a passion."

"Well, I hate the paperwork. I hate it with such a passion. And you can do paperwork on most days."

"I can," said Melissa. "I can do the paperwork here. I can do sitting, or even semi-recumbent. I want to help so very much. I'll do it while you're away and you can help with the sad remnants. I still hate this," said Melissa, "but I'll hate it less if you let me do the paperwork."

"Your illness sucks," Hal said honestly. "And sometimes it becomes unendurable. Let's get Mum's move out of the way."

"Okay," she said. In her mind was *These pictures are going to be for Hal. They're going to say something special to him, for I need to make up for this, for everything, for my whole damned life.*

Melissa hadn't been that certain about applying for this fellowship that had appeared temptingly in her email. She'd filled the form in anyhow. Time away made Hal's life less difficult. It would, this time, give him space to sort out his mother's stuff. That had to be done before it got out of control.

Hal never made her feel bad about it, but Melissa was an impediment.

She hadn't only applied for this one place. Every single fellowship, every single retreat, every single support she could ask for, she had applied for. They had done their share in pushing her over the edge.

The others had all returned negative responses. This was the only missing answer. The issue was not having heard.

*How could they plan everything that had to be done when there weren't so many choices? Should we ring? Should we consider some-*

*thing else?* These questions went back and forth between the two of them as part of their life-juggling. Nothing could be dismissed until a "Sorry, no" had been given.

Melissa distracted herself with her work on the books. She would create book covers that were abstract and convince herself she saw people in them. They could slide over a paperback and make it special.

"Look," she'd say to Hal. "This is for a Narnia book. What do you think?"

He would see what she saw. For Narnia, a lamp in a forest. For Middle Earth, a swirling and dangerous ring. For the brumby books, light shining on eucalyptus leaves.

"Books are portals into the world of the novel," she wrote in her description of the new category for her site. "Use these covers and you can go to the world of the book."

"Only if I have a hangover," argued someone in the site's comments, but everyone else bought them.

Melissa delved into her own dreams and added words to the website.

"Before I make these," she wrote, "I look into the novel. When I looked at my Narnia books, I wished I and my husband could be King and Queen of Narnia for a day. We wished that we had people to do all the housework for always, but for the rest of being royalty a very special day would give us forever-memories."

Hal looked at this and said, "Actually, I'd settle for a nice bottle of something."

They both got drunk.

The next day, Hal worried about Melissa to her face, because his hangover hurt. Melissa pointed out that hangovers were nothing more than her usual. In fact, it wasn't even a bad day for her.

"Oh my god," said Hal.

"That bad, huh?" asked Melissa. "Let me get you some painkillers and a glass of orange juice."

"If you feel like this every day," Hal said, not for the first time, "how do you avoid becoming an alcoholic?"

Melissa said obstinately, "I promised you I'd show you my reactions to things, even if they made you uncomfortable."

"Days like this I wish you reacted the way pop culture says you will. That way I can feel superior and helpful. Can I add hating social media to my list of things that are intolerable?" he asked.

"What is it?"

"Someone's telling you how to run your life."

"One day we'll tell the world that you're not sick and that I let you use my name on social media."

"And all the young men will stop explaining things to me as if I were a five-year-old," Hal said sadly. "And where would the fun be in that?"

---

"This is not the way to get my promotion," Zelda admitted to her one and only daughter. "I keep thinking that if I do, everyone will mistake me for someone junior."

"How do you figure that?"

"Why did we send you to the US anyway?" Zelda grumbled. "'How do you figure that' is not an Australian way of speaking."

"So?"

"So, if I become an associate professor, everyone will assume it's the same as an assistant professor."

"Like, you're a baby lecturer instead of an old hag?"

Zelda threw a biscuit across the table and the once-a-child-always-a-child caught it far too easily and ate it instantly.

"You're still starving?"

"Always. What's the problem you were talking about yesterday? You should list these problems and stick a bloodstained dagger in each of them to kill them when you're done."

"I've got enough publications in theory, but I need one more. Something glitzy."

Zelda was enjoying this conversation. Normally they talked about the problems in society and joked that they were the dread Social Justice Warriors. Zelda wanted to see the range of definitions used to describe Social Justice Warriors. Until she did, all she could do with the term was joke with her daughter, because they both cared so intensely about the state of the world. Yes, it was odd that the conversation now was about the state of her own career. Appallingly self-indulgent. She smiled.

Her daughter looked critically across, not deceived at all by that smile. She knew internal brain-wandering when she saw it, Zelda thought. "And when did this become a problem?"

"When I applied for that damn retreat that Bettina applied for. It makes my book real."

"And the contract that's waiting for you to sign didn't do that?"

"It didn't. And now I'm going to rural New South Wales, where they might not have internet."

"Oh god, you'll die!"

"Maybe. I've got to meet all my academic deadlines before I go. And I've got to finish almost all the book while I'm there, and get it sent to my editor two weeks later. Can't rely on online work at a retreat."

"But getting that fellowship solves everything. One book this year, one book next. And a fellowship."

"Maybe. Bettina's the famous one. She's the artist and I'm just the academic. Mine doesn't even have money attached."

"You've got a six-digit income. I bet she's got a low five-digit one. And you've got the job and you're getting a better one 'cause … fellowship! Glitz! And Cambridge University Press for your other publication since you dumped that lower-scoring publishing house and, and ..."

"Ssh about those publishing houses. It's ... just the way things work. I've made you into a shadow academic."

"And Dad made me into a shadow lawyer. Accept it."

"I maybe should just stay here and work. I can do it."

"Glitz! Good on the CV. Another tick for the promotion so that everyone can stop nagging you about your wealth because they think you're on much less."

"I'm not wealthy," Zelda excused herself, almost automatically. "And I work very hard. And I had to leave my favourite committee because the ugly one is more likely to get me that promotion. I sacrifice myself, you know."

"I'm going to stop advising you," threatened her offspring.

"Okay, I'll go. I'll do the wow-to-self thing. I'll add it to my application before I go and I'll get my promotion and finish the book and meet all my damn deadlines and it won't drive me crazy at all because you've already driven me forever-crazy."

"That's entirely right."

"Do you need to be driven anywhere?"

"Nah, I'm meeting Dad. He's been waiting outside for ten minutes."

"What're you mad with him about this time?"

"None of your business."

When her kitchen was quiet again, Zelda thought she should check the phases of the moon. She had intended to have a constant awareness of the moon, and develop an understanding of how women worked with the moon and question its relationship with portals, but mostly she forgot the actual object above her and did everything through her books. Her work was not the worse for that, but she always felt a bit guilty.

"Hah," she said. "It's a full moon again. Imagine. My kind of moon. A woman's moon and I'm a woman's woman. Precisely feminine. Femininely precise. The full moon might be my metaphor for a portal."

Or it might be a real one. Or it might not be anything at all. Her project wasn't about her own personal experience with portals and mysticism. It was how different parts of the Celtic world explored them. She'd spent two of the draft chapters that had won her a publisher explaining how the ancient Celtic world translated itself into modern life and how other scholars wanted to break it down by time and by region.

Zelda felt an odd little tugging. It was telling her to go in a different direction. But she couldn't. She had found her path, opened the door to it, and she was already walking it. At her last conference, she'd come out as someone who was following a trail bound by myths and old stories. Post-colonialism in Europe.

From Australia, one could see everything if one looked carefully and interpreted with wisdom. That was enough justification. She had to work out what resources she needed to take with her, what research had to be done before she left, and how the hell she was going to finish a year's work in the next four weeks. *In some ways, academia never changes,* she thought. *And I say this, me, on the brink of an everything-change.*

At that moment, the phone rang. It felt anticlimactic.

---

"Hi, it's Bettina."

"Oh, good, I was going to ring you. I heard about that fellowship," Zelda said.

"What happened?"

"I won one." Zelda turned this into a calm pronouncement. "The one with accommodation but no money."

"Me too," admitted Bettina. "That's why I rang. I won the flagship one."

"We can travel together. I'm on your way."

From the tone of Zelda's voice, Bettina guessed that Zelda already knew about both fellowships and had planned everything that needed planning. This was a problem. Bettina didn't like to correct her, but this once, Zelda was wrong.

"I've got to go south first. My mother left me something in her will, and I have to collect it from near Eden."

"Pick me up at Moss Vale, then."

"Unless I'm coming up on the coast road. It'd be nice from Eden."

"Moss Vale is better. A bit further for you, but we'd arrive together. Share a car." Yes, Zelda had made plans. Malleable, but not past a certain point. Some things never changed.

"Share a car?"

"The train goes as far as Moss Vale—I'd meet you there. It means my girl can have the car."

*Ah,* thought Bettina, for Zelda's insistence finally made sense. She put her thoughts of a leisurely drive on the coast on hold. She could visit the coast another time. The Pacific wasn't going to go away, after all.

"Okay," agreed Bettina.

"Thanks. I really want to leave her the car this time. She's old enough and responsible enough, and she's so scared about next year. I want her to have a bit of confidence before she reaches university."

---

They wrapped up the conversation by planning every detail of the journey. Zelda was thinking about her daughter, so the conversation wasn't as long as it could be. When she put the phone down, Zelda found that her mind was clear. These two weeks would be time off from worrying about her daughter, worrying if she'll get into university or whether she'd be stuck being taught by her own mother.

*It wouldn't hurt her if I had to teach her,* Zelda thought grumpily. But the girl wouldn't do Celtic studies, even though she adored them, nor would she do anything close to them, for she didn't want to create a family business or be taught by anyone her mother might have been rude to. Except it wasn't rudeness. It was a vigorous conversation. *Mind you, I'm pretty glad I don't have to bring that side of work home. Better if she goes somewhere else. It would've been nice to have her in my field, but ...* She wasn't sure about her daughter's other choice, which was physiotherapy. The health professions were her husband's area, and she didn't see why the statute of limited access only applied to her own subjects.

# ELEVEN

Fatigue creeps. I want to say "the fatigue". I most certainly want it not to creep. It affects how I react. When I'm not polite, when I'm angry and let that anger out through the floodgates of my mouth, that's a bit more of the fatigue, and a bit of me fighting that damned fatigue.

I got a letter from Bettina. It took two weeks to reach me. She was telling me about fellowships to that place in Robertson. Why does it tire me to even think that if I hadn't applied earlier, I would've missed it? And that I've missed it anyhow. Not knowing means I can't've got it.

If I weren't so very damned tired, it'd just be funny. I'd ring Bettina and say haha lookwhathappened.

I wish I could sleep off the fatigue pain carries.

I need to remind myself that this week I'm better than last week and that last week was better than the week before. I'm entering an almost-tolerable phase. I hope it lasts this time. And that it leaves the fatigue behind. Way, way behind.

# TWELVE

Calm, peace, one step and a click, then another step and a click. Bettina was playing an old-fashioned computer game in her sleep. The name escaped her, as names do when words are fleeting and of little import. She sat at her desk, the keyboard in front of her. It was slow and steady and very soothing.

After a while, she realised (as one does) that in a dream her hands were not doing much. Her dreamself said to her awake brain, "It's almost as if we aren't playing."

That was it. That was when she realised her hands were tucked neatly into her lap, each one protecting the other from … what would they be protecting from? She watched the game more closely.

Dreams where she was aware they were dreams gave clues. The clues and the awareness were two of the indicators that the dream was a real dream. That she needed to know what it meant and possibly to act on it. She moved her head toward the screen and blocked out everything except the computer game.

Each piece being selected had a pattern on it. A pattern that moved just before the click. Closer, she looked until a small group of pieces absorbed her complete attention.

Then she saw it. Faint faces on each piece. Some familiar, some not familiar. One grimaced. One (a very metrosexual male, slender and beautifully kempt) looked angry. One smiled. Bettina smiled back and the dream shattered. She found herself awake in bed, wondering, "Why did the smiling face on that tile look like me?"

It was a real dream. That was for certain. Until she knew all the people in it, however, she simply didn't have the material to interpret it. She hated dreams. She hated that they told her important pieces of her life and what it meant, and that sometimes she never did sort it out. The Strange House dream was the biggest and best example. It kept her in a part of her childhood. And it was important.

She hated her dreams on mornings like this.

Today she didn't have energy to hate. Today she had stuff to do. Life stuff. Today she was meeting with a representative of the family that owned the house she was going to visit. Dream consequences could wait. It was her day to be important. The flag fellowship person.

Most places used the material in a proposal to do all the advertising. This place had a member of the family talking to the flagship winner in any group, and that person would write it all up and tell the world about it.

His name was Adam. He didn't look like an Adam, this representative from Robertson. In fact, he looked exactly like a face from the dream. She'd planned to let the House people know the truth, and to see how they would react. After all, the House was described as strange and magic and special, but seeing him there—looking trim and metrosexual and very needy—made her cautious.

When he said, "Explain the dreams you talk about in your application," she slowed down and thought.

What came out surprised her.

"These are the dreams no one really wants to have. In my

imagination, they reflect the world as it's about to be and give us insights into special events. For instance, if I had a dream about this meeting today, your face might appear on a tile, or your whole body as a chess piece."

"And you'd understand what it meant?" There was something odd in the way he prodded. She was rather pleased she'd kept it pretend.

"Not really," she said, making all her dubiousness show through clearly. "I'd have to interpret it, and the better I interpret it, the more understanding and control I have over the world I walk into every day."

"Ah," he said, "so the paintings give that capacity to interpret to anyone who sees them."

"That's it," Bettina said confidently. "The question of whether they are real or not is moot. The key is letting someone interpret and see if they can understand the next picture from the hints given in the first."

"Fascinating," he said. "And so perfect for an exhibition. I'll suggest that we sponsor one when you're done. Your proposal should concern the translation of your dreams into real life, using the house and its gardens as settings. That should go down well," he said. "Very well."

Bettina waited for him to say something else. There was that element in the air. Anticipation. Almost, from his end, hope. But it didn't come. Whatever this guy was up to, it wasn't obvious yet.

"I'll see you in a few weeks," he said finally.

The rest of the afternoon was all messages. The doctor and the chemist and the supermarket, and she was fine for a month with all her checks and all her medicine. Her stepchildren, with whom she was perfectly fine now that her father had taken them back and admitted that walking out on all of them wasn't the best of things.

Her mouth tightened as she remembered, back when she

was well, that only Zelda had understood what was happening. Zelda and her divorce were quite different and not as complicated, but Zelda had still understood. Bettina had never married and never divorced; she just had honorary children. Thank god Zelda understood, for no one else did.

"They're my children," Bettina had explained. "Even if I didn't give birth to them. But I can't take care of them by myself and with no money and with all the problems and ..." She had been trapped at a crossroads, unable to move forward. Her dreams had faded and she had a day job and it was as if her whole life was a nothing. A big empty nothing. She didn't have any strength when she got home and the children suffered from it.

Now the only problem was not seeing them enough. Their birth mother paid her share and their father brought them up and Bettina had a life of her own.

Her marriage had been such a mess. The thing her husband said that still hurt was that Bettina wasn't suited to relationships. Why did he barge into her life in the first place, then? And what a godawful day for remembering it. She always had dreams about that time, and they followed their own rules and haunted her life for a week after.

All had been well, and recently, she'd not seen him at all. Before then, she'd seen him on a regular basis and her woeful ex would push Bettina to have sex and boast about his new girlfriend. And now, it was not quite that she'd "not seen him". He'd cancelled time after time. Today she found out what had happened. It was one of those explanations, where he threw three lines of explanation at her when he dropped something off. His girlfriend had walked out. Bettina wanted to say "Much yayness," but he was hurting and she couldn't make things worse. She had to make it as good as it could be, which was difficult.

That evening, she rang Zelda. Once a week they talked to

each other. Even when one of their lives was falling to pieces, they chatted. Most of the time they chatted about things other than lives falling to pieces and other than work.

The good thing about Zelda was she didn't talk about the bad things in life. She talked about her research and her life and the colour of the day and … Zelda talked. And she understood.

That was enough.

# THIRTEEN

It's a skin day. I don't write them down normally because they're part of other things. Always part of other things. A friend says skin days happen when we run out of spoons. They're the body saying we need to be less sick. I tend to agree with her.

When I get sick, my skin gets sick. If it's not too bad and on my face, I can hide it under powder and do work as usual, the way I always do. I shove being sick into the background and keep on going. On days like that, I wear cotton and soft clothes.

And why haven't I ever written this down? It's a minor thing, I guess. No biggie compared with everything else. It can happen when I'm moving toward a good part of one of the cycles, or can plague me at a bad time, so it's kinda an inconstant constant. And I can work with it. It isn't as if I'll infect anyone, after all. But if it's too bad … yeah. I disinfect it when it gets infected and I change clothes a lot and I wear certain types of clothes and I wince when someone pats me on the back if the problem is on the back this time and … now it's written down for the doctor. Some written and some dictated down and edited into sorta okay.

Today's not a writing kinda day, but I tried.

The sores I hate are the weeping ones. All the rest I can handle, in my own way. Except the ones that get in the way of sex. Those annoy both of us so much. We joke about it, because joking's how we get through, but oh my god it annoys us. And it hurts to sit and to wear pants and ... yeah ... mostly it annoys ...

Why am I telling myself this? I'm sick of being sick. I'm getting out my stuff and gonna marble paper for a bit. It's hard, but I need to find out if I can still do it. I miss my crafts. I thought I'd never say that. I thought singing was everything.

My drawer is empty. No more thank you presents. I hope no one needs thanking for helping me until I can go shopping. I hope there's money. Today is a day when everything is cast in iron: tough and dark grey. I want to be able to make presents again. Presents for everyone, every time. I want my damn body back.

I need bedrest. Not gonna happen for 90bloodyminutes. Can't take medicine till then and can't rest until the worst is under control. All I can do is sit at the computer and pretend I'm actively engaged in social media. Can't even play games when I'm like this.

In 90 minutes, I will take meds and everything will improve just enough for a bit of a sleep and then I'll be better for a bit and thinking about it is making it worse. Watched pots. Hurt.

I hate hurt. I hate clocks. I want the bath to pour itself and give me some pain relief without me having to damn well climb down into it and hurt my knees getting out of it. In my next life, if I'm stuck in a body like this, I want to be rich, please. To take away rough edges.

# FOURTEEN

Paris was a good dream. Paris was one of the dreams that made it safe for Bettina to go to sleep. Too many of the bad dreams, the real dreams that held horror, and she would never get to sleep. The thought that maybe tonight would be a Paris dream helped, always.

Last night's Paris was different. A train. A surface train and not the right kind. More like a tram. Space and seeing people she thought she knew who weren't people she knew at all. White with touches of dull green. Drab and plastic and soft metal and too much glass. She needed somewhere to stay and got out at a stop unexpectedly, hoping to find a cheap hotel. Crossed under a bridge where the landscape was rubble. After the trashed buildings, there was a square. Very Paris. Haussmann. Nineteenth-century. Stone and gilt solidity.

Someone came up to her and put arms around her. A stranger. They were both looking for somewhere to stay and they found a hairdresser. Bettina decided to stay there with another miscellaneous traveller, and found herself sleeping in the middle of the bed.

"Plenty of room," the hairdresser-who-rented-rooms said. "You don't have to know each other."

But it was cheaper than dirt and the haircut turned Bettina blonde and younger, with hair framing her face and settling softly on her neck, and it was all worthwhile. She woke up with the memory of leaving her body to take a puzzled look at herself, her solid chin and her wonderful haircut and brash blondness asleep in the middle of a triple bed.

She couldn't fathom what it meant at all. This was the biggest puzzle. She could prophesy weather from her dreams with no effort at all, but every other reading they gave her was obscure. Sometimes Bettina wanted to have great power from her dreams and sometimes she shrugged her shoulders and said, "Meh."

This morning, she was caught between the two.

# FIFTEEN

Today I'm dictating from bed. I'm only doing this because I must.

Today's a misery day. The doctor would tell me it's time to see a psychologist or counsellor, but that requires more energy than I have. She won't give me tablets for depression because she says it'll get better as I get better. Then, next visit, she admits I may not get better for years. Or ever. Not until we know more about things. And she sends me for tests and forgets the depression. I think, "Do I go back and remind her?" But what if she says "It'll pass" again? I shall stay in bed and whimper gently to myself instead.

Hal brought me hot chocolate when he came home for lunch. I'm over the worst of it. The miseries have subsided to their usual faint rumble. It makes it worse to talk about it at great length. It's like falling into a hole and exploring how deep the hole is rather than getting out of the hole.

This is why I stayed in bed this morning. I spoke with Bettina on the phone and she told me to be more active. I was too tired to explain.

Let me try something. A pronouncement. Here.

Whenever I get that bad, let me merely tell her (or someone else), "I have the miseries." I don't know if it will help me out of it faster or not, but it's worth trying.

Side effects can be bad. I saw that with a friend whose heart gave out because of the medicine she was taking for six other illnesses. The doctor forgot to check everything and she ended up nearly dead.

I'll write it down—"I have the miseries"—and document how often it's too bad to get out of bed. And the doctor will see it. I don't have to accept Bettina's medical advice.

I hate it that there are no easy means of handling my body and its crankiness. That all the procedures are for known and simple ailments. My friend who ended up nearly dead from heart trouble was much better with the heart trouble (why she survived) than with the six other things wrong with her, for the hospital knew what to do with the heart once it was diagnosed.

You can tell I'm feeling much better by the direction my complaints take. Now I'm angry. The hole is still there. The hole is always there when I have pain, so the hole is easy to fall into, every single day of my life. I shall try harder to avoid it. Though how I can do this on days when my physical strength fails and the pain overwhelms me, or when I've hurt in a gentle way for so long that I can't conceive of a life without the hurt, I have absolutely no idea.

Bettina's comment reminds me of something that happens so often. When I can drive, I park in the disabled parking spot because I'm disabled. I have a sticker on the car. The doctor tells me that I don't need to hurt so much, that it's okay to use a sticker and hurt less. She tells me and tells me and I always hate myself for parking there because there must be people who need it more. People who hurt more. I can drive. I can push the trolley to the car. And I can walk a little. Some days I can walk a lot. But she says that I don't have to hurt on the days I have to do things even when I hurt. So, I have a sticker.

I get yelled at for using the parking space. "You're not disabled," people tell me. "Get out and do some exercise."

The doctor suggested that I get a walking stick. I have a stick and I take it out of the car and pretend to use it, then people will stop yelling at me. I need to pretend to have a different disability in order not to be yelled at.

I want a Dantesque Hell and I want a whole level for people who make the lives of people like me worse by being noble warriors for those who may hurt more. That level can also include all the people who try to tell me what I should do to cure myself, or what parts of my life I should give up, or how Hal is so damned amazing for being able to handle all this and for every single person who wants to make themself feel great by making me feel like dirt.

Move on, now. Nothing to see. This is just an ordinary shopping day.

# SIXTEEN

Bettina's dream predicted thunder. The thunder took three-quarters of the day to arrive. This gave Bettina enough time to shop for a child's birthday, to finish the last of the sketches, and to write herself a series of very rude notes. She'd been putting off doing work and it was accumulating.

"What I want," she told her fifteen-year-old stepchild when she delivered the present, "is your sense of humour."

"Why?" he asked plaintively.

"My life would be so much more interesting if I was even half as funny as you are."

"How about I cut it in half and we share it?" He went to a drawer, took out a huge pair of invisible scissors, and pantomimed cutting something in half. "Here, eat this."

And she did and asked, "Am I funny yet?"

"Give it time," he said. "Give it time."

"I was hoping the scissors were to cut your height down a bit," she admitted. "I can't see past you anymore."

"Why do you want to see past me?"

"I like watching the window in case something comes up that would help my sketches. You're in the way."

"You do realise," he said with assumed patience, "that you've finished that set of things. And I know what you're going to do next."

"You do?" Bettina was fascinated.

"I do," he said confidently. "You're going to make a set of Tarot cards."

"Why Tarot cards?"

"My teacher said they're used to predict the future these days and they used to be used to gamble with. This makes Tarot the perfect set of cards."

"You know," said Bettina, "Tarot cards would be a very good outcome of my residency."

"You'll print me a set," he demanded.

"For Christmas," she promised. "As long as you show me how to use them."

"Which use?"

"Both. Christmas gives you time to learn."

"How did you know I had no idea?"

"Life is full of mysteries," Bettina said in the most droll voice she could find.

"Still not funny," her honorary son declared. "I'm taking back my sense of humour. I want that Christmas present, though. It'll be perfect."

# SEVENTEEN

The doctor wants a follow-up visit because she is worried about blood clots. "Just a small adjustment to your medication," she said on the phone, "and we're fine. I want to talk it through."

Blood clots terrify me. I was in hospital once because they thought they saw one on my lung. Twenty-four hours of peaceful misery in a white bed with whiteness all around.

I turned up to see the doctor, just as she asked.

She did a lot of talking.

The doctor wondered if I have fibro. "The original diagnosis took so long," she said, which was a very polite way of her saying that no one listened to me for years, "that it's possible. Overlapping symptoms can help us pinpoint different illnesses."

"Why didn't you think of fibromyalgia earlier?" I didn't remind her I'd asked about it. I wanted to.

"I was looking for one thing. Recent studies have shown that when symptoms include inflammation it's not unlikely to have more than one illness."

These aren't her words. These are mine, pretending to be her. I made it sound nicer, I hope. I was flattened but also … I dunno … It'd make sense if I had more than one thing wrong. If

I had symptoms that overlapped and my body was a Venn diagram.

Other people think that doctors cure things. These days I'm happy with a clear diagnosis and maybe something to quieten my symptoms.

Pain is a part of my life the way my right leg is.

Today is a translation day. I can choose my clothes, but I'm stuck with my right leg and I'm stuck with pain.

From now on, whenever the idiot side of life tries to take over, I shall declare a translation day and keep everything where it belongs.

Today it's easy. I can't walk much or do much, but as long as I'm sitting down, I'm fine. I can work! I can dream! I can't cook dinner.

"Translation" is a powerful code.

# EIGHTEEN

Melissa had agreed to be a part of the old school event. Not just to turn up, but to help organise.

"You've got time," others had told her when they read her bio. "Not like your bosom buddy Zelda."

"She's a real success," said Melissa, taking the implications on board and deciding that this was a once-off. Her old classmates liked a certain amount of success only and enjoyed stepping on those who were down. This had been true when she and her friends had been the brightest among them, and it was no different now. As a public good, she let the other ex-students walk all over her. She did not, however, tell Hal.

"I'll be glad it's over," she said to him. "And I promise I'm not going to help with organising again. What I'm going to do is use this lunch."

"Use it?"

"To move on. You and I do well, my body does appallingly, but the reason they all asked me to help was they thought I had time."

"You don't." Hal was stubborn.

"But no one can see it but us. I shall learn from Bettina and see about exhibitions and may, if the body permits, try running a few classes."

"What about that Etsy shop you use for craft?"

"I can't do the craft anymore."

"Don't sound so miserable. You do it, just a different it. Put more photographs online and let people decide."

"That's a lot easier physically," she said. "It can fit the less-pain parts of the day."

"You can always find out about events when you're ready. But it's—"

"One step at a time, as if walking on quicksand, I know. I'd say you've taught me well, but that will lead to a Star Wars joke."

"As lemon follows fish," Hal agreed.

Melissa stopped enjoying working on the lunch a few days in, but she knew this would happen. It was never comfortable when people told her to do this and that precisely when it suited them, and didn't listen when it was difficult for her. She wasn't in paid work, they thought, and she had no children; her time was everyone's.

She also made it to the lunch. It took a lot of work from both her and her husband, but she made it. It was only the second time she'd been to a school function since school finished.

She looked around for old friends and saw vaguely familiar faces, but none of those people she'd spent time with that wasn't dictated by teachers. More than anything, she missed her two best friends. No Zelda and no Bettina. They must've had reasons. Travelling too far, probably, and too busy. Successful careers. Families that took priority. Reasons.

Melissa missed them. She travelled all the way and her two closest friends weren't there. Messages from people were read out, however, so her friends were there by proxy. Zelda's message was clever and witty, of course, and Bettina's was from the heart. It was almost like being with them, for a fraction of a second. They both talked about career and life. Zelda's update was the one that caused a mild reaction. Senior Lecturer. Specialist in Celtic Studies. Had lived in Brittany and Wales.

"I wish I did the cool things other people did," said the woman sitting next to Melissa. "Only the ordinary people turn up to school events."

Melissa didn't know whether to argue her out of the statement or to … no idea, in fact, what to do, so when a couple of other school friends who she saw from time to time grabbed her for coffee she said yes. That was her biggest mistake of the day. She was therefore very pleased that her best friends had not turned up. If ever she saw them, there would be no weight of idiocy upon the meeting. She ate all the foods she should not and forgot to walk when she had to, and this is why a simple school reunion set her back for days.

# NINETEEN

Several days' worth of notes to add here. I'll just say which days, not when.

Day One: I had lunch with old school friends. I got there without any help and I did a couple of messages before I met my friends. This was despite everything. Some months the full moon hurts and this was one of them … but I was dealing. There's something deep inside that lights up when life turns out to be possible despite things. I was chuffed. Very chuffed. It may have escaped that I was pleased with myself over my day.

We were talking and the other two were feeling superior. They talked about other schoolmates as if they weren't quite good enough. Hadn't done this or that. Had been given more than they deserved.

Guess where this led?

One of my friends told me, with that confidential look you get from someone who is half-hiding behind the coffee cup and is empowered to take the conversation that one step further, that she knew I was sick, but, really, I should stop making a thing of it. Apparently, I exaggerate my illness and act as if it's special when I do perfectly normal things and all it did was make my friends feel stupid and it was a very bad thing to do. The other said, just as the first was paying our carefully calculated bill that we'd each put in for, "You're an old liar, aren't you? You've never looked sick and you always say you can't do things. You just want attention. Well, today you got it."

The bill wasn't split at all evenly. In the end, I paid.

I wish I had a bit more energy and could argue with people who do this kind of thing. I wish I'd gone home instead of having lunch with those ... those ...

I'm going to start a list of people I should avoid. Ones who want me to tell them things then either don't listen or don't believe me or don't ... I dunno. People I love but am going to avoid forever and forever.

Day Two: Today is a translation day.

Day Three: Something about these notes appals me. I hate it. I hope I'm wrong, but I don't think I'm wrong.

I was listening to other people online. They were talking about chronic illness. Lots of different illnesses all crowded into a single week-long discussion. When we talked about symptoms, about doctors, about the cyclist who shouted at someone who had trouble walking to "get out of the way" even though it wasn't a cycle path, about so many things, so very many things ... we all sound the same. Not quite the same, but close.

I think the pain creates shudder that infects our speech and stutter that controls the rhythm and when it's rare to have an hour free of pain the illness becomes the fabric of whatever we do. There's no existence that's free of the influence of our illness and so whenever we talk, whatever we talk about … it's influenced. It's changed.

One moment was odd. A famous person was in our midst and we were very polite. They started talking about their illness. At first, we were reassured. Someone famous who shared our pain. Except he didn't. He was visiting to get pats on the back for how brave he was when he suffered so—his illness was maybe a tenth of the average of everyone there. His pain voice was put-on; it was for show. He wanted us to orient our discussion around him, because he was important. Not his pain. Him. That's a luxury most of us don't have.

One by one the conversation faded as people drifted off. We'd been speaking with the same voice and the same hurt and he changed the tone by wanting the conversation to be about him. He wanted to leave the fuzz of everyday hurt behind. He talked about climbing the Sydney Harbour Bridge and was about to go walking for two weeks in Iceland. All the trendy kids go walking in Iceland right now. But who of us has the luxury to be a trendy kid?

His determination to own our pain and make us cheer for him determined me. I will do something. I don't know what yet, but something.

I can't change that shared voice. I'm stuck in the chasm that is constant hurt. But I still live and next time he raises his voice I can have something to talk about or even think smugly about. "Oh yes, I went to this place." And then he'll be forced to talk in our terms, because I'll bring the conversation back to the level we needed to be on, to deal with our ordinary lives. How to get out of a car when the hip isn't working properly. How to climb stairs when one isn't strong enough. How long before one has to get out of bed on a bad day, and what cheats one can do for meals. How much time each week is spent on medical appointments and long phone calls that are waiting for answers to simple questions relating to the public sector side of the chasm.

It's not my voice when I whinge, I've discovered. It's *our* voice.

I keep wondering if, maybe, it's the fact that the famous guy has so many choices and can do so many things that made him sound different. I thought it was because he assumes the world revolves around him, and not in the same way that the rest of us do. For most of us, it's a survival thing. For him, it was more that he was important.

I'm not clear. I don't know what I'm saying. Except that I share a voice with other sick people. Except that I hate it when someone who ought to understand doesn't understand and uses people who are more sick to get ego kicks. Why this has made me decide I want to kick up my heels and live the life is something I may never understand. Just as I may never understand why my left foot decided to cramp and scream at me just now. It's an oddity.

Still, I think I will. I'll save my spoons and think about what I can do. There must be something. Not just to take back into the chat and say, "Well, it may not be Iceland, but look what I did." Something that reminds me that my life is bigger than the pain that governs it.

# TWENTY

Bettina had one of those dreams she hated. All the vistas opened. Then all the vistas were lost.

Sometimes she stood at the top of a cliff and admired the universe and, before she could own any of that universe, her own feet took her down a narrow path back to an old grass hut she knew was home.

Sometimes she stood on the shores of an ocean, dove in, swam straight into the smallest and most quiet bay, and then got out of the water, not looking back.

This was a new one. She was climbing a mountain. It was hard work, that climbing, and even in her sleep she could feel her body puffing away. It was, as all of these dreams, somewhat lucid and she told herself to breathe more deeply and to enjoy the high air. Bettina reached the top and saw the water from the mountain trickle into a stream. It created the landscape she watched and that landscape welcomed her. The rivers and the lakes were hers. All she had to do was walk down the mountain in the direction she was looking. There was a path. Everything was easy. Easy and safe and she was lucid enough to try to make herself walk those first few steps.

Bettina pushed her dreaming self. “One step,” she said. “Take one step. That’s right.” And her dreamself took that step. Then another. Then another.

Then the dream turned to dross as she turned around, went back those three steps, and then went down the wrong side of the mountain. On that side were stunted trees and deserts and more red rocks than anything green.

Bettina was so angry at herself that she woke herself up. She’d rather be awake than ruin her night. She made a huge pot of tea and sat up the rest of the night, watching two different versions of *Pride and Prejudice*. There was safety in Jane Austen movies.

---

It was a full moon night.

Zelda loved them. She and the moon had a special relationship.

Next time, she’d be seeing it from the mountains. From near the Giant Potato. The thought of the Giant Potato made her shudder. She decided that she’d borrow Bettina’s car one day and get away by herself. She could do almost anything that day. She could spend a day at the coast or visit the local waterfalls. The fellowship wasn’t at all in her corner of Australia and it’d give her nice breaks from work if she could get away. Bettina wouldn’t mind, since they’d already agreed that Zelda would lend her car to her daughter for the fortnight.

“All meals are provided and everything you need is within walking distance,” the email answering her questions had assured her, but giant potatoes weren’t on Zelda’s lists of need. The full moon over a waterfall would be perfect, however.

# TWENTY-ONE

More notes. Lots.

Day One: Today is a translation day, even though I don't want it to be. I want to drown in a mire of despair. Painkillers aren't working. I'm not tired beyond bearing, but it hurts to do almost everything. Even breathing. I want to deny this thing's control over my body. I don't want it as part of me.

Translation is easier when I'm stuck in bed all day or when I can't walk but everything else is fine. Through a fog. Not through this mist of razors. I walked outside on the way to the doctor and the rain pierced everywhere it touched. It opened minuscule wounds and my soul seeped out.

The doctor said, "We can't control this symptom. Rest till it goes." Resting doesn't help. My legs wander around the bottom end of my bed, trying to find a place that doesn't hurt. I want to sleep until it's over, but when I sleep I suffer soul-sucking nightmares. Translation is tough.

. . .

Day Two: Today is a translation day.

Day Three: I have the miseries.

Day Four: My legs felt restless and kicked everywhere. I can't walk on them much today. A few metres at most. But they kicked everywhere when I was lying down and they refused to let me sleep and now my eyes look as if I've been in a prize fight and lost and it's almost four in the morning and I need to sleep to bring down the pain and I can't sleep because the pain has made my legs restless and they kick out when I sleep and they wake me up and my mind won't do anything else but circle around the problem. I've taken medicine and I should be able to sleep. Except I can't. And if I can't then tomorrow will hurt properly. I have to walk tomorrow. Have to.

No water. I'll take the water bottle out of my handbag. I need a tiny bottle for times like this, when carrying things hurts. And it's a camera day. I shall hide behind my craft and it will be my very own personal excuse for not walking far. Three steps and a whoops-I-need-a-picture.

I can't sit it out because my shoulders slump into the keyboard. That's the reason I'm typing instead of dictating. It stops me from melting into a tired puddle onto that keyboard and it means I keep going.

I'm going to try my "other medicine". Just three mouthfuls of liqueur.

It might help. It won't hurt. Sometimes it calms the legs down and numbs the pain a bit. Sometimes nothing will. I hope this is a day when it does, for sleep is going to bring down the swelling and make it hurt less. Sleep and no supermoon.

I don't know if I should blame the supermoon for this. I have to blame something, is all. I have to blame something.

On nights that feel like this, pain is my big shadow. My body is in broad daylight right now and the sun is so very bright that my shadow is vast and capable of eating me up. Except it can't. It just goes in and out with me, never never leaving me to live my life in peace.

That hour the other week made me so very happy. I started to hope that there'd be more of them, that every day I'd get an hour without these kicking legs and forsaken shaky pain. Without the hard skin and changed ankles. Without …

Someone said the other day that I was either a whinger or depressed. I am not my shadow. My shadow is a mere echo, a textured and subtle echo full of pain but an echo.

It's not serious. Not translation. Just a damned nuisance. Not even the worst of me. A blip. No more. No less. And I'm going to bed again and I shall sleep through and the shadow will be less dense. It won't trigger my normal symptoms. I say this to it with profound firmness. The kicking legs and the lack of sleep need to not make everything else bad. Not. Not. Not.

# TWENTY-TWO

It was phone night. Bettina wasn't able to talk about the giant family events yet. She wanted to tell Zelda that her man was getting married, that he was still talking to his mother, but that half the family walked past as if he didn't exist. She normally didn't really care about sharing secrets, but she wanted someone to talk with who wasn't dependent on her. Every single person involved in this regarded her as the post on which they could hang their emotions. Every single one. Even her ex's fiancé.

It felt good in one way—she was loved and needed and between that and her work her life was pretty full. Put like that, to suddenly require a conversation partner was stupid. Bettina put the thought on hold and, for as long as she was on the phone with Zelda, the fellowship was the big thing in her life. And it was. A prestigious fellowship. Two weeks focused on work and with her best friend there the whole time. Perfect.

Because it was a conversation with Zelda, it followed certain regular paths. The first stage was talking about what they needed from anything and their reasons for being there. That was easy.

"Same as it was when I applied," Bettina said. "My project. Time focused. A bit of a new environment. Time with you. Did I say how pleased I was that you received the academic fellowship?"

"You did." Zelda sounded smug. "And yeah, all that. I'll also be glad of a break. Too much teaching and administration in my life right now. Academia's changed. Everything's harder."

"You know what else I want," said Bettina, doing her usual trick of finding a way of being honest about her emotions without revealing anything she shouldn't reveal. "It's going to be simpler there. No rest-of-lives. Nothing complicated. Fewer crises."

"Amen to that," Zelda agreed. "That's what I meant by no teaching and admin. Academic life is all crisis right now. I'm glad you understand where I'm coming from."

"I'm glad you're my friend," Bettina said honestly. "I can tell you about my dreams." Not that she did, for the most part. And not that she intended to tonight. She wanted to keep that door open. No one knew that Bettina thought the dreams were more than dreams, and one day, this might be important. She needed to prepare herself, just in case the secret had to be spilled.

"You can," said Zelda. "We can interpret them together. You tell them so very well, too. I love listening."

They chatted about the dreams, but not for long. When Bettina's voice started to take on a serious tone, Zelda suggested that the dreams might be better left to the side for a little, and that she focus on the real work for the retreat.

"Reconfiguring," Zelda called it. "Using your art to connect your life. Both our projects focus on that, you know. Connections. Doors."

"Portals," said Bettina. "I love that word."

"We should take a book or two for reading while we're there."

"What a good idea," said Bettina. "You don't just mean any

book, though, do you? Your voice has that special meaning kinda sound."

"You are so right. I was thinking we could find books with portals in them. Like the Narnia books. For two weeks of our lives, everything will be in delightful perfect harmony."

Bettina laughed. "I love that idea. I'll have to talk to the librarian, though, because I have no idea which books would work."

"I've got enough portal books for an army. I'll bring you two, shall I?"

"Can you bring three? Just in case things get boring?"

# TWENTY-THREE

Day One: Today is a translation day.

Can't keep head up straight. Neck bows with toomucheverything. This is me telling myself even if bed hurts it's the only solution. Do everything later. Pizza delivery for dinner. Yuck.

Day Two: Remembering to say I have the miseries is another burden. I'll just skip it. Sorry doctor, but I need to keep my life manageable. You said. And having a thousand things to remember and no easy set of instructions to follow makes the miseries worse. So I shall not document them anymore. Maybe exceptionally, sometimes. Maybe part of other things. But mostly leave them out.

It's really hard having a body that's so fallen and that the medical professionals all say "Keep an eye on this" and "Do that." Some things are easy. Some things become a burden. Bye-bye one single small burden. I need to get through my everyday more than I need to document this one element.

# TWENTY-FOUR

Such a big day were Sundays. So many things happening. Before the phone call with Zelda, Bettina had to handle breakfast with her two men, lunch with her two children, afternoon tea with three of the relatives who wanted her to explain what on earth it meant that their gay dear one was getting married (and, it turned out, the fact that he was gay). The hardest part of the day was her eldest, at the door on the way out from lunch. He didn't want to see the relatives and he wanted time with her.

"I thought now," he complained, "but they're invading in an hour. And I hate them."

"They're being better than we ever thought they would."

"Some of them are, but that's not good enough. It's as if they're doing us a huge favour by not hating Dad for being who he's always been. I can see why he never wanted to tell them. God and his little sheep, can I see."

"You've not told them about you?"

"And you won't tell them for me. Promise!" He was angry and upset.

"I don't blame you," said Bettina. "I won't tell anyone. I'll wait until they tell me, and that way I'll be certain you've told them."

He unwound a bit. “Can I see you? I need mother time.”

Bettina felt a knot of fear she didn’t know she had and it was unknotting and pretending it had never been there. “I’m talking to Zelda tonight. How about I text you when we’re off the phone and you can come and chat late.”

“You don’t mind late?”

“Normally I do, but you’re a night owl and today maybe it’s important we use your time.”

He gave her a big grin, reached into a hug, and said, “See you later.”

Later, she had the call with Zelda. This was her Sunday. Emotions with family followed by unpicking life with Zelda. Except that she’d cheated for a while and unpicked other things than emotions. This Sunday, for instance, she pushed both of them to talk about plans for the trip and about everyday life. She admitted things weren’t good. Zelda protected her when she said this, knowing her health was chancy and her finances had their ups and downs. Zelda was her safe place, she reflected.

This time she decided to do a reveal-much.

“It’s the new family,” she said. “I need to sort them out.”

“Not the children?”

“Not even their father. His fiancé isn’t so easy to deal with. He came out when he was a teenager and is full of judgement about me interfering in his love’s life. He’s even more judgemental about the ex-wife, but then, everyone is judgemental about her. Sometimes I wonder if she isn’t a nice person after all, and all these things we say about her are inventions to make our lives better without her in them.”

“Surely he doesn’t think that about you?” asked Zelda.

“Yes and no,” she answered. “He’s okay that we never married or slept together. He’s very not okay with us never having had a relationship and the whole world thinking we do. He loathes it when either of the kids calls me ‘Mother’. He will stop the conversation in its tracks and lecture them. 'Just a friend of your father's,' he says. 'And a demanding one at that.'"

Bettina wasn't perfect with her in-law-to-be and he was very not-perfect with her. What she couldn't explain to Zelda, because it was so difficult to explain to herself, was that he didn't accept that the relationship was true.

This is what she wanted to explain to her friend. It was so important to talk about how distressed the kids were by this.

Before she had rung Zelda, however, she had rung the fiancé. She explained that she was going away for two weeks and would he please take the time to think, because she'd be happy to consider him a friend, or a brother, or a cousin, but she didn't want to lose her family and be entirely alone in the world because he was unable to deal. This was why she felt the need to spill everything on Zelda. Alone, she couldn't cope.

"I told him everything. I said, 'The stuff your fiancé has done is part of his past, and cutting him off from his past isn't going to help. I'm so proud he's come out. It was exceptionally difficult. Most of his real family are a bunch of hairless bigots. He's got very few of them left, but they're hard work. And you're saying I should walk out on him. That he should lose the one adult who's been with him throughout?'

"'For his own good,' he said. Such a young guy. So certain about everything. You know how I normally bite my tongue and don't tell people they're wrong? I couldn't. Not tonight.

"'I know you keep telling us that it's for his good. This is the third time you've said it. That's what I want you to think about. Why you keep saying it to me, about my relationship with someone I care about so very much. Me never seeing him again or the kids is not for my good, certainly. And I don't think it's for his good, either.'

"I told him about the fellowship, Zelda. I told him, 'You've got until I come back. Don't pressure him. Work it out. What you actually want. If you want him without me, then you're hurting the kids.'

"'I don't want to hurt the children,' he said, and I felt a blip of triumph. Because none of us want the children to hurt, and I was where they got their washing done and asked for emergency meals and rang up when they'd been locked out at …"

"You are their surrogate mother."

"Very much so," said Bettina. "Anyhow, I told him then that none of us wanted the children hurt, so I was giving him time to think. Two weeks. 'Okay,' he said, "'Okay, I'll think.'"

There was a silence. Zelda started to speak and Bettina said, "I'm so sorry. I'm just … I need a few minutes. I'll ring you back."

"Take as long as you need," said Zelda.

*He didn't even leave a contact number. That will teach me,* Bettina thought, but didn't tell Zelda. She'd said enough. She'd asked for permission to say it, but it made her miserable. It was him saying he'd think without leaving a contact number that set off the tears. He might think, but he wasn't thinking yet. And he might not think at all, and ruin several lives because he'd found his true love.

The trouble was that there were no models and no stories for this kind of thing. All the silencing and all the possible hate of gays and of Jews meant they'd worked out their lives behind the scenes. Bettina knew she'd given up stuff she really shouldn't, just to keep Dov from having to deal with the family, and now he was dealing and that was good but … Bettina might end up alone.

Not completely alone. The kids would visit. Just not as much. Just not as family.

Sometimes Bettina wanted a damn true love. Truly she did.

And what about the wedding? How could she be a witness if she wasn't supposed to even be speaking to them? She hoped time would help, because right now, life was such a mess. Her dreams weren't helping. Maybe dreams weren't the answer. Maybe they lied.

Bettina wanted to cry. She put on the right clothes and did the right thing. She ran and she ran and she ran. She came back just in time to talk to Zelda. Dinnerless, but no longer in tears. There'd be a lot of pain for this tomorrow, but she didn't care. She didn't. She was going to deal. She was. She rang Zelda back before those tears returned. Only just before, but time counted.

Zelda sounded cautious on the other end of the phone. Bettina knew that Zelda would do what she would always do at time like this: she'd take the emotions out of everything and make life liveable. She did this by talking.

She told Bettina all about her new academic paper and which part of her larger project it fitted into and exactly what stage she was up to. Then she moved onto her teaching and talked about two different classes and what work they were doing. Then she finished, as she always did, with an entertaining story. This time it was about her whole online class plan falling down.

"I blamed the staff member who did that kind of thing, but it turned out nothing had fallen down—I just went to the wrong page." The two laughed and Bettina felt cheered.

As she went to sleep, she wondered why Zelda never talked about her own husband and child. Maybe once a year, she'd talk about them, but otherwise they were creatures of passing mention. Bettina knew that the daughter was most of Zelda's life. Her daughter and her university job and her research. Maybe it was because Bettina's situation was so very unusual. Maybe Zelda just didn't want to make Bettina uncomfortable?

"How odd," thought Bettina, "that I don't know. She's my second best friend, after all. Especially now, when my first best friend is getting married and I'm in danger of losing him and the children, especially now I understand it. But she's never brought me into her home life. How very odd."

# TWENTY-FIVE

More notes anyway. Because I've gotten used to them.

Day One: Hal is, of course, out of town.

Friends sent me a message. "Out at a special restaurant for a special anniversary." Fucking yay for them. My last anniversary was spent in hospital. Last major birthday, I hurt all the fucking time and had to smile to keep everyone happy and it was one of these two who came over the next day because they'd forgotten it and wanted to see me.

Do they have to rub it in? Maybe they do. Maybe this is supposed to keep me happy, like coming over the next day and saying, "I just want a cuppa. Don't go to any trouble," when even standing up and walking over to the damned kettle hurt. Maybe knowing I'm alone tonight and that I hurt makes them feel extra special about their fucking day.

Except it's not that at all. They think they're being nice. That being happy for them makes up for me never getting to be happy for myself. Like that not having to make scones to go with the tea meant that the tea was easy and didn't hurt.

Maybe they like me but think I whinge and are staying round for the count, and being nice and sympathetic despite the fact that I never seem to get on top of things.

They have no fucking idea, do they?

Day Two: Something in the air tonight makes the pain feel nostalgic. It took me years to realise that pain is not one simple thing. It changes over time. Some types of pain require bad language. Some require dreamy eyes. Tonight I feel the same as I felt a few years ago, and so memories are flooding me. Memories of what happened when I felt this particular way most of the time.

Before Hal sorted out how to make home work for me, we thought that the government helped with this sort of thing. The government does. But only if you're almost too sick to need it. I was damn lucky I have a supportive husband.

I was less lucky in my family. My brother managed to get government help with his bathroom when he was in a bar fight and got injured. I don't begrudge him this. He recovered, and that was probably because he had the help when he needed it. One thing I've learned over the years is not to begrudge anyone appropriate help. Even my "bother".

What I'm not so impressed about was the way he shouldered in front of me for everything. He was so sick. And the family treated him as special. And I sat there at dinner thinking, "Maybe I'm not as sick as he is. Maybe I'm kidding myself."

Except I wasn't. I don't know if the impossibly slow diagnosis was because it's a chronic illness or because I'm a woman, but it tore me apart and the family helped with the ripping. I had to be there for them. Not them there for me. And when the bar fight happened and my brother was injured, I was expected to take care of him because I knew what to do.

I don't know what would've happened if Hal hadn't said at

that moment, "Excuse me, but Melissa and I are going." And we left. Just like that. And he turned to me in the car before he turned on the engine and said, "Melissa, I love you with all my heart but your family sucks. Can we divorce them?" And I laughed and we hugged and kissed and … yeah … I could keep on going. Best moment in my life was running him down when I was jogging. Back when I could jog.

I need a drink to trick my body out of this dream world. I can't afford to live in the past.

# TWENTY-SIX

Zelda nearly didn't pack for her retreat. There was too much to do. She had too many obligations, too much responsibility. *Also,* she thought, *I don't deserve this.*

For her, it was time out. She would have written her book anyway, she told herself. She would have done this and she could have done that and she ought to have done the other. Her daughter needed the car, however. That was the reason that convinced her to go. Not a theoretical need, but a big need. If she had the car, she could drive herself to her social functions and to shops and to anywhere. That would help her get over what happened last year. It would give her the capacity to leave if someone at a bar or a party tried what they should not. Taxi fares weren't doing the trick right now. Taxi drivers were also men.

All it took were four boys from her year to set up such a mess. Such a hot damn mess.

Zelda convinced herself, while she packed and unpacked and packed again, that these were lessons all women had to learn. That they were better than getting raped or beaten to a bloody pulp at home. She really didn't want to be away while her daughter sorted those lessons out.

Except she had to. All women had to learn how to walk in safety and play in safety and live in safety. It was part of being Australian. This was her daughter, and her daughter ought to be safe. Always and ever.

Zelda wanted to swear, but realised that she got that from Bettina who had adopted it from Melissa when they were all teens. Such an odd influence Melissa had been on their lives. She'd say it anyhow. Damn. Damn! Damn all ratbags.

She felt better. She could leave now.

# TWENTY-SEVEN

More damn notes. I take them on my phone and find them a few days later. "Oh look, notes! I guess I can translate them to the computer now.

So Bettina's admitted she stopped inviting me because I get sick and have to cancel. She doesn't think what it means from my end for her to think I don't need a social life anymore. But then, she's never asked me what kind of social life would work for me.

A flexible one would work. A caring one would work. Not one where the whole damn friendship depended on me being able to do everything predictably. Turn up to dinner carrying a dish of my best cooking, and being awake and alert and amusing and not in any pain for a whole evening, and then not having to spend three days recovering.

I used to spend three days recovering, then I learned that the others at dinner would make jokes about it. When I started bringing a bottle of wine with apologies about not being able to cook.

The jokes stopped and I didn't get to the dinner parties. Which dinner parties? The sort that those Bettina and Zelda are talking about online now, with such happiness, as if they're the only dinner parties anyone goes to.

Old friends who leave you out when your life gets hard can be the worst friends. All people need friends who listen and remember and pay attention. Not friends who leave them behind because it's too much damn work for their fragile flutterbrains.

# TWENTY-EIGHT

"At least it'll only be three weeks between thinking and knowing," Melissa had told Hal, but she had to give up entirely before she heard about the fellowship at all. She was honest with herself about such things, and she never won anything. Not ever. Except a raffle. Once she'd won third prize in a raffle.

Melissa already knew she hadn't got the fellowship. She'd been told over the phone, and also told that an email would arrive within two weeks, informing her if she was successful. Until then she'd be put on the back-up list, she was told, and heard nothing and nothing and nothing.

Hal was no help. He was busy with his mother and with an ongoing argument at work. "That's not a good reason," Melissa heard him say. "You can't make decisions in that way. Rethink this or I shall kick the whole thing upstairs."

She didn't like to bother Hal, so he never knew how frustrated she was by not knowing. Her whole life was being spent not knowing things, and this one felt like the last straw. Except it wasn't. Melissa knew that. Just a really scratchy straw, annoying her and needing to be taken off her camelback.

Then came the phone call. She was told "weeks ago" that she

had received the fellowship, the guy said mellifluously. Except she hadn't been told a damn thing and the person on the phone wasn't interested.

"All I wanted to do was find out what time you're arriving and what food restrictions we need to address."

"I wasn't told." Melissa was obdurate, but polite.

"I'm sorry, the email must have gone astray. Anyhow …" the voice on the phone raced on. This was not someone who wanted to talk about what hadn't happened or shouldn't happen. "Someone pulled out weeks ago and we have only two fellows. Would you like to be our third?"

It was not a short phone call and the man at the other end kept assuming she'd read the missing email with all its detail. A few minutes in, Melissa realised he hadn't given his name.

"Madam, I'm Adam." Melissa liking the palindrome made the phone call less difficult for a little.

Halfway through, Adam also realised that she'd not even been interviewed. "Well, that's not critical. It just means there are some details I need about your project."

Melissa talked through all the things she would have done if there had been an interview. She had to make most of it up on the spot.

And then came the admission that she was disabled. The thing she hated telling strangers. She had put it on her application.

Adam had said, "No problems," but had questions. All his questions assumed that she was in a wheelchair.

Her disability was the big thing. Adam's questions were answered, and so were hers. She knew how much Hal wanted her to take the fellowship and at the same time how much he wanted to be with her, so she was torn.

Quietly, while the voice at the other end informed her of more things (Adam had a very informative voice), she tossed a coin. The next time he paused for breath, she said quickly,

"I've thought about it. I'd be delighted to accept. Thank you."

"You don't have much time," he said. "I'll email you more information."

"Can we check my email address?" Melissa asked.

They had sent her emails to someone with a very different name. Adam looked her up and found that the email address was the duplicate of the one above her on the list.

Adam gave a near apology with much certainty, and, Melissa thought, the fact that this very certain gentle man said it so definitively meant that he probably ran the list and made the error and … Melissa stopped pushing herself into strange places and double-checked her email address and wrote down Adam's phone number.

"If I haven't heard from you by tonight, I'll ring back."

"Better make it tomorrow."

"If I make it tomorrow I will be coming with no clothes," Melissa said acerbically.

"I possibly should have rung the day the other fellow pulled out," Adam admitted. He was a piece of work, she decided. If he was there, she'd not take pictures of people for her project. She'd claim the error of her ways and take pictures of something else for her second series.

# TWENTY-NINE

I'm going. Hal agrees that if we work things out carefully, I can do it. He also thinks if I don't do it, I'll end up the way I end up every time I was off sick or on holiday. I love pretending I don't work, but when that happens, I'll pretend I do. I bet I do.

I've got this offer and I'm going. I can't guarantee the people who run this retreat will help when I'm less than well, but Hal says that he'll make sure they have his phone number so if something goes arse upward, he can come out to Robertson and rescue me. And work gave me time off without even a blink. Work will support a fellowship where they won't support a holiday. Have I ever written a note about work, or do I hate it so very much that I avoid thinking about it? The latter, obviously.

That's the short stuff. Need the long stuff, for the doctor.

I don't talk about work much at the doctor's. I probably should. There's always so much to talk about, and if I have more than three things that need sorting, the doctor gets tangled and my stuff is so complicated that I always have more than three things. Work gets left off.

I was so happy to get this job. Part-time. Desk job. Handling cases for ... I can't talk about it. Just deskjobhandlingcases.

That'll have to do. Writing it down makes me want to throw up. Not throw up food. Throw up paper and dry air and anger from what my desk-neighbour (DN) does.

The big thing is that I work by myself. That's so I can handle my illness. Boss is fine when I arrange my hours around my capacity, as long as I get everything done on time. DN isn't so fine. He wants me to do things his way. He's not my boss, but he sees himself as special. He's going somewhere. Doing Things With His Life. And he needs to tell me this and act out on this all the damn time. He'd make me get him coffee if he could.

A friend talked about having a Jekyll and Hyde boss. My DN is like that. One thing to everyone else and quite a different thing to me. He has a mental hierarchy and he sucks up to people who he thinks of as equal and I'm not equal. I've got a Masters and he hasn't, but he sees me as inferior. I dunno if it's because I'm female or if it's because I'm part-time or if it's because I came back last year after all that time getting my pelvis back and everything. Everything. Whatever it is, in front of everyone else he's sympathy and takes care of me and treats me like his cygnet in need of grooming and … yeah … grooming … that's part of it.

I resist being groomed. I put up walls against being bullied. And when he comes on sexually because the other things don't work, I am polite and say no, no, and no. We have an emergency code, Hal and I, and when I type 111 into a message, he rings me on my office phone. When DN gets to it first (helping me out), Hal explains I'm needed at home. Something's Come Up. I'm applying for new jobs, but finding them now, with me needing part-time work, with the economy sucking, with … yeah … with that. I just have to handle bullying. Or give up work.

Hal and I have talked about that. He says that if I can get a portfolio from the retreat and if I can show it and if I can start to make some money from the photography to top up my Etsy store, things could change. He says photos can sell more because they sell differently. Maybe that'll give us that financial edge so I don't have to go to that workplace. But I don't want to be forced out by a wanker. And I do like work, mostly.

I'm going on that retreat and I'm going to prove my art and my … other stuff. When I'm home, we'll talk about it.

"If only you could get employed for the other stuff," he said wistfully, the other day. "I'd love that."

God, I adore that man.

# THIRTY

"Put it to the test. See how long it is before anyone remembers to give you a call. I dare you."

Zelda sighed. Her ex was right, in a way, but he wasn't going to scare her off. It was a Grand Experiment. *It may be a house in the middle of nowhere,* she reflected, *but I'm not the only one in it. And my friends are bad at ringing me here, in Melbourne. They were bad at ringing me on my birthday and completely forgot me when I was in the US. And it's a house and there is my dream.*

"You don't have to dare me. I've already agreed to go. That's why you're driving me to the fucking station."

"Don't remind me," he grumbled.

"I just did."

He laughed. "It's not the way to finish a book."

"Nor is staying here and waking up every morning convinced I'm a failure."

It took him a moment to register this. They'd reached Spencer Street and everything was tight and slow and crowded.

"That's not the reason we broke up," he objected.

"You still said it."

"Oh, hold it against me, why don't you." He enjoyed sounding bitter. He didn't think about the consequences of that bitterness until she rammed them down his throat.

A wave of realisation made the whole city look brighter.

# IN THE HOUSE

# THIRTY-ONE

The house hid from the street behind a forest's worth of trees. Now Melissa was here, inside that heavy gate, able to see the edges the house presented to incoming visitors. The breeze blew crisply across the gravel path. She stood for a moment, convincing herself all would be easy.

Melissa jumped when a man's voice said, "Which one are you?" His voice was very deep. Gravel-deep, with a hint of the rustle of autumn leaves. It fitted the garden, somehow. So did his looks, when he slipped out from between the trees. He was different shades of brown and red, from his skin to his shoes.

"I'm Melissa," she said, tilting her head severely to look him directly in the face. He was very tall and very, very thin. If he walked over a crack in the path, he would fall right in and never come out.

The man took a hurried pace back, as if Melissa's thoughts scared him.

"Go straight in. When the path forks, take the right one, then the right again, then the east wing. Main door. Choose yourself a bedroom. Any one you like." He didn't give her a chance to answer. "When you're unpacked and you've read the papers, go to the main door and ask for Rachel." The man's voice rustled with the discontent of leaves about to fall. He wasn't comfortable with her being there.

In front of the house was a lawn. The second fork in the path split the trail to each side, keeping the lawn itself clear of everything except grass.

The house was red brick and white paint and old and had more odd angles than anyone could take in at once. There was a twisty tower on the right, and a big window facing the lawn, next to the central door. The window bulged out a bit and she could just see a window seat. It reminded her a bit of her grandmother's house. It was perfectly lovely.

Later was less lovely, but it wasn't the house's fault.

# THIRTY-TWO

I should've stayed in, but whatshername said I could walk, and I need to walk, and I did and that damned cyclist stopped on the path, turned around, eyed me, and asked, "Are you deaf?" Just like last time. Then she rode off. I'm writing everything super-fast. I want to use this writing thing to calm down, because I'm not at home.

I'm so damnedhappy to be sitting down that I want to make all the puns ever all day. This is one of those days when I need extra cortisone and will put up with becoming moonface just so I can move without wincing.

I was so furious. We were right next to the lights and I shouted after her, "I'm disabled."

"You should've moved faster," she shouted back. "I rang the bell."

Then she zoomed across the road. I was stuck halfway, because I can't walk quickly enough to cross the wide road. Not when everything hurts so badly. I shouldn't walk at all and I shouldn't've walked as far as the main drag, which is also the highway. I got all my evil drugs, which is the main thing, and will take my cortisone when I've sat for long enough to quieten the pain from the shopping. Then I'll start dinner and Hal will come home and we will be quiet together. That'll give it all the worth.

Except Hal won't come back because I'm in Robertson and all I did was walk down the street when Rachel the manager was too busy to see me. I need to walk. I don't need to be shouted at by a cyclist.

I wanted to send all kinds of evil after that cyclist. Every step home vibrated pain. And I had right of way on the damned footpath, so she could've swerved around me.

I couldn't tell what she looked like. I could only see just ahead of me because of the pain. I was afraid to cross the road because last time it was that bad I nearly got run over, twice. Except I need to walk. It makes the hurt less.

"Just go to the chemist," Hal said last time there was an incident like this. "I can do everything else." His idea of "everything else" doesn't include much housework. Even Hal thinks I make it worse than it is.

I don't limit myself. I hurt. I miss him already. Missing him makes me think of all the wrong things.

I thought I saw something scurrying to my right, but when I turned my head to look, all I saw was a pastry someone had dropped. Pastries don't waddle or scuffle or move. Except it's gone now. Maybe I made it up. The side had berry staining that had seeped out. My imagination is very good at times like these, and the pain can't be so bad if I'm writing stupid stuff.

If I were home, the dishes would not get washed. The laundry would rot in the machine. But the hurt from sitting here is far, far less than the hurt from walking at all.

I can't do those fifteen steps yet. My great inner magnanimity means I won't actually curse the cyclist or whinge about my husband. I will put on some music and sit here with my eyes closed until the music shushes everything else. Then I will take ALL THE MEDICINE. And the pain will become subdued and I can do what I must. I will walk as far as I have to so that tomorrow will be better.

As far as I have to is to that main gate, in the side gate next to the big fence, through all those trees, and then right, right and to the main wing, where Rachel will be waiting. When I'm settled, things'll be better. And I don't need any more medicine. Even the stuff I left behind is now wonderfully replaced.

I thought I remembered packing it. If I'm going to quiz myself, I should start back. One step at a time. I'll get there. One step. Then one step. Then one step.

# THIRTY-THREE

Later took a while. It was also confusing. Melissa found Bettina and Zelda in Rachel's office, meeting Batchette. Batchette was a cat, given a batty name for she had flown into Rachel's life as an adolescent the exact moment Terry Pratchett died. And because she stood on anything she could climb up to and jumped on heads and shoulders, or reached out with a paw and gave a gentle swipe.

There was barely time for polite surprises at Melissa's end. The best she could do was keep the conversation straight. This time there was food and Melissa took her tablets quietly with her tea once she'd had an elegant cucumber sandwich from an even more elegant tray. Her painkillers and cortisone were obviously going to be more powerful when drunk from a cup with golden flowers around the edge.

Between Batchette and everyone explaining to Rachel that Zelda and Bettina had been to school with Melissa, there was plenty of time for subterfuge. Neither of her friends noticed the tablets, but she caught Rachel watching. Her imperial slimness winked.

"I thought I saw you both in Moss Vale," Melissa said, trying to shake off Rachel's wink. "But then I thought, how can this be?"

"And it was," said Zelda, a satisfied look playing around her lips.

"You should've called out," said Bettina.

"I couldn't." Melissa was genuinely regretful. "You were too far away."

"Must've been quite a way—remember how you used to run to catch us?"

"I can't do that anymore," said Melissa. "The wonder of age."

"Well, we're all here. Just like school camp." Zelda looked under Batchette's dark corner into the grand hall that led to corridors and hosted staircases. "It's such a big place."

"It looked smaller from the east wing," Bettina commented. "But here it goes on forever."

"This place does that. I never go exploring when I've got to be somewhere in a hurry," Rachel explained.

"You haven't been here long, then?"

"I've worked here for, let's see … nearly a year."

"And you still love exploring it." Melissa smiled.

"Not if it's going to hurt, I don't."

Melissa looked at Rachel, directly into her so-slender face, and realised that she had winked because she had understood. It was as if a weight was taken from Melissa's shoulders. Being somewhere new wasn't such a pain-free thing anymore, but Rachel understood. This helped.

"Did you ring your husband?"

Melissa blinked as Rachel's conversation turned directly to her.

"Not yet. The chemist took longer than I thought. He'll still be on the road anyway. I'd better wait."

"You should've left him behind completely. I left everyone behind. Caught a train to Moss Vale," Zelda said complacently.

"Yeah, well, I'm not that mobile." Two times in a day it hadn't shown. Melissa supposed she should be grateful; instead, she felt like being sarcastic. She bit her tongue.

"We'll wait for you," said Bettina.

"Thank you—I'd really appreciate that."

While Melissa rang, the other three chatted, moving gently away from the sleeping kitten. When she came back into the conversation, it had shifted. There had been time, obviously, for Zelda and Bettina to get used to her.

Zelda explained they'd missed her and welcomed Melissa as if she was the long-lost vagrant but still-loved child. Melissa withdrew into herself to process this, because she was not the one who had gone out. The four of them walked to Rachel's office together, with Rachel silent and a little to one side, watching.

Zelda explained that she and Bettina had come to the office before, but Rachel wasn't in.

"You didn't wait?" Rachel asked.

"We didn't know we knew the third fellow," said Zelda.

"You're a pair, aren't you?"

"What?"

"No worries. Let me show you things. Batchette is fab, but she came with me. Had to be medically cleared! Not part of the furnishings. Acts as if she is. Acts like a bat. Likes being up high and leaping. Hates the sun. Let's do the sitting down stuff till you're okay with walking." She said this to Melissa, and smiled at the look on Melissa's face. "I read the notes."

"Oh," said Melissa. "Okay. I can walk slowly right now. But it will hurt for a little."

"Then we'll start in a little."

Bettina tried to explain that she was the sick one. Rachel nodded and said, "You let me know if you can't walk, too. Easy."

House rules, house map, house dreams. All were the same as the ones in their rooms. Where to go for meals. When to go for meals. Number for emergencies.

"Simple," Rachel said. "There are two of us when Big Sis gets back. Then you can ring anytime. Now it's anytime only for real emergencies. No 'I lost my toothpaste.'"

Rachel showed them the garden near the house, the dining room, the main work areas. Some parts were friendly and nineteenth century. Others looked older, which was hardly possible. Robertson was located in mountains that had not been crossed by any European until two hundred years after one room was built, if that room was real. It was probably a quite real fake. Melissa luxuriated in it and patted a big wooden chair on an arm supportively. It had the best carvings. That chair looked as if it came straight from an English country house.

It all looked cared-for. And big. More than Melissa could take in. It matched her first impressions, however. There was something almost fairy tale about the house and garden.

At the end of the tour, Rachel said, "Any unlocked doors are fine to enter. Use the rooms. Any locked doors, ask me. Some I can let you into and some I can't. Except for that wing." Her arm gestured vaguely to the left. "That's family stuff. None of us go in. Only the housekeeper."

"You're not the housekeeper?" asked Zelda.

"Co-manager," Rachel answered. "Papers in your rooms explain all that. They don't tell about Batchette, is all. That's why we started with her. In case she flies into you at night. She likes hair."

Melissa liked Rachel. "That'll teach us not to roam at 3 am," she said cheerfully.

"It will," answered Rachel. "She's never leapt into my face, but. Big Sis says she likes to swoop like a magpie from beams, but I don't believe it. Cats can't do that."

Zelda interrupted with "Excuse me," and it was back to basic questions. Although not walking in the main part of the building at night unless one had to was maybe a must-know. And the basic questions were interfered with by the fact that the three already knew each other. Zelda made a joke about the three of them being the Three Little Maids and sang "Three Little Maids from School are We" to illustrate her joke.

The third time she sang those lines during the tour finally got Melissa's goat. Rachel was the one who asked, "Why are you singing it again? Do you like it that much?"

Zelda told her about Melissa's great career in music and Melissa was forced to admit to the medication losing her the career. Zelda was silenced.

Melissa wondered what Zelda thought had caused her to abandon her great dream. Then she gave a mental shrug. It was a very Zelda assumption to make, that she had left music behind by choice. Melissa felt she was still the third maid who didn't get a full part to play. *How odd,* she thought, *that the last little maid is the only one who remained married.* Later that night she wrote Hal a postcard saying this, and that he must be the son of the Mikado. "It explains everything," she wrote. "Especially your first girlfriend." Laughter was the best medicine for the Zeldas of the world.

Melissa had read all the papers, but obviously the others hadn't. Pity. She really wanted to know so many things. Why were some doors called "portals" and others called "doors" on the map, for instance?

She tried to be subtle. "Is there anything we should know that's implied in the papers that's not spelled out? I'm not good at subtleties."

Rachel looked at her. She was so slender and so very young. Her slenderness was nothing like the leafguy's. He'd take root in a wind. Rachel would blow right away.

"One thing. Political. The family is not united. Don't ask Metroguy or any of the family for permission or advice. Ask me. Or Erin, when she gets back. Erin is Big Sis," she said slowly, for one of them had obviously looked confused. "The other manager. My BFF. We're avoiding her name right now because of … stuff."

"Because they'd give different advice?" Bettina had obviously focused on the family side and was puzzled. Whereas Melissa had focused on the do-not-name side and was fascinated.

"Because they can't agree and some of the things they can't agree on might be dangerous. I've got the keys, remember. That's why."

"Is Metroguy Adam? He sounds like a metro kind of bloke," Melissa said.

"He looks perfectly civilised," said Zelda.

"Metro is civilised," said Bettina.

"I don't know his looks," Melissa defended. "We did everything over the phone."

"Yeah," Rachel said. "I heard about that. The muck-up over your application doesn't make you less of a fellow, Melissa. It just means you knew two days ago, not two months ago. The grandmother to end all grandmothers made a decision that you'd all be equally fellows. Uber-granny said to tell you to ask me if there's anything you need, because she would lay odds you didn't get a bring-this list."

"I didn't," said Melissa. "Not in writing. But I asked on the phone and wrote it down."

"You might be missing things, then," said Zelda. "We can help."

"Nah," Rachel dismissed with a breeziness that made Melissa feel very much as if she belonged. "Our fault, our solutions. Come to me. Besides, the old lady said to ask … something."

"Something?" asked Bettina.

"Something private. She hasn't said what yet, so I can't tell you."

Melissa wanted to lay odds that Rachel wouldn't tell any of them about things that belonged to someone else. She intervened. "Whenever you like. I need to walk everything with the map to get oriented—can I do that tomorrow?"

"The pain get in the way of the walk today?" asked Rachel. Melissa wasn't at all used to such openness.

"How did you—?"

"BFF calls it symptom overlap."

The rest of the conversation before dinner was centred on Zelda's research. Melissa had no idea why. Zelda wanted to talk about stones and so they talked about stones. It was interesting and made her think about Europe quite differently. It also made it easy to sit back and watch. She was interested in Celtic stuff, but didn't want to inquire. Not tonight. Tonight was for sitting back and absorbing the feel of things. For watching. Watching was something Melissa excelled at. Watching and noticing.

Rachel reacted to the stones. At one stage she asked, "Are stones your thing, then?"

"Mostly. Sometimes it's water, but stones and forest are more interesting."

"How about you?" Rachel turned to Bettina.

"Light. Without light, I couldn't be an artist. I guess if we're talking about the four elements, that makes me an airhead."

Everyone smiled in polite denial, while Rachel turned to Melissa.

Melissa had assumed no one would ask her. She had just taken a mouthful of roast potato. Rachel held the room quiet until Melissa had finished. It was impressive.

"I didn't know until a little while ago, but water. Water and anything liquid gets me through most things."

Rachel nodded and said, "Womenstuff," to no one in particular, then turned her attention to her own roast dinner.

Bettina filled in the gap. "I was expecting a meat pie. It's Robertson, after all."

"Not Robertson," Rachel said. "Outside. Our own world."

Melissa tried to shift the subject sideways. "Someone in

Robertson dropped a pie of some sort. A fruit one. I was going to pick it up and bin it, but I had trouble getting up and down and must've misremembered where it was, because when I looked it was gone. I keep thinking about it, sitting there on the roadside. Poor pie."

"A pie," Zelda said blankly.

"They're a bit of a problem," said Rachel. She had scrunched her eyes as if she was trying to deny any part of a problem she had created. Maybe she gave away pies? No, that didn't make sense. "I'll get Metroguy back on it. He keeps telling me it's sorted. Chasing pies will keep him out of mischief. Maybe." That last was said with great dubiousness.

"Chasing pies is such a lyrical turn of phrase," said Bettina.

"Yeah, nah—it's how he catches them."

Melissa smiled. Rachel had said this with great seriousness and the other two had taken the whole pie conversation as a joke.

*I'll find out, thought Melissa, but slowly. Let this place reveal itself in its own time. There's something about it that reminds me of my book covers. And water. It's greener than the rest of Robertson. And it's a different palette. I will find out why. I bet Bettina works it out first. All those shades of green. She's clever with colour.*

Dessert came upon the four (it was fruit salad, not pie), and the topic changed, then Rachel excused herself.

The three stayed at the table. Finally, they were properly face to face after a very long time.

Conversation followed the usual paths. Melissa tried to say more after her usual two sentences, because there was so much more to say and surely these friends were the ones she could tell, but the sentences finished inexorably and left her no opportunity to introduce changes in her life. There were no questions about what Rachel was talking about with those strange pronouncements, either. There were so many possible conversations that couldn't happen if the conversation continued just the way it had been since school.

Two sentences for Melissa, then talk about Bettina's art and her life, then all the rest of the time was Zelda's. It was a path they'd mapped out years ago and the others felt safer for it. "How is Hal? Are you still at that job?" and that was it. Onto other things.

Melissa was disappointed in Zelda and in Bettina, for she could see no reason why they wouldn't ask her why she hurt, at least. She'd ask, if it were them. They may not have noticed anything else Rachel had commented on, but the fact that Melissa was obviously not well ... But they didn't ask. They never asked.

She stopped herself in mid-thought. She hadn't asked either, had she? Bettina was also chronically ill and they'd all been silent about that, too. So she did.

The floodgates opened and Melissa paid great attention to the torrent of words, but her attention was grounded by quiet fascination. She knew that each and every person who had chronic illness had a different life, but she didn't realise so very much about the nature of difference until her old friend released all that dammed water.

The bit of conversation she remembered and wrote notes on later was quite possibly not the aspects Bettina herself considered critical.

"A doctor told me once," Bettina had said, "that all the pain is because I'm sexually repressed. Religious upbringing, he says, does it every time. He ignored the scans in front of him and all the test results. For him, it was all about sex. He extolled his theory and he preached it and I thought, 'Oh look, he's trying to convert me to something.' I'm not sure even he knew what."

They'd discussed this from dress to rags, and it was worth discussing from dress to rags—the doctor had entirely missed that part of Bettina's hurting was due to one leg being shorter than the other. They enjoyed mocking the doctor.

"That was ten years ago," Bettina said almost wistfully. "So much has happened since then. And at least no one's telling me, 'You're too young to be disabled anymore!' I hated that."

"I thought it was cool. People telling you that you didn't look sick." Zelda still discovered the theatre element, Melissa noted. Zelda was shiny. Destined for fame or glory or at least a regular income in a good job. In this, she had never changed. Zelda had always been shiny. The universe had always given her small gifts because she was Zelda and she had always assumed that this was normal and to be expected. She could afford to look for glamour in discomfort.

"They made me sound like a charity case. Anyhow, these days I get that I don't sound disabled. Or someone takes my photo to put on the internet because I am in a disabled parking spot."

"Did they ever put it up?" Melissa was mildly curious. She'd given up driving after the event with her back, and it all sounded dreadfully theoretical now.

"Once. I persuaded them to take it down."

"How?"

"Simple evidence combined with an even simpler offer to get a lawyer onto it."

"Your boyfriend?"

"Dov was even more angry than me."

Soon they moved onto rocks again. Celtic stones.

"I was looking at the architecture, and dinner was so early," said Zelda. "We've got maybe an hour before dusk. I wanted to see if there's any Celtic inspiration in this building or the grounds, just to get me started. Coming?"

There were so many doors. Corridors and doors. Doors and corridors.

Melissa didn't speak much, because she was too busy

noticing the doors and the corridors and the fact that each walled environment had a different feel to it. She would follow her friends down a corridor or into a room and a few steps in the taste of the air changed. She tasted the difference first, which was odd, as Melissa considered herself very visual. The air was almost liquid in some rooms, green in others.

Walking became a synaesthetic experience.

The walls looked perfectly normal until she noticed them clearly and then it was easy to see that the sides of one corridor held a shimmer, and both walls and ceilings of a drawing-room carried the sense of old forest in the oaken brown. The house still felt as if it was loved, but in an eccentric and even enchanted way.

The doors were different, she decided. More than anything else, it was the doors that changed as they moved from one space to the next. Why had it taken her so long to recognise this? The last corridor had old wooden doors, and in this room they were made of dark glass. When she had walked through a wooden door from the oak forest room, it gave her a feeling of warmth and growing things.

The glass made the air taste cold and silken.

"Someone's office once," Zelda said thoughtfully. "I could work in here."

Bettina tried one of the doors and found that the dark glass led to a stone-lined corridor with an immensely long red-brown Belouchi rug lining the floor. "How bizarre," she said.

"Interesting, though," said Melissa.

"I guess. The stones are an odd thing in a house. More like a tunnel. But there's no light. Not for my type of work. Not the light I need."

"And it smells dank," added Zelda. "Even from here." She hadn't entered the corridor.

Melissa asked, "D'you want me to see where it goes?"

"Later," said Zelda. "It'll be a greenhouse and we can add that to the outdoors bit. Come at it from the other end, so to speak."

There was an expression on Zelda's face that Melissa was unable to fathom. It wasn't fear. It was a type of determination maybe. Melissa found out the cause of the determination a few minutes later. Zelda skipped a corridor that didn't appear on the map and went straight through the wood-panelled room with its interesting wooden door.

"The architecture's so odd," Bettina said happily. "And every single region of this house has its own palette."

"I wish the map had all these doors," said Zelda. "That's all. I want to find my working space and it hasn't showed. We've had two extra corridors and no library."

Bettina strode ahead and opened the next door and looked in and stepped right back. "This is your library," she said. "Without doubt. And it's mostly purple."

"A nice shade of purple," said Melissa. "I could work there."

"Well, it's mine. You're doing outdoor photographs."

"If you need privacy, I'll find a table somewhere else for my inside work," said Melissa. The library looked almost Fibonacci—it would be especially magic to use it. She dreamed of a little workspace, nestled inside purple bookshelves. But Zelda was right: Melissa had other choices. And that look on Zelda's face—she was seeking her private place to do her special work. But still …

They moved on, not even going into the library. If the room was going to be Zelda's, then exploring it now wasn't an option. Zelda shifted from meander to brisk walk. Walking slowly wasn't an option either, it seemed, now that the coveted work area had been discovered. Melissa lagged further and further behind, for brisk walking was something she was only capable of for maybe twenty steps. Eventually, she caught up with her friends in the sitting area near Rachel's office. Rachel wasn't visible, but Bettina and Zelda had found comfortable chairs and were talking about her.

Bettina, most of her body hidden by plush maroon upholstery, was saying to Zelda, "You won't be quite alone in the library."

"What? How do you know?" Zelda was sharp, almost unforgiving.

"I'd forgotten. I had hours with Adam for briefing and he was trying to fill in the time by telling me things. Adam thought we'd all be in the library, so he told me stuff about it. About the collection. That the door leading out of it goes nowhere. And that there's another guest. You'll see him in the library, possibly. Don't bother him and he won't bother you. He's a friend of Adam's and will do his thing and get out. He knows it's a favour, him being here."

"Why didn't Rachel tell us?" Zelda asked.

"None of her business. He's in the family wing. Doesn't interfere with the public side."

"There's politics between parts of the family and between the admin side of things," said Melissa. "I keep seeing it. It isn't just Rachel saying, 'Talk to me about things'—it's big."

"Those politics aren't going to affect us," said Zelda. "We're not here for that long and we've got our work to do."

Melissa wondered about this, given the late decision about her fellowship, but she kept her doubts to herself. Arguing with Zelda was a waste of time unless one had enormous amounts of strong evidence. Quiet concerns weren't evidence.

The next day was the trio's full first day. That's how Melissa described it to herself. She liked the description so very much that she began her notes that way.

Since her photographs were not going to be shown in chronological order, the notes would be critical to her display, and she was determined to make them fun as well. Numbers and part days, she decided, were the way to go. And sketches.

Loads of sketches. If her hand held out, notes and sketches. If it didn't … photographs. Clever Hal, for giving her the camera.

It had been easy enough to settle into her room, but Melissa felt that her room was not where she needed to be settled. Zelda had the library. Bettina had … Melissa didn't know.

Bettina acted as if she knew exactly what she was doing and where she was going and she didn't want to talk about it. Not anything to do with her work.

She explained why when asked, at least. That made the whole thing less like being thrown out of a conversation halfway through. "Before I've started, I can talk about a project with anyone. That's what I did on the application for the fellowship. I talked and I talked and I talked. Once I get into the project, though, it's as if my wordbrain switches off. I can't talk. When I try to, everything falls to pieces and I have to put it back together again. I won't do that. So I don't talk."

"I know a narrative specialist who would call that being in story space," offered Zelda. "Story space for writers is the world you create from. If you get into the right part of it, everything's easy and if something jolts you out of that, you've got to get back in again. I didn't believe it when she told me. It sounded like excuses, but it seems to me …"

"It's what I do," Bettina finished the sentence. "It's a good description. I can do other things when I'm in that space. I'm here, talking with my friends, for instance. And I can do everyday life stuff. I just don't want to challenge my story space or shatter it."

"Fair enough," said Melissa. "I'll listen when you tell me things, but I won't prod any more than I have to."

"Any more than?"

"If we're using the same physical space, I might have to talk about it a bit." Melissa felt far too apologetic. She'd accepted the technical term with no difficulty, but pushing her own work as equally important to Bettina's was more difficult.

"Try not to," advised Zelda. "You can do it." She wore her teacher stance and sounded as if she was giving advice from on-high to someone who had no experience, not much knowledge, and needed basic encouragement.

Melissa decided at that moment to avoid her friends unless the moment was a social one. Meals, excursions—these would be fine. For the rest of it, she would be better off alone. She could manage her pain levels without anyone observing and being informative about them, and she could avoid Bettina's story space and Zelda's ego.

This was school project time all over. They'd been surprised when Melissa got good marks because they'd never seen it coming. Been surprised, but claimed a share anyhow. Friends were an imperfect phenomenon, Melissa decided.

Her thoughts had looked like affirmation to Zelda, obviously. Quiet agreement rather than suppressed annoyance. The other two decided that it was a good moment to go to their rooms and do more planning. Melissa decided it was an even better time to learn the kitchen and make herself a decent coffee. She asked the others if they wanted some.

"Ooh," said Bettina. "Your coffee is always good."

"All that Mediterranean ancestry," said Zelda.

"I'm a walking stereotype." Melissa smiled reluctantly. "Do either of you want coffee?"

"Me," said Bettina. "I'll be there in ten minutes."

"Not me," said Zelda. "I intend to write a thousand words before dinner. Fifteen hundred if I can. Otherwise, today will be completely wasted, and I don't have time for that."

Over coffee, Bettina and Melissa talked as if they'd always been best friends. It was odd, reflected Melissa, how different Bettina was when Zelda wasn't there.

Melissa made sure to avoid the subject of art, however. Bettina had a confidence about her art. She'd earned it, too. And

Melissa didn't. And hadn't. Her chief confidence, she reflected wryly, was about living.

"I am alive and able to do things, despite my stupid body," she tried explaining to Bettina. This was another subject they should avoid in future, she noted, although the conversation that afternoon wasn't wince-making in itself.

Bettina focused on what was wrong with herself and didn't want to talk about Melissa. What was wrong with Bettina was small and annoying. One ailment that could be controlled given care and self-discipline. This ailment wasn't pushing slowly toward a complete change of life, but it was certainly affecting Bettina's joy in life. Melissa listened and sympathised aloud, but quietly she thought, *What about me?* Her inner voice turned that question into an old pop song. It might not be fair, but it was something that had to be lived with.

Melissa turned the conversation again to something much safer.

"Do you remember the day our English teacher threw a big volume of Shakespeare at Crow, instead of giving him detention?"

"It was detention before and detention after," Bettina said with relish. "But that day it was Shakespeare."

"That was just before we found out she was some sort of sportswoman, wasn't it?"

"Olympics—that year. We thought she was fat, but she was scary-strong. All muscle. And she threw that book at the exact spot she intended. Scared the hell out of him, but didn't hurt at all."

"And Crow copped it."

"Without complaint. Why do you ask?"

"I suspect it's the reason Crow got the English prize in Year 12. He's a travel writer now."

"Shakespeare changes lives. I've always thought this."

"These days a teacher would get into so much trouble for something like that."

"Even with someone like Crow."

"Even with someone like Crow."

"What about ...?" And they were off. Melissa and Bettina reminisced until they were called into dinner.

"So there are two kitchens?" Bettina was surprised by dinner coming so soon after coffee. It hadn't. The two had been talking for four hours, but there had been no sign of cooking. Maybe story space did things to the mind. Maybe it was just Bettina in her normal state.

"Five," said Rachel, who was waiting in the dining room. "One kitchen for guests and one for Erin and me. One for catering. Two in the family wing. But dinner comes from Robertson while you're here. We shop for your kitchen and then bring dinner in. It's easier."

Melissa summed up the day in her journal. For her, it had been about exploring, both together and alone. Rediscovering the past, re-evaluating who her friends were in the present. The house was an unknown quantity, despite the exploration. She could see that simply walking corridors wasn't what was needed. This was her second project, then. Her first was her photographs, her second would be discovering the house. Sometimes she'd do it walking. Other times she'd find a space and explore it sitting and staring. She would always be doing something, however. Her condition wouldn't get in the way of her fellowship at all.

She typed up her diary entry and texted it to Hal. She also told him he'd be getting a postcard one day, when she'd found where to post it.

"Sounds good," he replied. "Don't forget to eat."

"Catered dinners," she texted back. "Cupboards to raid the rest of the day. I'm going to eat like you and not like me."

"Extra good," said Hal. "Moving going well. It helps to be able to focus. Text like this, once a day? Better than postcards."

"I miss you," texted Melissa.

"That's why I want to finish here. I want to be finished when you finish. I miss you so much. Love you."

"Love you too. Once a day, then. But with much missing."

Melissa slept well that night. She woke and turned to tell Hal, but he wasn't there. It was odd to miss him and to wake up rested. Her life should have both.

Neither Zelda nor Bettina were around at breakfast time. Rachel was cleaning the kitchen and putting some new cheese in the fridge.

"There's a neighbour who makes the best fresh cream cheese," she explained. "And I thought you'd like it, but it only gets delivered in the morning."

"So I can eat it now?"

"Of course. There's some new bread today, too. I like it when we have three guests. And look, I'm talking whole sentences!"

"Whole sentences?" While they chatted, Melissa buttered a piece of bread and added the cheese, tasted it, and decided she needed another one. Much nicer than the cereal she'd thought would be an easy breakfast.

"Erin and I interviewed for this job together and she told me later that I never used a whole sentence. She told me that I wasn't capable of using whole sentences, not even to save my life."

"So you've been practising."

"Yup." Rachel was abominably cheerful about it. "Now I have dialect for me and my friends and proper English for everyone."

"I bet the dialect's more fun."

"Takes less time," said Rachel. "More sarky, too. Got plans for today?"

"I'm already mostly there. Look, my camera." Melissa pulled it off the back of the chair, where it was resting with her handbag. Her handbag was full of stuff she might need, like water and evil drugs. That meant she could spend the whole morning without having to go back to her room unless her body needed to lie down. The room was a pleasant and cosy place, but the lure of pretending to be fully mobile and seeing things was so intense that she'd prepared for it, in the hope.

Some time later, she was sitting on the ground outside, eating one of her emergency Wizz Fizzes. The house was a bit far to go and, anyhow, she didn't want to see anyone for a bit. She wanted to think. Emergency sugar would permit her to do just that.

The wall was made of granite boulders and hadn't been there yesterday. If it had been, she would have seen it. It was near the entrance and was unavoidable.

This was the last in half a morning of surprises. The reason this surprise triggered the sherbet hit was because the others could have been her misreading maps or not understanding or ... every time she had encountered something, she excused it. Blamed herself. Blaming oneself was easy. But this ...

It wasn't just an old-fashioned stone wall. There was a hole in the wall and she had walked through into a tunnel. The tunnel had led to other tunnels. They were all built of stone, but the type of stone changed from tunnel to tunnel. It was strange and wonderful and had not worried her until she came through the other side, having stuck to the only route with enough light to see sans torch. Out the other side was a glare of sunshine. That glare was reflecting from a lake.

A kilometre or so long and a couple of hundred metres wide, this lake could not possibly exist in the dry hillside of Robertson. It was surrounded by green turf and elegant elms and, on the far side, she could see a fake Greek temple made of what looked very like marble. The whole scene belonged in a Regency romance.

Melissa had the presence of mind to take pictures, but then

she turned around and went right back. She didn't look behind her, just in case the hole in the wall had closed. It felt like the kind of thing that a hole in a magic wall would do, after all. Then she sat with her back against the wall. This set her up so that she couldn't see a thing out of the ordinary, and she pulled her emergency rations from her bag.

When she was settled and had finished her sugar, she took out her Notebook . She keyed in her thoughts, as if that would turn them into a fictional narrative for her photography. She wished she were a novelist, or a travel writer like Crow. Mostly, she wished she could make sense of stone.

What she decided, after several deletions, was to turn everything she had seen into a fantasy land. It was shockingly real. That was undeniable. She had heard a bird cry as it swooped over the lake. Earlier, she had smelled roses where no roses had been, and her eyes were still echoing with the light from the water. If she made it pretend, she could handle it.

*How does one build a fantasy land?* she wondered to herself. *If it were me, I'd start from the land underneath. Soil, that's the trick. I saw so many different types of soil this morning.*

She'd photographed most of them, too. Melissa scrolled through her camera's memory, looking to see what she could see.

It wasn't just soil. It was soil and water. So many different types of soil and so very many different types of water. She had expected some landscaping and had prepared for this to a degree, but not to the degree she had discovered. One door in an outside wall had led to falling water so heavy she could not pass. That water still sang to her. Another had led to a stream burbling over rocks and around ferns in what she assumed was a nearby forest. *I need to see the forest near here. There are waterfalls. This might be one of them.* Melissa knew already that this was something else, but she wanted more information. She didn't trust her own senses.

*If I were turning this into a story, I would make it allegorical,* she decided. *That would mean …* Her fingers slumped as she looked through the fringe of trees and into the perfectly normal garden. The garden was also English-looking. It was made for afternoon tea and big hats. It was a place of dreams, in its own way. The sort of thing that Australians imagined belonged in their past.

*I can make this make sense,* Melissa declared to herself fiercely. This isn't a normal house and these aren't normal doors.

The map with doors that say "portal" was the key, she realised. *It's a portal house. It's a place that leads to other places. It's also a refuge. It's a place where some things are stored and saved. They give us fellowships because it's a place where stories start and where art can blossom.*

None of this was true, but it felt good to describe it this way. She typed that much into her notes.

It wasn't something she could share, of course. Maybe with Hal eventually, but never with Zelda or Bettina. Not unless they saw it too.

She betted Zelda would see it. This was her special area. Zelda would use it for great intellectual interpretation and would bring magic and portals and all the wonder into other people's everyday. This is what Zelda did and this house was sitting here, waiting for her. Not for someone like Melissa.

The house was here for Bettina just as Zelda was here for the house. Their fellowships was a given. Melissa's wasn't. This gave Melissa freedom.

She wasn't going to tell the others her theories because they were garbage theories. The magic of her book covers helped her understand that what she saw today was quite real but she didn't trust her capacity to explain things. More than that, she didn't know what to explain. All the theories in the world didn't mean a thing without enough evidence. She didn't know how to marshal that evidence. Zelda had taught her so well.

*It doesn't matter.* Melissa was defiant. *This explanation is for me, and I need it if I'm going to work here. And I have to work here. Hal can't come and get me until the retreat is finished because he's fitting a lifetime of sorting and cleaning into a few weeks. And I can't get myself home. So I need to make myself fit. I need to think this through.*

So she did. Melissa sat there until she had a working definition. Then she calmly put everything away, stood up, brushed herself off, and went to lunch.

*The soils are different here,* her notes read, at that moment.

*The sheer variance in the soil quality and type in this place tells a lot more about the house and its grounds than you might think. Each flowerbed is coded. Each corner has its own landscape. Each landscape echoes design and reflects the house's purpose.*

*Every section belongs to somewhere quite different from every other section. They unite because they're part of the same property, and they share that ultimate purpose. They're like the animals that came in two by two onto Noah's ship. This house is like a ship, an allegorical Noah's ark. It's saving all these places and all these scenes, but not necessarily for the world in which it precariously perches.*

*Why Noah's ark? Water falls, or fades, or drips at the end of every trail except the entrance. I shall explore the inside of the house bit by bit, but I bet there is water there too. Why do I think this? I haven't explored so far inside yet. I don't know. I just think it. I'll change my Noah concept if they don't. If doors lead back into the house, or if it's really a maze. Right now, I'm going on the outside, and every gate and door and hole in the wall but one leads to some sort of water.*

---

Zelda didn't like the fact that she hadn't explored the library. That was why she'd said "Mine" so firmly. It was not that she needed more research, but there were books and she hadn't seen them.

She gave herself two crystal-clear excuses. The first was that part of the house looked eleventh-century and had possibly been built in that period in Europe (and transported brick by brick, like Captain Cook's cottage), and the manager had said that the house was much older than it should be. She wanted to see if there were any documents to show exactly how it was put together. Her proper scholarly excuse, of course, was because the house had a much larger collection than she had realised. It wasn't documented as an important collection, but she'd noticed quite a few rare early editions of works in the description of the library that had come with the fellowship materials, and it would be good to be thorough. What if among the early editions were otherwise-lost works? Private libraries were magic for material that wasn't in databases.

"I shall work in the library," she told Rachel. "If you don't mind."

"I don't mind at all," Rachel said. "There's a bloke who comes in from the town most days right now. A friend of one of the family. Just so's you know."

"Using the library?"

"And wandering around a bit. He's thinking of writing a history of this place. Hasn't got permission yet—putting together a project outline for the family. If he becomes a nuisance, tell me."

"You don't like him?"

Rachel shrugged. "Some blokes, yanno, just aren't solid. He tries to hook people up with other people."

"That's romantic." Zelda smiled.

"Not romantic. Nasty. Don't let him. Always bad stuff happens." Zelda noticed that Rachel's fine English shattered whenever she was emotional. This didn't make her look trustworthy but … one of the staff members—now gone—had liked placing bullies with victims. Thought it was alternate love. So she couldn't blame Rachel.

"I'll be careful," she said.

There was one reason she hadn't told Rachel about doing her work in the library. Maybe, she didn't say to herself but the thought was there, lurking behind the official reasons, she also wanted to know how her friends just went out of sight when she turned her head. She'd asked Melissa, but Melissa always looked vague and then spouted rubbish. There were no doors to other worlds and no lakes and no giant waterfalls.

When she opened the old oak door (*Oddly large,* she thought, *and why oak?*) and walked into the library, she wished she had her camera. The light was on and the first thing she saw was a ceiling painted in black and purple. No straight lines. Everything about the ceiling was swirls. And everything about the shelves swirled. Different shades of purple clung to the curves and created a maze.

The eye pulled one into the pattern and Zelda almost walked forward. She stopped herself and regretted not bringing her camera. She had her phone, but only Melissa had permission to take pictures and Melissa's pictures were only for her art project.

Zelda would have stood at the door absorbing the room and its tens of thousands of books and impossible curvature forever, except that the curves beckoned her in. She sighed and made a mental note to document the design of the floor and of the ceiling. Maybe those curves created symbols. The note was to check for threes and for spirals. The Celtic symbols, for that way she could ask for permission to photograph.

At first, there seemed no order to the library and no way of finding anything. Whatever the order, she amended to herself, it was neither Dewey nor Library of Congress. Her fingertips caressed the painted wood with its delicately carved edges. Flowers and figurines and fancy. Impossibly imagined and beautifully crafted. The carvings didn't show from the front door—they only became clear when Zelda came close. They cradled the books in nests and aviaries and gardens. Within those aviaries and nests and gardens, the books were shelved straight and were in some kind of order. Partly alphabetical, and partly by topic, Zelda deduced. But how would she find anything? She stuck to her right and walked along the outside edge. The tug from the painted design was from the middle, but she had a theory.

Every now and again there was a crack in the curve, and a window would peer in. The windows had oak frames and the desks at the windows were also polished wood.

Right at the back of the room, near a larger window providing the light that tried to draw her through the centre, there was a noticeboard on one side and a door on the other. No desk.

On the noticeboard was the list of subject areas and the library's map.

Zelda tried the door, but it was locked. It only led to the garden anyhow, she thought as she peered out the window.

"Excuse me," a male voice said. "You're blocking the light."

"I'm sorry, I just wanted to see what was outside." She moved to the noticeboard and took out paper and pen to sketch where her topics were.

"I didn't mean to stop you looking." As the voice apologised, it came closer, and before the end of the sentence a man had emerged from one of the curves. "It was such a dramatic darkening of the ways that I felt I had to comment."

"I'm Zelda," Zelda said, and, shoving her pen and paper back into her bag, held out her right hand.

"Frater," said the man, and shook it firmly.

"Is that your first name or your surname?"

"Nickname, I'm afraid. Or title, maybe."

"You're in orders?"

"Nothing regular and nothing limiting," he said cheerfully. He was about her age, and only a small amount taller. Thin, but graceful. His shoulders bunched forward a little, as if he read too much. Except that there was no such thing as too much reading. Zelda told her students that every semester. She smiled at him.

"I can call you Frater, then? It sounds very … brotherly."

"You know some Latin?" He didn't sound too pleased. Whyever not? Why on earth would a knowledge of Latin worry anyone? Just in case he was one of those men who were irritated by intelligent women, she hid half of herself. This wasn't something she did at all happily. But she was used to dealing with strangers, and annoying them by admitting to being a lecturer and having a doctorate was not a good way to start. It was odd, though, finding these reactions in a library.

"I've got a fellowship," she said. "I'm writing a book about mythology."

"This library will be very useful, I'm certain." He didn't sound certain. In fact, his look suggested that he was terrified she'd steal his ideas.

Zelda sighed. "Mostly I'm in the library to write up earlier research. I want to look at a few books, just for fun, but I won't be using the collection in any serious way."

"You'll be using the Latin one," he said with firmness, and Zelda had to laugh.

"I doubt it. I'm a Celticist."

Frater's body language changed again. Now he saw her as a potential possession. Zelda knew his type. They'd both be better if they stayed clear of each other.

"I don't like to be a pest, but I'm on a deadline. I really only have my two weeks here to write the book. I don't like to be rude, either, but if I can just get a handle on the library layout, I can get to work. If you wouldn't mind showing me your spot, I'll choose somewhere far enough away for both of us to work without interruption."

"Very nice of you," said Frater. His face was almost radiant.

All it had taken was Zelda knowing one word of Latin to make him happier with her not too close. Zelda mentally shrugged. At least she wouldn't have to face some of the other garbage, if he didn't want her near.

---

The three women settled into a pattern of work very quickly. They didn't see each other at all during the day. That was the time for their projects. They came together with Rachel for dinner and that was their time to talk. The time to pretend that the past had never changed them and that they were still schoolgirls together. Melissa didn't challenge this pretence. She didn't really care about it, one way or another. Melissa was busy.

Her theories of water and her wish to explore weren't what took up so much time after that first morning. In fact, she delayed her explorations because she wanted to set up her shadows first. Rachel was marvellously helpful. She was enthusiastic about being called upon during the day to talk about pictures. Melissa would take some, talk about them, then go out and take others. Having someone to describe her aims to and show the reality helped her find a path through the shadows.

It would take the full time in the house to develop a visual story using the shadows, but with Rachel as a sympathetic ear and with much time spent note-taking, it would all be done here. She felt rather proud of herself for that.

The trouble with the last-minute warning and with her health issues was that she hadn't believed she could do it. Three days in and she knew she could do it. A single person supporting her had always made the difference between success and failure and suddenly she had two people.

Every night, she updated Hal on the progress of her photo collection, and every night, Hal updated her on what he was getting rid of. He had found twelve boxes in the shed and they had contained old socks. He had no idea why his mother had twelve boxes of old socks. Some project she probably meant to do thirty years ago. His mother had no idea—she had forgotten so many things that the old socks were neither here nor there. Her memories were faint ripples in the water of her mind. Except now Hal had to get rid of the old socks. Twelve boxes of them.

She didn't tell him about Noah's ark, or the water. She didn't tell him about the strange lake or the waterfall dumping impossible amounts of wetness behind a perfectly dry door. That would have to wait.

What she talked about, every night, was her first set of pictures. How it was developing. How Rachel was advising. How she missed him.

On the afternoon of the third day, the leaf-thin gardener came into the office.

Melissa felt terribly educated. She knew that he was one of the owner's grandsons and that another grandson, who had been the other gardener, had taken a leave of absence to get married. This was why the other manager was missing.

She wished she had been at that wedding. She wondered what this strange house would have been like when the grandson married the manager. She wondered, because Rachel didn't tell her. She said "They got married" as if it was small and simple and easy, but her whole body looked as if she were suppressing secrets.

Melissa found herself wondering why the leaf man never had a name. Why he was so jumpy around her. So many stupid questions. She excused herself so that he and Rachel could talk, but they followed her outside.

This could be an extra session of photography. The rosebushes had shadows, didn't they? And that should be far enough away from Rachel and Leafman so that they had their privacy.

She focused her camera on the shadows, only on the shadows. When that failed, she took perfectly ordinary pictures of roses. Then she returned to the shadows and the rose shapes were much clearer for the detour via the real flowers. It was a matter of reframing the picture in her mind, then finding the right place to take the picture, not of saying, "I am taking shadows here." The shadows had to speak to her.

This wasn't a bad outcome of an interruption. Despite this and whatever she did, she couldn't help but overhear some of the discussion. No names were given and she only heard tidbits. Those tidbits were enough.

This house was a place to be desired. Super-uber-granny (whoever she was—Melissa had never found out) had left someone out of the inheritance line. Melissa had to infer this from everything else. The closest either person came to saying it directly was, "He knows this'll never be his. Why the f* doesn't he stop trying?"

Melissa instantly thought of how someone could obtain that denied inheritance. If it was a movie, one killed for it and lied, obviously. In real life, with a place that was as strange as this, movie rules would probably be ineffective. Her mind drifted through plot scenes, as if she were writing a novel. Or maybe telling the story behind her shadow exhibition.

One moment she was dreaming and the next she castigated herself for stupidity. These were real people, and her dreams were not theirs. Their reality was probably a lot stranger than her dreams.

"He's found magic that works here. His magic, not the House's magic." That was Leafman. The two of them were closer. Melissa stopped dreaming and tried to focus on her photography, but it was hard. So hard not to hear.

They knew she was there, though. Surely they did. Unless this guy was so damn dangerous that Melissa had been forgotten. Wouldn't be the first time. She shrugged inside and packed up her camera. Time to lie down.

"Tapped into the family stuff," Leafman said gloomily. Melissa wanted to call him "Puddleglum" at that moment, but he wasn't wet enough. Just gloomy.

When she was recumbent, her mind was too active to sleep. Melissa didn't actually need to sleep. The doctor said to lie down before the pain hit, when she could feel it coming, and this was precisely what she was doing with such virtue and such a roving mind.

When it was time to get up again and deal with the outside world (in the shape of dinner), Melissa had come to a set of realisations and another set of decisions. The first was that she had seen that pie on the side of the road. And then it had gone. She also suspected that Kangaloon Street changed a bit, with extra houses on her way back from the chemist. She knew her limits and she had stressed herself just beyond them in getting back from the chemist and not strained them at all going there initially.

She would get a lift next time. She'd already decided it, but she decided it again. She'd also count houses, and Giant Potatoes, and anything else that needed counting. She'd find out how far the strange world radiated out from this house.

Would Zelda and Bettina believe any of this? Probably not. Melissa would have to do the work quietly while looking as if she was doing other things.

Observe Robertson. Observe this house in Robertson. Explore all the doors and all the portals and make her own map. Find out if everything led to water. Work out if this was an island, or an ark, or if she was reacting to medications and hallucinating. That conversation made the last impossible, but she kept it on her mental list. One had to, in order to deal effectively with suckitude every damn day, Melissa explained to herself. Just as one had to get behind all strange things and understand them. Patiently, but understand them.

"I'll hide behind my camera and see what I can see."

This led to her being left behind by Zelda and Bettina. That may have happened anyway, but Melissa suspected it didn't help. It was a night following day thing. She only saw the pair at dinner, but she noticed they got together other times. Three nights later she told them about the waterfalls and asked if they'd like to go and explained it needed the car. *I get to spend time with my friends this way, without having to negotiate here, at Ground Zero.* Melissa was happy with this.

She wasn't happy with the notes she added to her little archive over that same time period. All these happenings were on top of pain. Of course they were.

---

Bettina was just as busy as Melissa, but more focused. She knew what she wanted to do and she had explained so many times that she didn't want to talk to anyone. Bettina wanted to paint. She made exceptions when exceptions had to be made, but with reluctance.

"This is about translating my dreams into a project," was all she could tell the others, for she was past words. Inside, she had a not-very-defined wish to use her mother's gift and to shift herself sideways into the right sort of story. That was the dream beneath the dream. She wanted to be in her story. And only in her story. If there was another right kind of story, then she didn't want it. She didn't want to know. It was like those long arguments when her mother told her to follow the dreams the night gave her and to become something else. Bettina knew herself and wanted to remain herself. Her project would cement that. It would bring her to where she needed to be.

What had her mother given her?

Inside the box her mother had sent her to collect was another key. This key was made of glass. The colours of water flowed through the glass as if they had formed it. A part of Bettina wanted to find a door for it, or another box. Most of her decided that it would be the trigger for this painting. She would use the key to bring her into the right space, to remind her brain to shut out the world.

*One day I won't need this,* she thought. *I'll have my own narrative. Then I can lose my mother and be free.*

The next morning, and every morning, Bettina placed herself where she needed to be in the garden, played with the key for a few minutes, and she would paint. She had alternate places for wet days, but they were always in the garden. She would become the garden and translate the garden and interpret the garden and put it in her dreams.

---

Zelda did something similar with the library. While she claimed the whole library when her friends dropped hints about it, all she wanted was a private corner of it. She always did this with her research, found a place that became hers for the duration and would stay with her for the rest of her life.

It took careful exploration to find the perfect spot in this library. It was curved but it had a sloping desk and flat places to put books and papers and anything she might need. The slope hid a nice deep under-desk where her legs were comfortable. And it had lights. Ideal.

She loved her curved niche in the library. There was a reading slope and flat space to put books and even carved curves for her pens. She could write straight to the computer and have books and paper on both sides. It was made for her.

She didn't notice Frater at first. She had meant to write up what he looked like, so that she could blog about her research, but the moment she didn't see him, Zelda discovered that she had forgotten what he looked like. Odd, but she decided this meant the man was not for blogging. She got on with things.

Nevertheless, each time Zelda left her desk to stretch, to walk around the library for her legs, to leave for a meal or a cup of tea, there he was. He did a lot of standing at this shelf or that, looking at a book.

There was no logic in the books he was looking at, given how he moved around.

When she wrote seriously, often something small would attach itself to her mind and serve as background. A theme for her writing, she called it.

Zelda had been certain that the theme for this writing would be the library itself. Every time she walked into it she felt the pure beauty of its lines. It spoke to her in a way the garden never had and in a way the unpredictable corridors and odd doorways never would. The library became the backdrop, however, and the real theme was Frater.

He avoided looking at her directly, and they seldom spoke, but he was in almost constant communication with her. He'd leave a book open on one desk for her to glance at as she walked past, or he'd leave a book on her desk for her to read. If she left the library to get a cup of tea and then came back, all these books were gone. One of them was a rare book on Ogham inscriptions and she knew it was not one she needed, but it was a book to covet. After Frater had put it back, she couldn't find it.

She left him a note asking about it and he left her a note back. His writing looked very much like that of a Humanist scholar in the seventeenth century, Zelda thought. Or at least the way she thought such a scholar would write, for really, she knew nothing about old handwriting. She knew a little about Ogham and was deeply disappointed when the note said, "I looked, but I couldn't find it." She didn't believe him. She also didn't believe that he had to (as he claimed in his next note) put everything back so quickly.

Frater was playing with her; Zelda found it amusing.

All this took two days. Frater's intercessions were Zelda's refreshment break and she didn't notice what became of her friends in those hours. She was focused on writing and writing and pausing to recover and Frater was a part of this process and her friends were not.

On day three, they started chatting in those breaks. The man was never intrusive and never … personal. Friendly and helpful and insightful, but he gave Zelda her space.

Zelda teased him about it—that he was safe to be around. He smiled at her, complicitly, for the first time letting any real expression show through. It was as if they had a game, and that Zelda had just explained one of the rules to the person who invented the rules.

Every time she was in the library, Zelda undertook her own small exploration. It took her back to her childhood. The three of them had done that. They could never agree which part of the neighbourhood they liked or where they wanted to go, so, unless they had a message to deliver or wanted to buy sweets, they explored systematically. Zelda planned, Bettina drew, and Melissa dreamed. That was how Zelda remembered it. She'd used the system in libraries ever since.

Today she was looking in one of the many alcoves. This one didn't have a desk, but the shelves had pull-out sections. She took advantage of this, for the books were all plays. Old editions. No one was around, so she could spend a happy few minutes reading aloud. Performing old plays. That took her back to her first university years, where she'd spent a lot of her time in the student theatre. She'd moved into Celtic landscapes from there. *Juno and the Paycock* had been her moment of truth. As she flicked through the plays on the shelf, she remembered.

The fake accents that gave the performance the air of a farce.

The extraordinary nationalism of people like her who had never been to Ireland and knew next to nothing about the Troubles.

Ancestry was supposed to be enough, and she was discovering that ancestry was never enough. She had felt sick when she'd seen the way certain audience members had shifted uncomfortably in their seats. She saw that shifting time and again, for she had watched them from backstage—she was no major player.

Later she saw the Abbey Theatre perform the precise same play. When they did it, the characters didn't have accents—they spoke in a manner that felt perfect for the dialogue. And they were full individuals with increasingly troubled lives, not symbols on a banner. Zelda knew that her instincts were right, even when her grand intellect was very far in the wrong.

When her instinct flared into fascination at a particular volume, Zelda took it straight from the self and commenced reading. O'Casey might have sent her to a set of cultural traditions that were ancient and satisfying, but that was then. Right now, he was sending her to a French play.

Her French sounded so very wrong, for she didn't have as much of the language as she admitted. She could read it (mostly) but she couldn't speak in any of the range of proper accents to save her life. Back to accents, then. Not people.

She didn't know this work. So what was it that made her keep it off the shelf?

Zelda kept reading aloud obdurately, and gradually her French sounded almost passable. "Back-brain, work." She stopped to admonish herself. Then she looked around.

That was odd. Frater wasn't there.

Zelda stopped reading and took a closer look at the title. It was an old edition of Rostand's *Cyrano de Bergerac*. She knew the story more from the Gerard Depardieu movie—the one with Tom Stoppard subtitles. The one she'd told generation after generation of students that they could learn everything from, if they wanted. Stoppard had made such perfection out of an old French play. Probably not even a very good French play. Not that she knew. Her French was too little. Instead of reading aloud, Zelda looked at the title and thought.

What was the play about? Cyrano courted a woman through someone else. And lost the woman in the process. Lost love was nothing to do with her life, but then, she was a modern woman. She wasn't being courted for sex or love or anything nice, she was being courted for knowledge. For influence. For—

Frater clattered as he dropped something and bent to pick it up.

Some moments, Zelda hated men. All men.

"I need to find out more about Frater," she told herself viciously, and shut the slim volume with a very faint slap. She put it back on the shelf so very neatly that no one would know which plays she'd looked at, then took out *Juno and the Paycock*. It not only had an excellent cover, it would remind her to look for the truth, not mimic others and live a lie.

Frater was not at all interested in her answer when he asked about her reading. What was he interested in, then?

---

Melissa had a run-in with Frater that same day.

She had decided to try a door or two. There were things she needed to see and a map she had to create, after all. Also, the first two doors marked "portal" were close together. She could get the hurty bit of her daily walk done, with the doors as natural stopping points.

It was another of those rather problematic days, when her old doctor would have said "stay in bed" and "take prescription pain relievers". Going slow and stopping frequently often helped the pain work itself down to a manageable level. If it didn't, then her old doctor's words helped. She didn't want them to hold in this place. Two doors, close together, would help her decide how to manage the rest of the day.

Melissa was so slow that it was obvious when someone was following her. A bloke. Probably the bloke Zelda had mentioned was in the library. Metroguy's friend. Metroguy's guy was how she would explain it to Hal in tonight's text. Her follower pretended he hadn't seen her and so she mentally shrugged and went on with her self-imposed task.

She skipped into her first portal and found a delightful garden. It was tropical and damp and full of ferns. The warmth and wetness seeped into her and unknotted some of the ache. She wandered there slowly for ten minutes and more of her unknotted. When she left the ferns and the flowers and the wet, she closed the door gently behind her.

Metroguy's guy was gone.

It didn't take long for pain to return, but it didn't return to the level it had been prior to the fernery. Melissa stopped to note that down on her pad. This was a much better solution for pain than lying in bed feeling miserable or taking such big medicines that they warped her brain and body. It wasn't an everyday solution, but it would help her during her residency. That was something.

The next portal was plastic. Or a type of glass that felt like plastic. She tapped it and listened carefully to the sound. Plastic. Pale blue plastic. She slipped it open and walked into a plastic room.

Behind her came a faint "mmph" then a male "Help me!"— sharp and scared. There was a hand stuck in the door.

Melissa opened the plastic door again and the hand slipped out. Not in. She went out to investigate.

"How do you even see those things, anyway?" Frater grumbled at her.

"You don't see a door?" Melissa asked, curious. "Was it your hand?"

"Of course it was my hand. Look!" And he waved the injured member at her, as if she had hurt him on purpose.

"You should find Rachel. She's got a medical kit. Or go to a doctor in town."

"I want to go into that room."

"You know where the door is. It won't go away." As she said this, she wondered. That stone wall with its tunnels had come and gone. But this was on the map and the wall wasn't. "It's even on the map." Melissa added her thought to her scold. "Go get that seen to!"

He gave her a look. Such a look. Then he turned away and went … maybe to Rachel. Who knew? What Melissa knew was that something about him made her ill.

She turned back to the door, curious, then went into the room. Pale blue plastic. Pale green plastic. Sculptures and vessels holding water. Very modern art. Lovely lines, but dull. She spent the rest of the morning doing photography. The shadows made her think of what might be underground.

That afternoon, she checked a cellar. It had a portal. She opened the door and there was a tunnel. Another tunnel. This one was lit with fungi that glowed green and blue. The same colours as that morning, but turned to modern art. *I will explore this tunnel another day,* she thought. *I need to get back into the sunshine. Also, I need more pain relievers.* These were excuses. She was finding everything disturbing and Frater's presence changed things.

As she left the cellar, Frater caught up with her. He grabbed her shoulder with his damaged hand. Obviously he healed quickly.

"Ouch," she said.

"Where have you been?" he asked.

"In the cellar," she replied.

"Why?"

"I'm a photographer." Melissa exaggerated her camera expertise in the hope it would shut him up. “My project is taking pictures. The cellar is full of shadows. Too full. They’re not going to work for me at all. I had to see, though.” She wondered why she was explaining this to a man who made her so very uncomfortable.

“Show me.” He was abrupt and rude; nevertheless, Melissa opened the door to the cellar and indicated down the stairs.

“Not enough contrast,” she said as he clambered down. “I’m not going down there again. It will hurt and I can’t get pictures.”

He turned right at the base of the stairs and walked right past a door as if it weren’t there. She watched him prowl through the open space.

“I’m photographing shadows,” she explained, so that he didn’t think to look for the door he couldn’t see. “They’re very dramatic in sunlight. They’re the whole scene here. I don’t need this cellar for my project.”

He nodded and Melissa could see the spark of interest disappear. It was totally worth the long time it took to get to her medicine and to bed. Totally worth it. She hadn’t actually done anything, but she felt she’d saved the house from … something. All her numbness and worry washed away. Even if she hated the plastic room, she still loved the house. Melissa felt benevolent as she rested.

She resolved to stick to what she said she would and to photograph those shadows. This didn’t mean she’d skip seeing the waterfall and exploring for other things. This house was amazing. It meant she’d have an excuse for being almost anywhere, for she had two sets of photographs and they covered most conditions. That meant she could stay away from Mr Frater. He wasn’t interested in her work, and if she was doing her work, he wouldn’t follow her trying to find … magic. There, it was out. This was like her water-coloured books.

She left her bed and found Rachel. Rachel was with the other manager, who was back for the afternoon. She confided to them about Frater and apologised for thinking stupid things when he probably wasn't any problem at all.

"Your instinct is terrific," said Erin. "He should not find the water features or the doorways and he should not even be looking."

"He must work for Metroman," said Rachel. "Must. Dammit, now I sound like you." She turned to Melissa. "Don't worry. I'll get rid of him. He can come back to Sydney with me and if Metroman asks, well, I can say he bothered one of our fellows. You don't mind, do you?"

"Of course I don't mind. I'd feel a lot better without him around."

# THIRTY-FOUR

Migraine—I call it migraine 'cause it fits the description, but I think it's like the bad skin and linked to my body being on the edge of a chasm and it's when I hurt because I'm clinging onto a branch so hard to prevent myself tumbling down. Everything hurts because of the clinging. Some of them might be real migraines. How can I know when the doctor doesn't?

I'm shoving days and days of notes together here. That way the doctor can find them. I'm honestly not sure it's useful anymore, but if I put them all here then I won't remember them as happening every damn day. That's what the notes were doing.

I didn't know I had this mental capacity to obliterate some of the everyday awfulness and get through it emotionally by strange sublimation. When I read the note or write the notes or both, I turn the pain into concrete and put my feet firmly in the middle. More sequences. Not hours apart. Sometimes a day apart. Sometimes a few days apart. And when I realised what I was doing to myself in turning the symptoms into an aware part of my life, I stopped entirely for a bit.

This, then, is just to remind me and the doctor that this was a very bad idea. A very very very bad idea. Got that? Good. This is the last sequence I'll do. I'll only note down pain when there is a real need. And symptoms when they're new or present differently. I live with them enough. I do not need to spend valuable spoons making everything worse.

If it was going to make it better, it would've by now. So there.

Migraine.

Today is a translation day today is a translation day today is a translation day. Dammit. Work!

Today is a translation day.

Today is the day I stop taking notes. Unless I forget. I hope I don't forget. My life is bad enough without commemorating everyday disaster.

# THIRTY-FIVE

When the sun shone on the property, it shone quite differently in different places. Today there was smoke in the air. Melissa savoured the eucalyptus scent, then felt a twinge of guilt. If she were allergic or had breathing difficulties, she would be tasting discomfort and even danger. She once knew someone who would have to go to hospital if he had taken such a deep breath of the fragrant air.

*That's the trouble with constant pain,* thought Melissa. *It distracts me. I am aware of what hurts other people. I am aware of what hurts me. My mind hovers on awareness, always. It's tiring. And it brings a kind of emotional exhaustion, which carries its own burden of a nagging depression. I don't need that. I need ...*

Her thought trailed off as her word-brain switched off and her sight-brain took over.

Melissa saw the sharpened close images, with the colour of the trees deeper and stronger from the change in air quality. If she could see the mountains from here, they would be hushed and gentle. The Blue Mountains would be very blue today. All the mountains would be blue today. Every single one in the region would be part of another world.

This light she saw, this golden sunlight, softened by the slight haze, made warm by it, was telling her something.

"I'm in another world," she said aloud.

That was it. That was what she had been looking for. Shadows and light that showed different worlds at different times of the day. That used the different qualities the smoke in these mountains gave the air, and the purity of it when the smoke blew away. Even days without sun gave the whole of reality a sense of shadow, so that would be another world entirely.

Melissa walked very slowly around the garden. Every now and again she'd pick up the pace to give her those stretches and walks that would make tomorrow a little better, but for the most part she stayed within her comfort zone. When she hurt, she used that as an excuse to stop and take pictures.

It was a bit random, but it was effective. She trained her eye to see beauty or squalor or danger or joy from wherever she stood. Shadow was sharp against the almost tangible warmth of the bush sunlight.

That was the thing. The faint smoke brought the bush into this very cultivated garden. It eroded its barriers. Melissa was fascinated by this notion and walked a section of the brick fence that was one of the borderlands, taking pictures of the shadows that reached from the fence into the garden. If the shadows were long enough, they'd reach the house. There was a story in that, and she needed a story for her photo collection.

Melissa stopped for a moment, leaned against the wall for support, and took out her phone to make a note.

"Ask Hal to write poems that will tell the story. How the shadows crumbled the borders of reality and what happened then." If only she painted or drew well. Then it would be perfect. But if she noted the patterns of the shadows with her camera, they could tell a story.

This is what she loved about being with Hal. She grumbled

about his perfection from time to time, because she didn't marry him for perfection. She didn't marry a nurse, or someone who would deny his own life to give her less pain. His continuing support and love made her feel so guilty sometimes. She wasn't always sweetness and light about it because she hurt, because she was humiliated by her own helplessness, because ...

Shadows. These were her shadows. They breached her wall of sanity. They turned her from who she had been as a child, that supportive girl that had rounded out the trio, to the stronger but very different adult.

*I wonder if I can tell this in pictures? I wonder if I can document my own learning with these shadows? I wonder if I can stop worrying that my friends don't treat me as an equal and start accepting that Hal and I have just as good a relationship now as always, and that my physical condition is a part of it and not a humiliation.*

She had no idea how she'd do this. Not with shadows. Not with anything. Bettina's grand talent might manage it. Zelda's brilliant analysis might succeed. But Melissa wasn't either Bettina or Zelda.

She made notes of all of this. "Start with the shadows" were the last words she keyed in before putting her device away.

"It's not a device," Hal always chided. "Give it a name if you don't want to give it a product type. Other people give them names."

"I prefer device," Melissa had said then, and, at the memory, she wondered if she should call the device "Zelda" for its memory. Once she'd dropped the device into the toilet. She felt the sunlight deep inside her as she tried not to think of how to tell Hal. "I dropped Zelda down the toilet. Can you help me get her out?"

When she was warm enough and had sufficiently got even with Zelda for the latest unwitting put-down, Melissa turned her camera on again.

The most interesting shadows here were along the wall, in

fact. There was a row of gravel and it was sparsely scattered with succulents and bushes. Everything else in this place was so above the ordinary. The main garden with its resident Leafman ("Sort-of Puddleglum" was now her alternate name for him). The orchard with its thirty types of apples, each with its own name. The other strange fruit: medlars and damsons were the labels on the little posts by each tree. The flower garden, in which, when she stepped into it, she felt that her clothes ought to transform into those suitable for a 1930's garden party. This was none of those.

"I've seen this before," she said aloud. She had been in Sydney for a medical check and Hal said, "Meet me in Wollongong and I'll drive us home the fun way." Robertson had been a place they went through then, she supposed, and hadn't noticed. What she'd noticed was the wall in the car park of the train station. A red brick wall, more boring than this one. This wall had colours and shades and a sense of industrial importance. It was a superior brick wall. But the plants next to this wall and the gravel … they had migrated from that station car park.

That was it. The starting point she needed. The other pictures had been finding her voice. Now she could begin the ones she'd use to connect any others.

Her baseline was the midsummer shadows at Wollongong station. They'd been grand and ghastly and Melissa had been very relieved when Hal finally turned up, deeply apologetic for being so late. Those shadows had given her nightmares for months, until she discovered that the nightmares were from her new medication. Whenever she saw shadows of a certain kind, they reminded her body and she had nightmares again.

That internal sickness, that faint horror—those were what she could use the shadows on this wall for. It would be the connecting thread throughout her photo story. They would grow and change and consume all, even if she had to reorder them to make them do this.

The pictures they would connect would be the light and dark she saw in all the parts of the garden. Colour would be background: light and shade would meet to give the story life.

Melissa developed a plan so that she could see everything, do everything, and hurt the least possible. Every day she'd make sure she walked gently. That would be her inside exploration and her outside exploration. How much she did and how quickly she did it would depend wholly on the complaints her body made to her. The only time she would leave the house and gardens was when she saw the forest and waterfalls. Which she would. Somehow. Every single day she would have a minimum of two new sets of pictures from two different times of day. And she would enjoy herself and tell Hal every evening she missed him but that she was enjoying herself. This was her plan.

Before then, she was going to see a waterfall. Bettina and Zelda had promised.

---

The day started well. The three met after breakfast, loaded into Bettina's car, and went to the waterfall first thing.

"We want the early light," said Zelda, "which Melissa would know, being a photographer." Melissa did know, but she wondered why it was so important for this to be announced. Maybe Zelda didn't believe she knew anything about light. Maybe Zelda needed more coffee.

Most probably Zelda was simply being helpful, but it rubbed and Melissa spent the whole car trip thinking of ways to explain to Zelda how she used light and what her art was and all the things she could never say. Illness set up problems with verbal transactions, she had discovered. *Once one can't talk about the everyday pain, it's hard to talk about other things,* Melissa admitted to herself, as she sat in the back seat and didn't say a word.

The waterfall required walking. That was okay. She had

taken extra pain relief in case, and she could go slowly. The others went slowly, too, for it was a narrow path and tourists had arrived before them.

Melissa tried to take photographs of everything, but there was a group of people who stood at the best corner of the lookout and talked and talked and didn't look and just took up space. Melissa took all the pictures she could elsewhere, as did Zelda and Bettina on their phones.

Bettina said, "Would you mind moving a bit so that I can get a shot? I'm an artist and this is the only time I'm going to make it down here."

They moved and the three swooped in.

"I'm impressed," said Melissa to Bettina.

"That I said I was an artist?"

"That you got them to move. They are such a close group," Melissa explained.

All the body language within that group had been internal. The outside world didn't exist for them. From the way Zelda held herself, it always existed for her. She protected Bettina from the world. She had taken her pictures quickly and then stood admiring the many-part falls tucked far into the cliff, and playing with the swimming pool one had carved, but her body language kept space for Bettina to photograph for as long as she liked.

Melissa didn't have that choice. Back seat of the car for travel, and side of the group for her pictures. But she had learned to deal with that years ago. Another side effect of being ill: one became contained. One did what one must in the time one had, in the space one had. With the friends one had. The everyday pain brought enough pushing and stretching and left no energy to say, "Please, can I have some more?" Melissa grumped at herself. Why couldn't she say that? It might be work and it might take her out of her safe zone, but why couldn't she? It would have to be done right, was all.

"How is the view from where you are, Zelda? Is there anything I could use?"

Zelda moved aside and Melissa got more pictures. Not enough. Not free range and fair choice, but more. She thought about a waterfall printed onto A3 card and then cut into bookmarks. That would go very well for sales.

They walked up to the car and it was difficult. Even Zelda was slow, for it was up stairs. The three of them made jokes about the stairs and they were over in an aching flash.

"I want to go on one of those walks," said Zelda. "Three or four kilometres isn't too bad."

"Good idea," said Bettina.

"How about I hang out near the car? There's interesting old growth here and the sun is so fierce and there's that tinge of bushfire smoke. I might use it for my portfolio." That was the best Melissa could do.

"Meet you at the car, then," said Bettina.

Alone, Melissa's world didn't shrink: it grew. The gnarled trees reached for the sky and Melissa found herself drawn to them, taking picture after picture of a single fantastically warped silhouette.

The faint smoke brought all the bush scents together. The undergrowth was stacked up with fallen branches and bark and lichen and scuttling creatures. She was on the path a mere fifty metres from the car park, yet she was moving in a new world. Or an old world. An ancient world that recrafted itself around the needs of tourists and park rangers.

Her camera clicked and shuttered and clicked and shuttered. It became the path from all her senses to her new world discovery. The sound of tourists blended with birdsong and rustles in the undergrowth and formed its own carpeted background for her work. She moved slowly, led by the camera until Bettina's grumpy "Oh, there she is" brought her back into everyday life with a snap. She turned the camera off, put it in her handbag so she wouldn't be tempted into staying in the alien landscape, and walked back to her friends. She was slow, because pain had started to attack her walking with its usual faint viciousness and, by the time she reached the car, all the "Hi—how was your walk?" questions had been posed and answered and there was only one thing left to say. Naturally, Zelda said it.

"Okay, we can go now."

The three went to the meat pie place. "It's tourist day today," explained Bettina, as if any explanation were needed. And they each ordered pies. *Of course we're doing this,* thought Melissa.

She looked at the dessert pie Bettina and Zelda had decided to share, and the tiny bit of juice seeping out the crack convinced her she didn't want one. The pie she'd seen in the street on her first day had been one of these. She imagined it walking by itself. Of course it couldn't've, but even imagining it scuttling or scurrying or sitting there in plain sight and then moving smoothly into hiding when she wasn't looking, even this imagining was enough to make her want to avoid it. She didn't want a pie at all now, but she'd ordered it and so she sat at the tourist table and ate her tourist food.

After that, they went to see the Great Potato and found a place to buy potatoes, as one does.

"How about we walk for a bit and look in shop windows and suchlike and then have a cuppa?" Shop windows would be slow walking, and Robertson was small and there was a car to take her back, so Melissa agreed. She'd forgotten how sharp the pain had become in the short walk back to the car after the waterfall pictures.

*It's as if the damned brain can't remember pain,* she thought as she found herself looking in shop windows for longer and longer, not quite staying still, keeping the movement of her feet going despite herself. What she needed was to lie down, but that wouldn't happen for a bit.

The coffee would help. *One has to sit down for coffee.* One foot then one foot then one foot then one foot then one foot and she could continue. One foot then one foot then one foot then one foot then one foot and she did continue. Melissa was very proud of herself.

By this stage, however, she was so far behind the others that she gave up on catching them. She would meet them in the café when she could. Hurrying wasn't worth the hurt.

The emotional hurt of being left behind for the third time wasn't worth it, either. Bettina was cosseted and Melissa was given tough love. That was how things had shaped between the group since the first day they had met again. These thoughts that scuttled in Melissa's brain were hardly possible, but they helped hide the pain.

Distraction was a great assistant. The camera had done that before; thinking how the friendships had changed and were developing did the trick now. One foot then one foot then one foot then one foot then one foot became almost automatic as she thought about old friends and how she no longer quite fitted into their world.

"What can I do?" Melissa asked herself out loud, then secretively checked. No one was close enough to even half-hear.

She realised that she hurt too much to think straight. The idea of parking all those blocks away from the café and having this nice refreshing walk in both directions had been such a bad one. And she couldn't get back to the house without the lift, either. She sighed. They'd wait for her, but she'd probably miss out on that cuppa.

How to turn this into something worthwhile?

Melissa's gaze turned from secretive to assessing. If she could find something to photograph, she could at least do work. And her camera would help mask pain. Win-win. She was at the house to develop a portfolio, after all, not to catch up with school friends.

This town was much more ordinary than it had appeared at

first. Nice. Good wide streets, friendly people. Everything was in the right place, including the Big Potato. The showground was not on the wrong side of the house.

All the things that seemed shifty and dubious had settled into acceptably normal in the clear bright sunshine of her friends' presence, she suspected. The sunshine was particularly clear because of the elevation and she slowed down her puddling walk to a halt, realising over and again that all this analysis was simply her self-distraction from pain. Sometimes a halt helped.

For a moment she shut her eyes. Her feet and legs were beginning to ease off and it wouldn't be long before she could walk at a reasonable speed. Just for a little. Then she'd have to slow down again.

Once pain was triggered, it came back far too readily. With her eyes shut, she focused on her body's state, assessing what she could do and how everything felt. When she opened her eyes to the bright sunlight, everything was much clearer. She could probably walk back to the house if she had to, but it would take several hours. Better not to have to.

What was there that she could usefully photograph on the way to the café, without losing sight of her friends if they left? She reflected on her body-feel and thought, *No bending or stretching.* The sun called her, the warmth reminding her again that it was a bright, bright day. *Shadows,* Melissa thought. *I could do a terrific portfolio of shadow pictures. Make them speak. Make them tell stories.* And she'd begun doing that back at the house, at the red-brick wall. *Might as well continue. Make those thoughts the reality.* This was not the first time she'd decided that. The pain triggered new decisions that were old decisions. She didn't care. The fact that it would work out was what mattered.

She took her camera out of her handbag and slung the bag across her body so that her hands would be free. She started walking toward the café as she set the camera up. Slowly, slowly would do everything.

As her brain came back into gear, she decided on sequences. How many, she did not know, but they'd all have their own character. She didn't know yet if they'd tell a fairy story or simply look charming, but if she divided the pictures into themes as she did them, either would work.

The first theme shouted at her. The lampposts and the electricity boxes and the occasional shrubs and trees made street-shadows. Another world that echoed this one, oddly and erratically.

She kept walking very slowly as she took each shot, only pausing for a microsecond. Melissa reassured herself with this pace that she would reach the café and have coffee and cake with her friends and that all would be well. Unlike last time. This time she knew she could get home if she had to, even if it meant she was very late for dinner. That walk scared her, but the fact she could do it meant that under the fear was a certain security. This was the feeling she took from the shadows: fear underlaid by security.

*I wonder if I can turn this into one of those handwavium things when I get time to myself tonight,* she thought. The controlled fear was fascinating. Two types of art from the one street experience. She very much wanted to do this. If only there was a way of recording the handwavium. *But maybe it's better not recorded. Just as it's better if no one knows about it but me. Yeah. I need to get the pictures perfect, then, because I damn well want to share this feeling. It's odd and fascinating.*

This brought her safely to the café. The other two were sitting there, waiting. Not for her, but for their coffee.

"Oh, here you are," said Bettina. "We ordered. You'd better go to the counter for your order. They're very slow and you might have to finish by yourself if they take too long. We need to be back a bit before dinner. Zelda has to email her kid."

"I'm not sure I can walk that far," Melissa told the literal truth.

"Well, tell the staff then. Nothing we can do about it."

Were they this daft at school? she wondered as she gave up on even looking at the menu and went to the counter. Or is it my crippled state that befuddles them? She paused until the girl at the counter noticed her.

"I'm with the table over there," she started to explain.

"Just sit down and I'll get to you soon," the girl said slightly impatiently.

Melissa decided that literal truths were good things today. "My friends will leave when they finish their coffee. They've got messages to do. If I don't leave with them, I'll have to walk back to the lodging place and it will take me three hours. Maybe I'll just skip coffee. Thanks," she said and turned away.

"Wait!" said the girl. "I'm sorry. I shouldn't take my bad temper out on you. How about I give it to you in a takeaway cup? And if you want cake, Bob can bring it over now." A young man was about to deliver coffee and cake to the table. The girl waved him back.

"Thank you. That would be wonderful. The chocolate cake you have on display would be perfect."

"Easy." The girl smiled. Genuine relief. She told the young man to take the cake with the others.

"One of those days?" asked Melissa.

"Oh, yes. And you're having one too. Wasn't fair."

"Let me pay for this and the biggest takeaway coffee you have and both our days will be improved because you can get rid of me and I can sit down."

"It hurts?" While they chatted, the total was rung up and Melissa paid with change and all the problems of the world were half-solved.

"So much. We're only two miles away, but …"

"You're at the estate. Wow. Are you a writer? I met my favourite author last year."

"Artist. I'm here to photograph things."

"Oh." And the girl's eyes became dreamy. "I'd love to talk about it."

"If I can come back another time and if you're not too busy …"

"Perfect," she said. "And here's your coffee."

"How did you do that?"

"I didn't. I messaged the barista and said it was urgent."

"You are a gem and a marvel."

Melissa took her coffee and her camera and felt her handbag to check it was still safely wrapped around her and she joined her friends. The afternoon had lost its fear now that she didn't have to walk back. And she had coffee and chocolate cake. And her medicine was just a feel away. What more was there in life?

There was something more in life: the Giant Potato was missing when they drove past it. Zelda was driving and didn't see. She had taken the wrong turn and took them several kilometres south of the town. This is why they passed the place it should have been twice and this is why, the second time, Bettina said, "That's odd. I thought this is where the Giant Potato stood."

"The Giant Potato?" Zelda was focused on making the correct left-hand turn and getting onto Kangaloon Road this time.

"Huge turd-like thing."

"Oh that. You just didn't look properly. That reminds me, I want to take some of those local potatoes home."

Bettina rolled her eyes at Melissa and Melissa passed her a note, as if they were in class.

"I didn't see it either," the note said. "But it comes and goes."

Bettina asked her about the note that evening, after dinner.

"I can't do more than a few minutes now," said Melissa. "But

I want to show you something." She took Bettina on a detour back to their wing.

"It's a nice door," Bettina said dubiously.

"Teak, I think. Probably tropical," answered Melissa. "Let's just see what's on the other side."

She held her breath as Bettina opened the door. She didn't know if the waterfall and the gully would be there. She didn't know if the streams would burble in the background or if that weird displacement of space would happen.

They did. Every single one of them was there and behaved as if they were always there and always did that thing.

Bettina and she stood with their backs to the rock face and looked at the door in the distance, almost invisible behind the veil of water.

"I need to think about this," Bettina said abruptly.

"I went to Rachel about it," offered Melissa. "I had to ask."

"Of course you did." And Bettina smiled. "You've made it all so normal."

"She said not to talk about it with people. If you couldn't walk through that door and through the water …"

"You wouldn't've told me."

"'Fraid so."

"I need to think about this." This time it was less abrupt.

"That's fine. I won't be exploring again until tomorrow arvo sometime. If you want to join me, just say. Otherwise … no worries."

"Explore? Here?" Bettina's arms waved a bit ineffectually.

"This is labelled as a portal on the map. I want to see—"

"More portals."

"I love finding out things." Melissa felt apologetic.

"Let's do one together tomorrow then." Bettina sounded suddenly conspiratorial. "I can keep thinking while I find out what another door does."

"Where it leads."

"And it's one you don't know?"

"I've not got very far," Melissa admitted. "I was mostly exploring outside, to take pictures."

"Let's get a cuppa."

"Yes, let's."

The next day was like the first day Melissa had explored a portal, only, maybe, stranger.

*There's something about the shadows at this wall,* she thought that morning. *They're not changing according to the sunshine, for I'm taking the pictures the same time every day. They're growing too fast.*

And they were darker than the tree shadows. They felt as if they'd eat the house up if they reached it. She photographed the whole wall line, not just the bit that looked as if it belonged at Wollongong station. Over the wall was Robertson. Inside the wall, the house's portals led to … other places. The portals had their defences. But did this wall? Did any of the walls? She was late to lunch because of her pictures, but it was a low pain day and she skipped her rest and it was all done. Melissa felt very smug. Also very worried. Those shadows felt hungry.

Or maybe she was just hungry for lunch.

That afternoon, she resolved, she would finish with the tree shadows quickly, and have a rest and visit a portal with Bettina, and either then or that evening she would sort all the shadows and find out if they were hungry or if she was just stupid. Easy.

She uploaded them to the cloud first, and she made sure her camera was with her.

Melissa's life hadn't been entirely safe. She never talked about it. She never even thought about it if she could. She made a nest for herself with Hal and dealt with complications as tidily as she could. She didn't let herself get too scared. She never let her past catch up with her.

One thing she took with her everywhere was the strong will to never let anything like that happen. Not ever again. Not to herself. Not to anyone she loved. Not even to her possessions. When anything of hers was even slightly in danger, she protected it.

Her room was not as she had left it.

Her computer was open and powered-up on the desk. One idea chased another round in circles. Someone had been in her room. Those shadows were haunting her.

Melissa sat still until she had found a way of handling both problems.

She would have to ace those shadows. That was all. And take pictures of them and … think about the pictures. Study them. Work out why the shadows looked like hungry ghosts.

That would be a good name for her exhibition, if she should get that far. "Hungry ghosts." Her grandmother would have loved that. A tiny bit of that Singapore childhood she had left behind when her father had helped build the Snowy Mountains scheme, creeping into Australia. Gently and softly, not like those ghosts. They should be gentle and soft, shouldn't they? It was all … disturbing.

Melissa ate lunch quickly, then did what she had to do almost perfunctorily. Pictures were important. Keeping up with things that needed keeping up with was important. Not hurting was desperately important. But they were all hard to focus on when she had ghosts nibbling at her through her camera. Her bag felt heavy. The camera felt as if it was hiding secrets. Which it probably was. Even in her room, trying to rest, she had her bag beside her and her camera safe. Melissa turned this thought over and over in her mind: she hadn't realised what she was doing.

*I don't want to be in this place again,* Melissa thought, and reached for her phone. Talking to Hal would help. But Hal had his mother to move. He had her whole life to sort and tidy and complete so that he and his mother could move to that next stage when Hal was in charge of the family. And this abuse of her privacy was something she could handle. She had grown a lot since her youth. *I can do anything. Not anything physical,* she amended, *but I can handle the big betrayals and the small betrayals and the strange stealing of privacy. First thing is to never let this idiot near my camera again. And the computer ...*

There was a way of making herself safe there, too.

She put a notice on her machine. One that would appear the moment it was booted up.

> Dear new friend,
>
> Thank you for looking at my cute little toy. It's free for you to explore because of the files linked to the desktop that tell people what medicine I need. If you play with that, we'll find out when I get raced to hospital. Know that it is on your head. All your fault. All my work is offsite, and my husband did all the passwords. Look, I'll make it easy for you. If you want to amend my medication and argue with my doctor, I'll leave you the printed list on the desk. What else is there for you on this machine? Not a damn thing.

She placed a spare copy of her medicine list very tidily on the desk so that it looked decorative. There was already one in her handbag, so she put one of the other spares in the pocket of her jacket, and the last she would give to Rachel and explain why. Easy.

The fact that she had four because she'd forgotten to change the quantity after the previous print job was immaterial. Also immaterial was her packing them all out of guilt. She'd intended to use three of them as scrap paper and take extra notes on her thoughts about her photos, but her photos didn't need hand-written notes. The pictures and computer notes told the story quite well enough. But now ... she would use them all. And she'd watch for someone being shamed. Or at least embarrassed.

It had taken a while for her to wind up and now it was going to take a while to wind down.

Time to move, even if it hurt. Some days it was better to move and hurt more than to let the distress build. Her room wasn't the safe place right now, and her work was. *I thought I was past this. Years ago, I was past it. I will get past it again. Work will calm me. And maybe old friends.*

Three minutes later Melissa was knocking on Bettina's door.

"Hi." Bettina looked tired.

"I didn't mean to wake you up." Melissa stepped back a little from guilt.

"If I'd slept any longer, I'd be up half the night. I didn't mean to sleep!"

"Oh," said Melissa. "I just wanted to ask if you wanted to check out a portal."

"Which one?"

"Any. I'm going to try as many as I can while I'm here, but I have no order to them. Does that make sense? I'm … not with it today. Someone went into my room and looked through my stuff."

"Mine too,' admitted Bettina. "I've locked up things I don't want anyone to see."

"Locked up?"

"In my suitcase."

"Good," Melissa said vaguely. "I'm going to tell Rachel."

"Tell her about both of us, then, and I'll come and find you in a few minutes."

"Can you bring your map of the house? I can't find mine."

"You can have mine forever and ever. Just give me a sec." Bettina ducked into her room for a moment and instantly handed it over.

"Don't you need it?"

"Everywhere I'm going regularly is easy, and for the rest of it —I'm going with you."

"Thanks. See you soon."

"Give me ten minutes," Bettina said.

"Take your time. I'll wait in Rachel's office."

"Okay."

Bettina took quite a bit longer than ten minutes, which was just as well. Rachel and Melissa had a lot to discuss. None of it led anywhere, but Melissa felt good about it. Nothing had been lost and Rachel had been angry and … it had felt like talking to an old friend.

Rachel never said, "It'll be fine."

Melissa asked her, "Why don't you say that? Most people do."

"It makes you happy right now, sure, but what of after? When things aren't fine? It's fake."

"I miss that word—fake," Melissa said slightly mournfully. "Modern politics has ruined it."

Before Rachel could reply to this soul-destroying comment, there was a knock at the door and in came Bettina.

"I hope you're ready," she said cheekily to Melissa.

"What're you two doing?"

"We're going to see if we can explore another portal," said Melissa.

"We don't go far," admitted Bettina. "But walking through a door and seeing stuff … it's special."

"Are you going to explore all of them, or just a couple?"

Before Melissa could say the obvious "As many as possible", Bettina had butted in with, "Just enough to know they're for real. They're a bit over the top for everyday, you know?"

Rachel looked across at Melissa and winked.

"Your choice," Rachel said. "Just as long as you don't take pictures and stuff beyond the doors. If you paint anything, you claim you made it up. It's kinda a big secret."

"I'm surprised that two of us can see these things." Bettina sounded a fraction acerbic, which surprised Melissa. She unintentionally stated the obvious. Her life would be so much easier if words didn't always appear the way they did.

"You mean, you thought it would be you and Zelda."

"It usually is," said Bettina, showing her virtue. "Still, it's going to be interesting."

"Yeah," said Rachel. "Sometimes it can be dangerous. Be careful."

Melissa was very surprised at this. Rachel had encouraged her when she'd reported in the first time. And she'd taken those photos and Rachel hadn't been worried at all. Something had changed. *Something's always changing here. Things are in flux. I'd better get used to it.* She smiled back at Rachel, who winked at her again.

"We'd better get a move on," was all she said aloud this time. She needed her walking. It could be slow and it could take a long time and it could include many rests, but if she didn't move shortly, then she'd pay for it. "Do you have any recommendations?"

"Do you want the surprise? If you do, make it random."

"I want a safe door," Bettina said emphatically. "I want something beautiful and safe."

"Where's your map?"

"Here," said Melissa. "It's Bettina's, though. Mine was stolen."

"It won't do them a scrap of good. Portals are marked, but that doesn't mean idiots can see them."

"Idiots?"

"People who are blind to portals, of course."

Melissa felt uncomfortable about Zelda.

Rachel moved on before she could ponder this. "Anyhow, you want this one." It was at the back of the house.

"D'you mind if we walk slowly?" asked Melissa.

"No worries," said Bettina, who took off down the corridor far too quickly. Melissa sighed and set herself to catching up without hurting. The result was a compromise. She caught up and only hurt a bit. Life with Bettina, even when they were children, was a little challenging, she reflected. Bettina lived more inside her head than anyone else in the world. Except Zelda. Always "except Zelda".

Finally, they reached the room Rachel had pointed to on the map. Finally, for it took nearly ten minutes to get there. This house grew and changed according to the time of day or the feel of the air. It was a pleasant room. Big enough to be a ballroom. Green and brown and glass and even metal. It had a greenhouse feel.

Melissa looked around and said, "This is the conservatory we saw at the back of the house."

Glass and metal brought the heavens indoors. There was a perfectly ordinary door leading outside.

Bettina opened it, walked outside, and said, "It's the door we walked past that first day. It's just that the conservatory is bigger on the inside."

"Was that a joke?" Melissa asked suspiciously.

"Oh!" said Bettina. "I didn't mean it as a joke, but it could well be!"

"I'm not sure if I want to be adrift in space and time, is all," Melissa replied apologetically.

"I'm not sure I never want to be adrift in space," admitted Bettina. "But I've got to know."

"Me too."

They pottered around the door for a moment, looking at the plants and the odd little sculptures tucked into the soil or turning small trees into displays. All the sculptures were of heads.

Bettina commented, "The eyes are upon us."

"That's not funny," said Melissa.

"It was until I said it," her friend defended, then changed the subject by saying, "We still haven't found the portal for this room."

"We need to find the thing that says 'Drink me' first, and shrink to fit."

There were several glass tables, small, with just two chairs for each. Two larger tables with more chairs. But no bottle saying "Drink me".

"So we're not in *Alice in Wonderland*," said Bettina, her confidence returning.

"I love it that we looked, though," commented Melissa. "And I bet that's the door, hidden there."

"There" was the internal wall. At that precise point, the brick wall was hidden by a thicket of bushes, which in turn filled a large carved stone planter.

"Why there?"

"Because there's no other place. And because the door we came through isn't in the middle of the wall, it's on the other side of it. If it had a twin door, that twin door would be there."

"Well spotted. Now all we have to do is get behind that megastructure holding the trees."

The planter was nearly a metre out from the wall, and, on its far side, all the trees were clipped. And there was a door. It was identical to the door at the far end of the wall. Melissa wanted to crow with success, since she was being so literary. She felt like Peter Pan—winning and adventure.

There was not much space to reach the door. Bettina went in first and discovered that the door opened toward them.

"It'll open enough for us to get through," she said doubtfully, from between the part-open door and the planter. "But we need the other side."

"You could leave it open and we could walk around," Melissa suggested.

"Good idea."

They only just fit. Zelda wouldn't get through at all, Melissa suspected, but Zelda wasn't here. Just as well, then.

The door led outside. There was a small overhang that sheltered the doorway and beyond that was water. So much water. Not thick water. A thin rain that looked as if it fell incessantly. Around it, the mist obscured everything.

"We have to walk through it."

"Only if we want to know what's there," said Melissa, who did want to know. She saw Bettina step back instead of stride through the veil of water. That had been what Melissa herself had intended to do and a stupid thing it would have been. Her camera was loose. She put it into her bag and zipped it up tightly. "Which I do," she then said, and suited her action to her words.

The rain was as thin as it looked. Two big steps and she was past it. Underfoot felt as if the rain didn't exist at all. There was brick that matched the wall.

She walked a little further and, beyond the brick, the land was soaked and splendid. In front of her were vistas of rocks and waterfalls and green ferns. The sun played among the rocks and danced through the water. It was a landscape of rainbows.

"I want to explore," Melissa said when Bettina caught up.

"I don't." Bettina's voice was short.

"What's wrong?"

"This is." Her hand swept across the landscape. "We've been outside the conservatory. We've walked around it. Rock piles and waterfalls and Amazonian ferns can't possibly exist."

"A portal isn't a door then," said Melissa.

"I guess not. It makes me uncomfortable."

It didn't make Melissa uncomfortable. It opened her eyes and made her heart dance along with the rays of sun.

"I want to photograph it," she admitted. "But I'm pretty sure my permission doesn't extend to portals."

"Surely it does."

"Remember what Rachel said? If you paint here, someone will say you've got a good imagination. If I take a photo, they'll know this house has secrets."

"Check then. I'm going back inside."

Melissa gave in and went inside too. She would come back another time. In the interim, she needed to check with Rachel, make sure her camera wouldn't be affected by the mist, and most of all, she needed to take some medicine and get to her next set of pictures. The tiny rainbows everywhere here made her wonder about the shadows. How dark they were. How dangerous. She had a sudden urge to find out.

She would come back to this door and she would explore, Melissa promised herself. The fact that she could just walk into it, even with pain, was a miracle. One step into a special life, rather than having it forever denied. This was the first door she had felt so strongly about. It was fascinating how each landscape was different. Even the ferns had been different.

She wondered why Bettina was so scared of the magic. Maybe she hadn't experienced any before.

Melissa checked her camera first, and then she found Rachel, for she needed to talk about magic. That thought had changed everything.

The next morning, she did her shadow work early. She photographed along the brick walls. That gave her the feel of the shadows she had photographed in Wollongong, which was her base point for the narrative. When the sun was high, she'd try a series in the trees next to the lawn. One wall had early shadows that were stark. Grasping. They extended from the wall, and the plant that produced them sat there in all innocence. *Good,* she thought. *This is going to be a lovely base to work from.* This was the wall she'd start with every morning she was here. Even on a cloudy or wet morning, the feel of those plants would change. They might become the centre of the picture, or they might diminish themselves even further. *This is going to work.*

That was the oddness of life. One could travel and live an exciting existence and not see those shadows. Not see that disassociation from the trail of succulents that grew so placidly next to the wall. Not see …

Melissa felt a sudden urge to become that exotic traveller, to see things that no one had seen and do things that no one had done. And here, she could do that. Or close. She didn't know who could walk through those doors or even where the doors led, but in this house, right now, she was the one exploring. She wasn't a South Pole explorer, being the first and dying to let others walk that ground. But she was part of a rare few who could see the doors and walk through them. Who were given access. Would that do?

It would more than do, Melissa decided. It would give her that profound experience of feeling special. Not special because she hurt. Not special because people treated her like a lonesome child who needed to be rugged up and left alone, but special because she was doing something fabulous.

*I can't take pictures.* That was a desolate afterthought. No one could see what she saw. But that was the point. It was like her book decorations where stories came from nowhere to decorate the cover in watercolours of special beauty. Each cover of a book filled the mind with joy, even in memory.

It took a while to prepare for walking through the door. Melissa had to pack up her camera and rest for a bit. During that time, her mind's eye dwelled on the covers she had created, but especially on My Polly, who found adventure in an ordinary world. *My world's never been ordinary,* Melissa's thoughts drifted as she faded into sleep, *but I like this new kind of extraordinary. It's special in all the right ways instead of special in all the wrong ways.*

It took her until after lunch and after her walk in the garden and after her next set of photographs and after all her pictures for the day had been uploaded to safety before she was ready. It might have taken longer if her friends had done more than be polite to her, but they were focused on their work and not interesting in chatting at all. That liberated time. That made it possible to open another door.

She opened the heavy door carefully and stood on the far side of it. It was a wooden barrier between one world and the next. Dark red teak. Old, like so much else in this house. The far side had a safe space, maybe a metre deep. The door led outside, but it had a tiny porch, and Melissa rested there and breathed in the mist as she surveyed.

The rain didn't look deep. It wasn't falling off the roof: it was regular and so light it didn't reach the ground. The porch framed a green world that was tinged by a glass-white veil. Melissa took a deep, damp breath and walked through that veil.

Beyond the veil was damp ground and rocks. She threaded her way through them until she reached a dry vantage point. Forty steps exactly. She leaned against the stones and looked back at the house. The porch was a nothing. A hole in a cliff. The corridor wasn't visible behind it, and the door was a mere sliver of wood visible to someone who knew it was there. The wet hid the fact that it was a door and a porch and the whole thing looked hundreds of metres away. Yet it was forty steps. Melissa had counted her steps so that she knew when she had to return. Forty.

The rain was the mist floating from the base of a waterfall. She looked upward, then upward some more, then so far upward that her neck hurt. The fall came from heaven.

Melissa talked to herself. Or to the landscape. Maybe it was to the landscape, she decided, while she was talking.

"I don't understand this at all, but I love it. I wish I could take pictures, but if I can't, I can visit every day and make it live inside me. You're so … perfect. The place of my dreams. Not possible, but here, anyway."

It was a warm afternoon on this side of the door and the humidity made her a bit sleepy. She could hear the sounds of other water nearby. She kept her eyes closed until she had deciphered the landscape of sound and then she looked again and realised that the rocks she'd walked across were water-worn. This was a dream on a dry day, despite the veil of rain and the murmuring waters. On a wet day, her messy cobblestone path with its hints of moss and mildew and slime would shine through a stream.

"I'll visit again," she promised. "But maybe I'll stop and check every time. I don't want to be caught up in a flood or to get my feet wet or anything."

Melissa thought she was being funny. She dropped in on Rachel to tell her about it.

"I'm glad you didn't take your camera," Rachel said soberly. "It's gorgeous. Not for sharing."

"I assumed that after what you said earlier," Melissa said. "But what about Zelda and Bettina?"

"If they mention it, then you can chat with them. I bet they don't. I bet they don't get there."

"Why?"

"You know this house is special?"

"I maybe and perhaps have reached that view," Melissa said ironically.

"Yeah, I know. Sounds stupid 'cause it's obvious. But, special."

"Special," agreed Melissa.

"People want it. There are politics and … stuff."

"I get that. Adam was very possessive when we talked on the phone. His decision to let me come. His way of handling it. He was very … 'this is mine'."

"Yeah," agreed Rachel. "And that's a problem. He's one of the family who wants to change things. Own it. But it's not his. Never was. He's just a cousin."

"What has this got to do with the water valley?"

"Defences," Rachel said darkly. "The house can protect itself. From a lot of things."

"It's a very special house," said Melissa, wondering if her camera would have posed a threat. She asked.

"I dunno. It depends on what you do with the pictures, I guess, which means you won't be drowned for taking them. But …"

"Better safe than sorry," Melissa said. "I can survive without the pictures. If I go through a door with my camera, I'll leave it in its case."

"What if there's reason to take a picture?"

"Huh?"

"I don't like imposing things. People are bossy around me. I don't want to do that to you."

"Common sense then, not absolutes?"

"Common sense works for me."

"To be honest," confessed Melissa, "common sense works for me, too."

She went back to her room to rest for a little and found her camera unbagged and switched on. Melissa examined it closely. Nothing was wrong with it. But still. She took out the memory card and examined it on her computer. All her pictures had been copied. Not erased. Just copied. All that had changed was the most recent time of use. When she had discovered this feature on her camera it had amused her. Now it made her very serious indeed.

She put her camera and computer in her big handbag—and went straight back to Rachel's office.

Knocking gently, she asked, "Can I see you again, please?"

"Sure. What's up?"

"This." She took out her equipment and explained it.

"How long was it in your room?"

"An hour. Or less. And my door was locked."

"That's good. I'm glad. It means it can't be any of the other guests. It has to be family."

"Isn't that bad rather than good?"

"Yes, but it's not your friends."

"You're right. It'd be dreadful if it was one of them."

"Can you take your camera with you always?"

"What if someone asks about it?"

"Then I've given you permission to take pictures anywhere. And I do. Now. 'Cause if there's something up, I want to know. Drop in on me 'cause we're really good friends, and we'll look at the pictures every day."

"Every damned day?" Melissa suggested slyly.

"I'll enjoy it," said Rachel, her voice coloured with pretend huff.

"But what about my computer?"

"What do you store there?"

"Not a damned thing. My husband's computer was hacked once and he always does other types of storage."

"Well, then, leave it behind and no one will know."

"But carry my other storage with me. Always."

"That and your camera. Also, I'll try to find out who went to your part of the house. Someone has to've seen something."

"Okay," said Melissa. "Let me know if you find something."

"When," Rachel said with dignity. "I'm going to ask Erin's new husband's replacement. He sees everything. I don't think he's human, sometimes," she admitted.

"Leafguy?"

"Him. No one knows how old he is or anything. Just that he's reliable. And he sees things."

"He's here as a replacement?"

"And he wanted to be here."

"He can't be the person who looked." Melissa was certain.

"Politics," said Rachel. "He's from the old branch of the family."

"Leafguy is from the old branch … I like that."

"So do I. Can I tell him you call him Leafguy?"

"He's scared of me."

"Not so much you. More ... that you see stuff. He's happier when no one sees he's different. Other people see what they expect—you see him the way he is."

"You want to use my seeing of stuff?"

"Kinda. I see stuff too. How I got the job. But three eyes are better than two. Six eyes. Four. Dammit. Just leave Leafguy to me."

"He looks as if he'll blow away every time I talk to him."

"That's why. He's a whisper kinda guy and you're a direct speech kinda girl."

---

While they were solving all the problems, Zelda was chatting with Frater. She found him in the library, looking at a computer full of pictures. He closed the computer when he heard her steps, so all she got was the feeling that someone loved plants a lot. She started with that.

"You like flowers, I see?"

"Very much," he said. "You know my friend, Adam?"

"The one who interviewed me for the fellowship?"

"He loves them, too. I'm pulling together a collection for him. I might make them into a book about the gardens here. They're very special gardens."

"Very pleasant." Zelda felt she had to agree, even though she felt a bit guilty for hardly going out at all. "You should talk to Melissa. Her project is photographing them."

"There are parts of the garden she can't get to, I suspect," Frater said in all seriousness.

"We don't comment on the trouble she has walking. It's better for her if she's left to deal with it herself. Besides, it's not so bad."

"So you don't make a fuss?" asked Frater.

"Would you?" Zelda felt a little sharp. She felt as if the man was insinuating things. One moment he was interesting, another moment he was attractive. And the third moment he made hints that intimated she was not a good person. He rattled her.

"When I'm in doubt about things like this," he said mellifluously and apologetically and very calmingly, "I turn to other friends. In my case, I always turn to Adam."

"He looks as if he does know things."

"He's here tomorrow, too. Would you like to take morning tea with him?"

"That would be rather nice," said Zelda, feeling flattered and also feeling as if maybe she wasn't so cruel to Melissa after all. Her mind moved on from Melissa. "In the garden?"

"The front garden. It's his favourite place. We'll have a proper English tea. Cucumber sandwiches and a silver teapot."

"Sounds lovely," said Zelda.

"It will be," promised Frater.

"Will the others be there?"

"Why?" Frater's right hand tossed a pen in the air as if it were a toy.

"Morning tea with five people takes so very long. It will get in the way of my work."

"Is that all?" Frater's smile glittered. "It's only the three of us. And I promise, it won't interfere with your work."

"I'm so glad," said Zelda. "I love the thought, but if it meant I didn't get my project finished, I'd have to stay indoors and miss out. That's typical for me. Life's that busy."

"Then this time you won't miss out. I promise. Nor will it interfere with your work. I can promise that, too."

"I'll enjoy taking tea with you both." Zelda felt halfway between relieved and cosseted. It wasn't a bad place to be.

---

The next day was interesting for all three women. None of them saw each other until just before dinner, however, and there was a strained silence when they met. It was Melissa who broke the silence, by telling a very bad joke she'd just received from Hal. As she told it, she puzzled about the kind of day they'd all had. The unreportable kind, obviously.

She'd had the cat sleeping on her bed, but wasn't going to admit to it. Batchette purring by her side made Melissa feel like she was being given a special treat that the others would have to miss out on. Even if Batchette had slept with them other nights, the cat wasn't going to talk.

Melissa had so many reasons for not talking. Most importantly, the others would nod if she told them she hurt and would change the subject. It was better if the subject were not raised at all on days like this.

The first was waking up to bad pain. This would be a day of doing what she had to, under duress. She took her camera, but emptied her handbag of everything she didn't absolutely need. She filled her water bottle and checked for the medication and her map and she locked her door with caution. She saw a note pinned to her door, and put it in her bag for later. Reading it could wait until she was in the bright outside. Sunshine made reading easier. Squinting into half-light hurt. Even turning the key and hearing the lock snip into place hurt on days like this.

Her walk was a slow hobble, but it helped. It might take forever for her to reach breakfast and then the garden, but she would do it. She would take her pictures and get the movement that would get her into a less-bad tomorrow. That was the most she could hope for on days like this.

Melissa hated days like this.

The path crunched underfoot and everything was so damn slow. Someone had once told her that the trick with living was to be in the moment. Always in one's body, always aware. At that precise moment, she wanted to body-swap with the nice person who had advised her of this wonderful method of dealing with pain. Give the pain to the one who couldn't stay in her own body without it and who didn't notice time passing.

Being grumpy helped. It shouldn't. Life should be achievable without an inner self-complaint. Her little whingey voice enabled Melissa to reach the garden beds, however, and to get into position to take her photos. By skipping the kitchen visit for breakfast, she'd managed to reach the beds at the precise right time. Little things can redeem bad days.

Melissa stood in the position she'd marked out for her first picture. Same place every day, to take advantage of the changing light. The sun was bright, so it ought to be a repeat of the day before yesterday. This is what she told herself. This is what she repeated to herself as she tried to find a better spot, for the shadows were far too long. She was in the position that had framed them perfectly every other time, yet today they reached out into the main garden. They didn't fit into her frame.

Melissa refused to lose her temper. Those shadows were simply part of a day that was going to stretch her capacity. She could deal. She found a sunny, shadow-free part of the wall and leaned against it. Time to read that note. It was from Bettina.

> I don't know about those doors. Let's give them a miss today. If I feel up to it, I might check one by myself, but I'm not sure. I'll keep my options about the doors open. Make up my mind when I'm ready. I'm going to be out most of the day anyhow, painting. It's a good day for it. See you at dinner.

This opened a floodgate of past messages from her and from Zelda. Melissa had forgotten that bit of school. Where they'd arrange to meet and then a note would come to her saying, "We can't wait", or "Sunday lunch is cancelled—sorry". That day in Robertson was part of a pattern. Zelda and Bettina had only ever really been her acquaintances and Melissa was so damn stupid she only just realised it. Now. After all these years.

She wanted to cry. She didn't. Instead, she let the pain and the realisation that her past was not what it had seemed trigger fury. And the fury overrode the pain.

Melissa ripped up the note, stuffed it back in her purse, drank some water, and then, filled with rage, went to photograph her shadows.

The stark shadows started reaching toward her. Converging on her. They were not real. And she wasn't going to be put in the damn shade again.

*Click*, and she took a picture of the shadows, clustering and converging on her. Another *click*, and they were fleeing. She went up and down that wall three times, clicking and letting her anger flow. Her wrath poured out through the lens.

Melissa looked at the now-normal shadows, peeking out from beneath the succulents as if it really were morning. Just enough shadow. They still contained an ugly, strange darkness, but Melissa didn't care.

"I'm going to sleep," she told them. "And if you don't behave tomorrow, I'll do this all again. I've years of range and layers of pain and you're welcome to it all." *I'd better tell Rachel,* her inner voice said. *But not before I've slept. My body can't deal with today without a sleep.*

She slept right through lunch and woke up, drained of fear and pain and anger.

Melissa went to the kitchen and grabbed a muffin, then took it to Rachel's office. Rachel wasn't in, so she left her a note. "Been photographing shadows. Strange stuff. Need to talk." Notes in Rachelspeak. Melissa was proud of herself. She went back to the kitchen and made herself some tea to go with the muffin. She was still slow and tired, but she was past the worst. This afternoon she had to walk.

Zelda's morning was all about books and morning tea. Zelda's whole life was about books, so she only counted the morning tea. Before morning tea she had the library to herself, so she took a quick detour to discover the part of the library Frater inhabited.

His desk was cluttered and she respected that. She'd been teaching at university for too long and had prepared explanations should he walk in on her. Zelda's best was, of course, one that held a part of the truth: she wanted to know what books the library held without interfering with his work.

The books in his alcove were mainly seventeenth-century. Some were modern editions, but most were impressively original. She'd never seen that many early volumes in one open place. It was intimidating. What was more intimidating was how many of them still had their original bindings and were in pristine condition. It was as if they'd been bought four years ago, not four centuries.

Zelda collected several volumes for her research. She simply hadn't expected to be able to obtain anything this wonderful anywhere in Australia. There'd be some useful new research in this, and it would complement what she already had. Not big stuff. Small highlights.

The volumes in Latin she looked at wistfully and put back. One looked as if it contained interesting stories, but she really couldn't tell. "Frater Diabolus" was a story in the volume, but since she couldn't read Latin, it went back on the shelf.

The volumes she took back to her desk to look at that afternoon were all books of people's travels. She could consult these easily, by checking major places that she was talking about and simply adding, "In the seventeenth century, so-and-so visited this place and said ..." Make her text prettier, so to speak. Not that it needed prettification. But she craved these volumes.

Zelda yearned after them. She wanted to hold them and read from them. These six books would give her the sense of being an historian or of travelling in time, even if it were just for two hours that afternoon. Such little books to have such a big impact.

Most of the volumes in this section were small. There was a whole series called *Mercurius*.

Then Zelda found the chapbooks. They were bound together into thick volumes, which had tricked her eyes into missing them the first time she looked. Solid leather binding held the most unsolid form of literature. Zelda almost purred.

There were just two collected volumes of chapbooks, so she took eight books back to her desk. Then she left Frater a note, explaining the gaps, and that she'd not touched anything on his desk or looked at his papers.

> I need to look at the England travel books for the descriptions of certain places that have strong Celtic history. There won't be much in each of them, so I'll be quick. I'll have everything back to you shortly.

She looked at the volumes spread over her desk and realised that she couldn't just leave them scattered. And she was out of time. The beautiful books would have to wait. She could especially not leave them scattered on the surfaces that weren't flat or that were too small. What if there was an earthquake, or someone jumped too hard?

That had happened, once. She had been reading rare books in California and everything trembled. "Nothing to worry about," the librarian had told her. "We've suffered much worse." But she did worry. None of the material she was reading was damaged, but it could have been.

Ever since then she had been very careful to make sure books were secure. Two lots of three made safe stacks. None of these amazingly rare volumes would be endangered in such small piles. Finally, she put them under the desk, to one side. They were invisible, but she'd remember they were there.

Six small books she could finish with in her time this afternoon, and they wouldn't interfere too much with her writing because they were mainly reference tools. She was hunting places mentioned inside them, not reading the whole volume. Zelda didn't know what the chapbook collections held, however, for there was no index. They'd take more time and would be tomorrow's extra work. They probably had nothing that reflected the holy and magic aspects of Celtic tradition. Almost certainly they had nothing. Mostly she wanted an excuse to leaf through and enjoy them.

*If they're tomorrow's treat,* she thought, *I have to earn them. When I finish this chapter and have revised my outline for the next one, I'm allowed the chapbooks.*

Zelda looked at her workplace and tidied it a bit more, then went to her room and refreshed her makeup. Refreshing her makeup was her secret tool for delineating work time from pleasure time. Everything else was done. Zelda smiled at herself in the mirror. This was such a very special treat. Tea in a garden in the middle of nowhere!

It was an elegant morning tea. The garden was beautifully trimmed and felt very much as if it belonged in the south of England. The garden of Australian tea-dreams. Zelda felt deliciously flapper. She was grateful she had brought exactly the right pants and top and even a sun hat. Frater was his usual affable and occasionally unctuous self and Adam was surprisingly debonair. She had known he was sophisticated, but debonair was a surprise.

The three talked music and art and drank fine tea and ate delectable small cakes and even smaller sandwiches. It was all very retro.

There was a moment when the morning's sun shone a little

too brightly and the green of the grass and trees and the pleasant lines of the path descended into farce. That was when Zelda told Frater she'd left him a note because she was reading books from his alcove. She explained it very politely and carefully and, just as she had in writing not two hours before, said that she'd made sure she didn't even look at the desk. Frater excused himself.

*He's going to do to me what he thinks I've done to him,* Zelda thought. *How amusing.* What was most amusing of all was that all he would find was that pile of books. She worked directly on her computer, which she never left in libraries or bedrooms. It was in her handbag. Some libraries didn't permit pens. Some didn't permit backpacks. A handbag-sized device was easiest. So all Frater would see was the stack of books. Not even all the books. The ones under the desk were virtually invisible.

Adam alone was delightful company. He was older than he looked and his age was not too far removed from hers. He cared about the politics she cared about and they were equally cynical and sarcastic. He was metrosexual, she admitted, and that was perfect.

Melissa's cynicism about him had left Zelda bewildered, and she entered a defence mode. Not defence against him. Defence for him. She leaned slightly into the conversation and it turned just a little flirty. Still political, still sarcastic, still ragingly funny, but with an undertone.

Eventually, she remembered that she had words to write and books to read.

"I really have to go because deadlines are deadlines," Zelda said. "But it's been lovely."

"Do you work in the evenings?"

"Not so much," she confessed. "I spend it mostly chatting. I've known Bettina and Melissa for years and it's like old times." She didn't mean to think *Boring as old times too,* but she did, and refused to regret it.

"Just tonight, after dark, come and look at the moon with me?"

"The moon?"

"For your research. It's a gibbous moon and terribly Celtic."

"Terribly Celtic," Zelda agreed, half smiling. That was what everyone said about any stage of the moon. They weren't wrong, but neither was it original. "Won't the mountains get in the way?"

"I know the best patch of clear ground, with the best views. Come and see."

"Okay, I will," Zelda said, surprising herself. This was a special time after all, and she should live a little.

When she reached her desk, in time to do a mere hour's work before lunch (not that she was counting the hours), she found a note from Frater.

"Enjoy the books," it said. "Leave them on the table just outside my alcove when you're done and I'll put them back myself."

---

Bettina's day began with painting. Painting centred it. Painting ended it. She made such progress that she wondered whether she even needed two weeks.

This was a surprise.

Every time she reached a point she should not have been for two full days, she explored a little. It felt like being Melissa, with that need to see everything, as if life were limited.

*While I love my friends,* Bettina thought, *I'm very glad I'm not them!* This thought carried her through the gardens. They were big and complex and delightful and she preferred them to the house. She didn't like the edges of the gardens, but she adored walking down the paths. It was like walking into paintings. All she did with her paintings here was to walk into gardens. It was perfect. The gardens took her somewhere else and she took her painting through doors into those places. Doors in each picture and beyond each door … something special. These were the doors Bettina was comfortable with. The one she saw and that other people didn't spring on her. She painted the gardens she enjoyed in this residence, but the doors and the detail she saved for when she was at home. Finding things to say wasn't what she was here for. She was here for the thinking and the gardens.

Or maybe she was wrong? Maybe she should find this out by checking something by herself? In the garden though, not in the house. The house was great when she was with Zelda or Melissa, but it didn't have a homey feel; it wasn't a place she belonged.

As Bettina cleaned up and put everything in its place after her first session, she thought about when she and Zelda had arrived. They'd walked right past a wall made of stones and in that wall there had been a hole. Zelda hadn't looked at it or said a word, but Bettina was curious. Maybe it was a portal. Maybe it led somewhere interesting. It was such a bright day that she left her things outside. *I'll move them to the next place when I'm ready.*

She liked the thought of the hole in the wall. Such a contrast to this day of saturated colour and slow warmth. She walked across the front lawn and waved at Zelda and her two men. They didn't encourage her to stop.

Bettina didn't like Adam. He had given her such a good introduction to everything that she had felt special. She knew what that meant, for it had happened before. With art people who wanted to be her or show her work or ask for donations of this or that. She was always flattered at first, because she never quite believed that she was the type of artist who thought she was going somewhere and would one day find out where. The type of artist who knew where she was going and was important because of that.

Bettina didn't kid herself: she was having a good run. But it could be for so many reasons. She looked below the surface when someone was too flattering, too nice. And that was Adam. Likeable but not loveable. Not someone she'd trust with her secrets.

It didn't surprise her at all when Adam waved a friendly greeting but didn't follow it up with a "Join us" or even with a "How are you?" It didn't surprise her, but it annoyed her. She hated the world where people were not authentic. Where they were incapable of being themselves.

*This is why Dov is in my life and not someone more demanding. The only thing Dov asks is the thing I want to give—authenticity. Myself.*

She didn't know what holes in walls had to do with startling insights. It was probably Adam's gloss that had provoked that one. She might be purely hetero, but Adam was not her type at all. Nor was the guy with him. There was a dark cloud around him. It distressed her. She nearly turned around to give Zelda some help, but when she twisted halfway, she saw the other guy leaving. Zelda liked beautiful men—she didn't need any help. Which was good, because Bettina, in painting mode, could fit in side trips to see things that must be seen, but really didn't want to shoulder emotional burdens. Her emotions were caught up in her work.

Still, a hole in a wall should be just interesting enough and just safe enough. Then she'd have time to start the next picture before lunch. Such a perfect day for the palette she wanted for the next one. The easel was set up to look at the trees and how they whispered secrets to each other. Bettina almost turned around and began immediately but she needed to walk and stretch and there was a hole to explore. Life was good!

It wasn't really a hole in the wall, she said to herself as she walked into the dark. It was an open doorway leading to … somewhere. The rocks were flat on the outside, where the sun reached, but here inside they looked more like builders built into some sort of megalithic burial ground. Bettina shuddered as she thought of this tunnel leading to dead bodies and their ghosts. She could almost feel the damp crawl of a ghost over her skin. Bettina stopped looking at the uncarved rocks that made the walls and ceiling, and she didn't look at any side tunnels (for they led into the dark). She walked straight ahead.

"I'll stop walking when the light runs out," she said, to fill in the silence.

Just when the darkness should have been complete, she saw a pale grey light peering in from the other end of the tunnel. She strode confidently and tripped over. Of course, she tripped over. *Big steps toward the light are still in the dark. I'm living my symbolism.*

The ground was dirt and her hands felt gritty and sore from the fall. So did her knees. She brushed herself off and leaned against the wall to sort herself out. The wall was no longer rough. She ran her right hand over it and the grit went back to where it belonged.

Her left hand joined her right and she wished for a flashlight. This wall wasn't entirely flat. It had patterns. She ran her fingers over it and her whole hand and then her fingers again until she discovered that the patterns were waves. Some were simply wavy lines, but some were waves like those she loved from Hokusai's woodblock print. She memorised the lines and then turned away, reluctantly, to see where the tunnel emerged. Probably into a field. This house was near the edge of town, after all. Maybe it came out into the showground.

That would be perfect. Bettina could paint from just inside the doorway and get a picture of the showground, where things happened. She smiled and walked toward the light.

Just before the doorway, she stopped. This was so wrong.

That pale grey hadn't been the rock shadowing the entrance. It was rain. On one side of the tunnel was endless sunshine and on the other was endless rain. Waves, then rain. It reminded her of the first doorway she'd seen with Melissa. It made her feet shift edgily. They shifted so edgily that they turned her body right around.

*This is stupid,* Bettina told herself. *I am stupid.* She took control over her feet and walked through the hole. Into the grey. The grey was cloud and faint rain. Nothing more. It had looked worse, but that was because the sky was reflected on a thoroughly charming lake. The lake had a Romantic Greek temple on its far side, surrounded by oaks and Dutch elms and the occasional sycamore. The scene she was regarding looked entirely planned and even more entirely English. Like someone coyly copying Capability Brown. Too pretty and too planned. Like the lawn outside the house. Not her kind of thing and … disturbing. How could a tunnel lead to something like this in a dry landscape?

It made her uncomfortable for so many reasons. So many. Her feet shifted beneath her again and this time she gave in to them. This lake wasn't on any map. The door she came through wasn't on the map. And besides, the portals inside felt safer. They did. At the same time as explaining how awful it was, Bettina fell in love with its mystery and Englishness. A door in her painting might lead to somewhere like this. Not here. Somewhere like here. Somewhere safe and English, not somewhere so very strange but looking safe and English. Bettina nodded and turned around and went right back. From grey light to the bright warm light she belonged in.

She spent the rest of the morning painting as if her whole life depended on it. She grounded herself in the scene, and let her innards deal with her short adventure.

Melissa didn't turn up for lunch. She was pretty unreliable on the regular events that created a life, Bettina decided. Bettina also decided it was time to talk to Zelda about the doors. "Portals" was pretentious. They were doors. Leading to odd places, maybe, but doors. And the places were probably terrifically artistic deceptions. Also pretentious, but so very well done.

How should she mention it to Zelda? Tell her they were going to look at a lake where there should be no lake, then throw stones in the water only to discover the stones ripping through a very clear *trompe d'œuil*? She didn't want that kind of embarrassment.

"Zelda," she said, as Zelda sat down with her coffee and salad. "Are you free for a short walk after lunch?"

"A constitutional?" Zelda smiled. "I don't have a lot of time, but walking for fifteen minutes won't destroy my schedule. Is there something you want to see?"

"I want to walk to the entrance and back. That stone wall looks rough and I don't think it is."

"You want a second opinion?"

"About the wall and any parts of it that might be of interest. Historians know stuff."

"I'm a Celticist, but yes, I get the point. We'd be looking for different things. Happy to. I ate so much cake at morning tea that I could do with a bit of a stroll."

"How was morning tea?" And lunch proceeded as lunches do.

After lunch, they walked to the gate, past the wall and back again. A simple enough thing. At several stages, they stopped and discussed the wall. Whether the stones were put together by someone who knew drystone walling or if they had invisible sticky stuff.

"Concrete?" suggested Bettina.

"Mortar," Zelda said with firmness, and then corrected herself. "How the hell can I know when I can't see it? I can't tell you a thing about this wall without more evidence."

The shape was either amorphous or classic and the stones were not local but Zelda didn't know what they were. That gave Bettina an excuse to be perturbed.

She wasn't perturbed because Zelda proved to know less about walls than both of them had assumed. Zelda learned by doing and would know everything about walls within a fortnight of this little adventure. Bettina let Zelda think that the wall's obscure nature was the reason she was upset. She wasn't going to tell her friend, "There was a doorway in this wall this morning. It led to a lake. The doorway is missing."

On the way back to the house, Bettina didn't let her hand leave the wall. Her hand was seeking an illusion: either a closed door pretending to be more rock, or a hole that looked like more rock or … something.

Nothing. There was nothing. Or rather, there was rock. Firm hard rock. If she tapped every single boulder there would still be rock. Her eyes told her this. They also told her where the door had been and she tapped the rocks in that place, pretending to find out how dense they were. Not pretending. She wanted to know. She wanted them to be hollow or fake. She pushed them. Nothing. Either the door was closed from the other side, or there was no door at all. If there was no door at all, and if there was no hole at all, then the other doors led to strange places. And she didn't want that. Bettina loved the feel of strange places in her paintings, but she wanted her everyday to be safe.

When Zelda went back to her books, Bettina went straight back to the wall. This time, it had a hole. A dark hole. A hole that led to a lake. And that lake ate all the stones she threw into it. Bettina wanted to throw the whole wall into the lake and lose the wall and make the lake go away, both at once.

Stone after stone she flung angrily, then sobbing, then just tiredly. The stones went splash. And splash. And splash again. Nothing happened. She turned and walked through to the house side of the giant hole in the wall and ignored everything. She ignored the waves carved into one end and didn't look for concrete or mortar at the other. She walked obdurately away from the wall, denying it and all its secrets a place in her life.

If her best friend couldn't see it and help her understand it, if she couldn't share it the way she had shared everything else obscure and difficult since she was a child, then Bettina wasn't interested. More than that, she felt betrayed. If Zelda couldn't see the hole and couldn't walk down through the darkness to that little spot of English fantasy, then there was a gulf between them.

Bettina refused to accept a gulf between herself and her best friend. She was not going to accept that hole or that lake. They were fictions.

---

While Bettina won an argument with her inner dreamer, Melissa was walking the walk and talking the talk. The talk was to herself.

She'd found the exploration with Bettina uncomfortable and she needed to know why. She could just have asked, but she knew the sort of answer Bettina would give. She'd given those answers so many times in all their pasts. That Melissa could deal with things, all she had to do was put in a bit more effort. And so on.

Also, the morning had left her annoyed. She didn't want to wait until tomorrow to feel better. She wouldn't feel better even then, but she was tired of carrying pain. She was no St Christopher and her burden wasn't holy and didn't make her special. And she couldn't take her pictures of the trees until Bettina had finished with that spot.

Bettina didn't ask. Not ever. She just said, "This is where I must be." And she took her place there and created beauty and joy around her and it really didn't matter that Melissa had been there first.

*I'll go when she has her tea break.* Bettina took breaks religiously, never worked through pain, and had earned her sick-but-not-too-sick status. It was hard work.

And Melissa appreciated all this. The talent, the hard work, and the generosity that life had shown her friend. It was just that she had to wait until Bettina was out of the way to take her pictures, because if she tried to do them when Bettina was there, Bettina would give her instruction and advice and guidance, without even knowing what Melissa was seeing through her screen.

It had been the same at school. Bettina and Zelda had both "helped" Melissa even when Melissa didn't need any help. She was their poor cousin because she wasn't Anglo enough. Because one grandmother didn't speak much English, and the other grandmother had the big accent and the big arms. Speaking hands. Melissa loved that about Nonna. Nonna would have said to just do what she needed to, and not get into an argument with the girls. They were always "the girls". If they couldn't see she was getting better marks than they were, Nonna said, they didn't need to know. "Don't make waves."

Melissa ignored this advice for the most part. She had made waves to be seen by Hal and she was very pleased with this. Hal saw her, though, which Zelda and Bettina had never really done.

No waves then. Pictures in between Bettina's work. For there were times for waves and this was not one of them. She really didn't think Bettina understood what they were seeing beyond that door. Beyond those two doors. Melissa did and it was wonderful. She wanted to feel the joy at the beauty. She wanted ... not to spoil something that was so very special. Rachel understood, so she'd tell Rachel later. She had to. There were things Rachel had to know. Rachel was out until 3 pm, however, and Melissa had to walk gently and get some movement back into her and expel the draggy dullness that the pain and anger and sleep had created.

A portal, then the afternoon pictures, then Rachel, and then rest until dinner. If she said this firmly enough, it would be possible. If she put one foot in front of the other when things became too much to do otherwise, she would make it. And if she walked gently now, then tonight's sleep would be less troubled and tomorrow would be less damn impossible. How did other people manage walking, when they didn't have to tell their feet to move, first one then the other then one then the other, on days like this?

All the time Melissa was talking to herself, she was walking. The portal she had in mind was downstairs, for that would give her the most movement. It was hard, but it was good for her. And she had two hours, so it needed to be something she could navigate. The thing about the stairs was she could use the rail to pull herself up if, toward the end, it became too hard. And she'd noticed a chair near the stairs, so she could rest afterward. She would manage. She would set her own pace and set her own emotions—and look, she was already at the cellar door. Self-talk, she claimed to herself proudly, can get one through almost anything.

The cellar was brick and spacious and mostly full of wine. Hal would love this cellar, he would love this wine. He went soft at the knees when he saw old bottles, and these old bottles had so much dust that she was certain they were the stuff of drools.

She sat for a few minutes on that nicely placed chair. She could lean on a vertical plane, behind which was much wine, and she could sit and let the hurt diminish. When she was able to walk again, she opened the door that was less than a metre away. It opened toward her and as she walked around it, she saw what she'd seen when Bettina had opened it for her and Zelda the other day. A strong wooden rail and clean stone stairs leading somewhere unfathomable. That last word was a joke to herself, for she could smell the sea. If she got on a bus and travelled over the mountains, through Albion and past many country towns, she would reach Wollongong. That was the closest sea to here, as far as she knew. The big industrial town never had sea that smelled like this. Not since the steel mills.

She was going into unknown zones and she was hurting, so Melissa was going to move so carefully, so very carefully. First foot on a stair, second foot joining it.

After a while, the stairs ran out. The bottom one sloped a little and flowed into the rock all the stairs had been carved from. She looked back up at them and realised they were all one rock. Thc light was much brighter down here than it was near the cellar door. It was luminous and a golden-green. And the scent of the sea was joyous and exuberant and made her smile. The rock might go on for miles, but a bare metre away a thin film of golden sand covered it. Sand that came from another rock, somewhere else. Wet transforming into damp. The tide was going out. The strange light was a glowing sea at night, and Melissa could see a little more every minute. Dawn would break in a little. She stood on the last of the hard rock and smiled.

The waves were very gentle. Melissa moved forward every now and again, to follow the tide. It moved quickly. This was not a beach that took hours to fill and empty.

Soon she could walk over the sand and toward the pre-dawn.

She brushed her fingers lightly along the wall. Sometimes it was smooth, sometimes pitted, and sometimes eaten by water. The feel that made her fingertips come alive showed her that there was more than one kind of rock, but that none of it was carved by humans. This was a cave, with sea-hewn rock. Once the water had filled the cave every day. Now, given the fact that the stairs had been dry and safe, it didn't even reach them. Unless ... it was a magic cave.

Knowing that she walked into magic, Melissa nevertheless smiled. She'd rather believe the sea had gone down over time. Somewhere, the sea had to be lower in height than fifty years ago. She would rather it were here eighty years ago, she amended. The leaflet about the house said it was built in the 1930s. Rachel had told her she had been made to visit a place the same age near Eden, as a joke by her selection committee. Melissa had pondered a selection committee that could make someone travel hundreds of miles for a joke, then stopped and thought, *I am here. Let me feel every second.*

She stood at the mouth of the cave, looking out. Ahead of her, the water was further away than it should be. She didn't look at an ocean, but at a wide beach. Dawn was sneaking over the horizon and shone a green light in the far distance. She wasn't sure if she would lose her way back to the house if she played in the sand, so she leaned on the rock, forcing it to reassure her she could get back to her room anytime, and she pretended to play in the sand.

She was in the middle of a particularly glorious sandpit, one that she could never manage in real life, when she realised the sun sat in pre-dawn. The tide had gone out, but the sun still shone a small green light across the water.

"You came at a time, you leave at a time," a man's voice murmured at her, like the sea. She was still startled. "That's how we keep visitors safe."

"Where are we?" Melissa turned to look the man in the face and was so glad that she had asked first. The man had scales. Fine scales. Supple like skin, fine and green-blue. Not all over. The way they glittered in the sun made her look almost hungrily. He was very familiar and also very alien. He was the sea version of Leafguy, with hair that matched dark algae the way Leafguy matched autumn in a forest. "You're not scared of me," she added unnecessarily.

"I can see that you would scare my brother," the merman said. "You're full of fire and light."

"Your brother?"

"Your mind is reflecting his shadow, and he's running away

from you like a leaf in the wind. He's not always scared. But you, yes, I could see you might make him jump a little." His voice was still soft and shushing and murmurous like the waves, but still filled with humour. Melissa liked this seaman. Her mind jumped ahead.

"Family," she said. "You're part of the family that owns the house."

"We're the part that protects it. Four men. Four women. I'm the senior man."

"And Uber-Granny," added Melissa. "And Rachel? And Erin?"

He laughed. "Yes, very much."

"Why do all the doors lead to water?"

"Water protects us. Water protects the house. This sea can flood right up in an instant and drown the cellar and sweep away any dangers."

"That's right. One day I may tell you my name, if you're lucky."

He was flirting. This was ... not nearly uncomfortable enough. It would be more uncomfortable if Melissa didn't find him so nearly familiar. Someone she should know. Or someone she could know. She didn't know which.

"Senior?"

"Of the men. We are more a clan of women than men. Only four of us are protectors."

"You, Leafguy, the guy who's married Rachel's BFF, and Adam?"

"Three, yes. Adam has chosen to follow his human grandfather."

"He's the one with a human grandfather?"

The man laughed again, and his scales rippled and became flesh and clothes. He now looked as if she should know him. Knew him well. Seeing someone she knew and did not know was doing her brain in. Melissa stopped looking.

"We all do. We're all mostly human. Our life decisions are

what make us suitable or not suitable at all to be part of the house."

"And Adam's not suitable?"

"His father wasn't, but he's still being considered. He enjoys some of the work, but the one you call Uber-Granny hasn't yet decided."

"I can't see him with scales."

"Nor can I." This man had such a soft voice.

"This sea ..." Her arms reached out along the beach. She realised they'd been walking along it all the while and she hadn't felt any pain. Melissa shelved this thought for later. "Is it real?"

"It's all real. Pocket worlds. Some of them lead to other Earths, some to other parts of Earth."

"The house is so special. And how can you even be telling me this? Surely it's secret?"

"Anyone who can see the green light at dawn over the sunless sea has earned the right to question. Which of the fellowship recipients are you? Bettina? Zelda? I was shown pictures, but on this shore, parents cannot even recognise children. It's a strange place."

That explained it. If she knew him, she wouldn't recognise him. Did she know him? Melissa didn't want to ask.

"Melissa." The man stopped, and Melissa stopped with him. "What's wrong?"

"Not wrong. Not precisely. I was expecting one of the others, given the interviews."

"I wasn't interviewed. I was included at the last minute because someone pulled out."

"Of course. Do you think the other two are likely to reach here?"

"I honestly don't know. Bettina went with me to look through another door. Two other doors. And she was really upside-down about it. And Zelda? I saw her walk right past a portal door and not care. But that doesn't mean she can't open a door—it just means she won't do it in front of me. She told us that this trip is all about research, and last time I saw her she was having morning tea on the front lawn with Adam and that friend of his."

"Friend of his?"

"Doing research in the library."

"Thank you."

"Thank you?"

"Something is happening. Something not so good."

"You normally talk about these things with random visitors?" Melissa felt protective of this strange house and turned to sarcasm for comfort.

"Not at all." Melissa could hear Adam in this man's voice. The smoothness was obviously a family trait. "The portals are not equal in where they lead. You came down here and the sea receded for you. If you'd not been someone I could trust, the sea would have lapped the stairs." He was hiding something. But the thought of the sea rising disturbed Melissa so much that she didn't pursue the mystery.

"How high?" Melissa wanted to know so urgently.

He shrugged. "As high as it feels like."

"Sentient sea." Melissa sighed.

"Protective water."

"Fair enough." She paused just long enough, then asked, "Can you tell me more about what's wrong?"

"I wish I could." Again the voice sounded like Adam's. "Why aren't you looking at me? Don't the scales match the suit?"

"Nothing like that," answered Melissa. "I'm married and a bit of a hermit."

"Would it help if I told you I'm gay?"

"Maybe," Melissa said cautiously.

"Pity. I don't feel like lying today." He was far too attractive. With scales and without. This was unsettling.

Melissa turned and faced him and saw his face lit up with

mischief. "You know," she scolded, "you and Rachel have exactly the same sense of humour. And it works much better for her."

"Really?" He paused. "I need to know. Or you can tell Rachel. If anything happens here that worries you ..."

"Like the sea climbing the stairs?"

"It's already decided it won't."

"I'm so glad to hear that!"

They walked along the beach together. It was as if they'd known each other for years. The sand was firm, as if the tide had just gone out. *Which it has, and that damned sun is still just peeking over the horizon. And it's still shedding that odd light.*

"There's something I'd like to ask about," Melissa said, to stop herself thinking about golden suns casting green light. "Yesterday, when I took my morning pictures, the shadows were all kinds of strange. Is that like the sea? I mean, are the shadows sentient?"

"There is no way they could be," he said, puzzled but firm. "Can you explain?"

"I can show you, if there's somewhere to sit."

"The stairs," he said reluctantly. "You'll have to go inside after that, which is why we were walking away from them."

"The stairs tell the sea to come back in?" Melissa guessed.

"Yes."

"Maybe they'll let me visit another time. I want to walk here, but I need to understand the shadows."

"As do I."

"Why is your speech sometimes archaic and sometimes perfectly modern?" she asked abruptly.

"Age is a thing, you know. And so is time shifting because one lives outside it."

"How much time has passed while I've been here?"

"Not as much as you think."

"Not a consolation. So not at all reassuring," she muttered to herself, but loud enough to be understood.

This muttering led to silence as surely as incoming tide follows outgoing tide, and the two walked companionably together until they reached what looked like a big rock, with stairs carved in near the bottom. It was only when they were seated on the stairs that the tide started to turn and the walls grew around them.

"This is strange," said Melissa.

"But important. I can't tell you more about it than I have, so show me these pictures."

And Melissa did. The shadows the first time, and the second, both before and after she'd let out her anger.

"What caused them to fall back, do you think?"

"I'd say I'd have no idea, but they reacted to me being angry at them. I was furious."

"Why?"

"Just one of those days."

"It's obvious why you're here, then, but not why Adam didn't notice that aspect of you."

"And the shadows?"

"You're photographing them every day?"

"Every second day now, because I mucked up this morning."

"Let's get you back in time for today's pictures. Take them. Don't get angry again, just take those pictures."

"I need the ordinary ones. For my display. I don't want evil shadows."

"Try, please." He reminded her of Hal. Maybe that was all it was. She yearned for her husband in that moment, but tried not to think about him. This was strange and it was important.

Melissa promised to try to find some sort of solution, but she was frustrated. First Bettina and the trees and now this. The world was conspiring to throw her into magic realms and to stop her taking the photographs and creating her display. Couldn't she have both? Just for a change?

"Can I come back and see you?"

"Not a good idea. Twice to this door would draw attention. It's too powerful. If young Adam's friend sees you … not a good thing. Tell my brother in the garden, or tell Rachel. Tell them I need to come and see you."

"I can tell them about the shadows."

"We don't need to scare Rachel. She's doing well, but she came here very vulnerable." Melissa wasn't sure if she would respect this wish of his. It sounded too much like Zelda being protective.

"So, then what?"

"I wish I knew." He sounded as lonely as she had felt a moment ago.

Melissa was aware of the water, gradually flowing in with the gentle waves. It was coming closer. "I need to go."

He looked at the water too. "You do."

"Do you have access to any other doors?"

"Any water on the estate will reach me."

"Easy then, I shall write you a note and put it in the water. Even if the ink washes out, you can find the note. I have no idea what you'd do after that."

"I'd find you. Don't put a note in the water, though. Put in one of these."

He reached into his pocket and pulled out a handful of limpet shells. "One each time you need me."

"I might not use them all."

"Now, no, but maybe one day." He didn't give them to her. He put them in her handbag, added the camera to the mess, and closed it with a snip.

"Maybe one day you'll tell me what to call you."

"Maybe I will, at that." He smiled down at her and stood up. He reached down, pulled her up, walked her to the top of the stairs, and then they both turned around to see the water had already climbed up one stair. No more rock. No more sand. No more sunshine. Just water in a dark tunnel. He opened the door and said, "Time to go."

When she was just through it, Melissa turned around and saw that his suit had become scales and he was diving into the ocean as if the stairs had never been there. The door framed this and made it less surreal than terrifying. She closed the door in a hurry and found herself in the corridor. Her aches returned as if they had never gone, but her bag was weighed down with seashells. Walking through a door one way took her to fantasy lands and walking the other returned Melissa to drab pain.

Time wasn't what it was supposed to be, either. She looked at her watch and saw that dinner would be on the table. Should she return to her room? Yes, for she needed to see if it had been broken into again. Not that there was anything to take, or any photos to steal, but because she wanted to know.

This time, the room was a mess. Everything had been turned upside down. Melissa stood there and looked and looked and couldn't think. Finally, she rang the mobile number Rachel had given and within three minutes Rachel was there, also looking at the mess.

"I was visiting the sea this afternoon," Melissa said. "Is it possible that someone hates me for that? Or have the other rooms also been ransacked?"

"I bet it's that. The sea. If you're talking about the cellar door. Not even all the family can go there. Did you meet anyone?"

"Yes. Leafguy's brother. He didn't give me a name, but we talked."

"He thinks I'm stupid," confided Rachel.

"He thinks you're fragile. He said so. Why do his scales come and go? I stood here and saw this mess and all I could think about were his scales."

"Never saw scales. He must like you."

"And someone hates me."

"D'you want me to get someone in, or can I tidy this now?"

"I'd rather do it myself, but I can't do the bed and move the cupboard back and …"

"You need a new room."

"I think … I'd rather. If it's not too much."

"What's too much is whoever did this. Or whatever."

"Whatever? No, I'm not asking. I don't want to be in a room with a whatever."

"I've got a room for friends who visit, in my part of the house. It's always made up, just in case. Why don't we move your things there? If you don't mind walking past the office to get there?"

"If I have to walk past the office then so does whoever did this. I'd like that. Very much."

Ten minutes later it was all done and Rachel and Melissa went down to dinner. Zelda was nearly finished, and Bettina was happy to see them. When Melissa sat down, she realised that she'd packed and moved her things (with help) and walked them to her new bedroom and she still didn't hurt beyond dull aches. The sea air had been good for her.

She wanted to go back. Not just for the air and not just for the lack of pain, but because there was something about her merman. The handbag weighted heavily, not because the shells were heavy, but because the emotions they carried were not light.

She'd not walk through that door again unless she had someone with her—it was too risky in too many ways. She loved the protection and danger of that sentient sea, and she knew she would dream that night of her new acquaintance. She resolved to ring Hal and tell him about … what she could. Bettina. She could tell him it was Bettina who had visited the sea. That would hide all the things she couldn't tell him. They weren't her secrets.

Rachel had to leave after dinner to sort Melissa's old room. Zelda absented herself without any explanation. This left

Bettina and Melissa sharing drinks and thinking about the evening.

Bettina was stressed. It didn't take long for Melissa to find out that being deserted by Zelda was intolerable and the unaccountable nature of Zelda's absence made it even more intolerable. Maybe the perfect friendship looked better from the outside?

Melissa did what she always had done when Bettina was down: she offered her something special to cheer her up. When they were children it had been an ice cream or a book to read. Now it was the cellar door.

The moment Bettina realised that Melissa was talking about another portal, she froze her out. Melissa couldn't tell Bettina about it, nor about her room being ransacked. She couldn't tell Bettina anything, because Bettina wasn't listening. They finished their drinks and went separate ways. Bettina walked as if the world was around her shoulders. Melissa walked as if life was a bit damaging. Not unendurable, but difficult.

That was the moment Melissa realised she hadn't told Rachel about the shadows. She hasn't asked Rachel whether she should do what the seaman told her, either. For the latter, she could trust her own judgement. The shadows could wait until tomorrow.

---

For Zelda, the evening and the night were perfectly simple. She and Adam saw the moon. She and Adam saw the fields and the vast horizon, for they had driven to a point where the world was theirs. Zelda then spent the night with a younger man, at a motel not that close to Robertson, and felt deliciously evil for it.

The next day, Zelda rebelled. There was a clear trigger for her rebellion. She was a very reluctant rebel. She found herself whispering this to herself all the rest of the morning, after the rebellion. After she'd gone to Rachel with a problem.

"It's a big problem," Zelda explained, "otherwise, I would not have let it eat into my work time like this. In fact, it's a very big problem."

"Tell," said Rachel, her slim self looking tired even as she sat down in a chair. "Wait. Coffee?"

"Not for me," said Zelda. "I need to get back to work. But you have some."

"It can wait." Rachel's hand waved the drink off, even though her body looked so tired that Zelda imagined a direct infusion of caffeine was essential. She pretended she didn't notice the fatigue. After all, it was none of her business.

"Let's get this over with then. I hate complaining. I hate making a fuss. But this was invasive and rude and I cannot have such things happen."

"Tell," said Rachel again, her eyes big.

"After breakfast, I went to my desk to do some work. I was a bit late, because I stayed out last night …"

Zelda was very strict about how her desk was set up. Her workplace had been turned upside down. Paper on the floor. Computer open and on. A message on the screen announcing the password was incorrect. Unplugged and running out of power fast.

"And the books?"

"They were all away. I try to finish with them the day I take them off the shelf so that I can put them back the same day." Except she hadn't this time. She'd forgotten the chapbook compilations. "Except two, which I didn't check for—I put them under the desk because I was scared they would fall."

"Let's check them then, and work out what to do about the intruder."

"It has to be Frater, but I can't think why. We had morning

tea together yesterday and he didn't ask me about my work at all."

"Why does it have to be Frater?"

"He's usually in the library when I am and I can see him watching what I do. He's fascinated by my work."

Zelda made this statement comfortably. She was never worried when people found her work fascinating. This was one of the side effects of Celticism. She was only worried when people tried to do the work for her, or to steal it. This time she wasn't so much worried—for her computer had bravely defied the intruder—as angry. Very angry. Her anger demonstrated itself in the loudness of her footsteps and the tightness of her body. She felt that she would burst at any moment, and held it all in. This was not Rachel's fault. Rachel shouldn't have to pay. Rachel was admin and admin copped everything and needed protection against the vicissitudes of life. Thinking of Rachel as admin got them both to the library without Zelda bursting into diatribe.

Zelda dove straight under the table and retrieved the two books. They were precisely where she had left them. They'd been easier to put down under the desk than they were to pick up. Old binding was slippery and the volumes needed two hands. Zelda hit her head twice on the desk, once for each book. She couldn't know if this was what had saved them or the fact that they were invisible, but she was very glad they had been hidden in the dark. Computers were replaceable and writing had back-up, but rare volumes were different and these ones were unique.

"I put them here because I was afraid they'd fall," she said again.

"I'm going to check the rest of the library, if you don't mind," said Rachel.

"I'll look through these books and see if there's anything in them, then. It will calm me down and get me some work done and I can put them away and ..."

"It'll all be a bit better. I get that," said Rachel. "I'll take my time checking. It'll take a little anyhow. Big library."

"Such a good library," murmured Zelda. "And I'm so angry at whoever's not respecting it."

"So am I," said Rachel. "And at whoever doesn't leave your stuff alone." She moved off and began walking through each and every corner of the library, looking for more evidence of malfeasance. After a long while, she came back.

"I'm almost finished," said Zelda. "Give me two more minutes."

Rachel moved out of earshot and got busy on her phone. Zelda sighed with relief at the efficient way Rachel handled this. And the fact that she stood in the niche across the other side of the room—privacy and efficiency and respect were her hallmarks. And she was going to finish the books with Rachel watching. Not only finish with them for work, but find out if there was anything in them that might be of importance. After all, if anyone wanted to know about her work, all they had to do was ask.

One of the volumes was political. It took Zelda minutes to slip through the pages and realise that the history of the Rump and other English quarrels of the seventeenth and eighteenth centuries weren't going to be of use to her. She couldn't see what interest they would be to a thief, either. They were very dull, and really only useful to certain specialists, of which she was not one.

One attractive feature about original chapbooks from that period was that they were quick reading because the print was big and there wasn't much on the page. Although she wasn't certain that these really were chapbooks. More like leaflets. Not that she knew. Not her area.

One book down. One to go.

The second book took her longer and by the time she emerged from it, Rachel was sitting nearby, silently watching.

"This is odd," Zelda began. "Stupid, but odd."

"Okay," said Rachel.

"It's stories. There are a couple in there that I need for my research, which is why I was so slow. I've taken notes so you can have the volume. Not that you'll need it, but anyhow, it's odd."

"How odd?"

"Just one story. These are cheap books sold by pedlars. For the not-very-learned. Popular stuff. Someone I met years ago put me on to them. Said her favourite was Sir Tom Thumb, Knight of King Arthur, or something."

Zelda realised she'd closed the book and opened it at the right page.

"This is the one that's of interest. Adam's friend Frater has called himself that. He says it's not his real name. And he's copied the actions of a character in a story. Frater Diabolus. Brother Devil? Brother Devil tempts good people into ill-doing. He promises men women and persuades the women to sleep with the men and corrupts them both."

"Why this? Apart from the name."

"Well, Frater is a friend of Adam's and we all had morning tea together yesterday. And guess where I was last night?"

"He chose the wrong woman if he wanted someone who doesn't talk about their sex life." Rachel sounded acerbic but approving.

"I don't see why women have to be so modest. It's social pressure. I had a fun night. That's all. I don't understand the need to frame it as this story. I don't know why he told me 'Frater' was his nickname. Why can't he own up to himself as a liaison between Adam and Adam's objects of lust."

"Would you've slept with him?"

"Dunno. Adam was direct when I saw him. I thought Frater was being more like the young man from Cyrano de Bergerac, and speaking on behalf of someone else. At no stage did I trust him as himself. He's too … wanky."

"We're going to find out if he did this—he's coming here in a few minutes."

"Let's leave the book somewhere he can find."

"Not this one," said Rachel. "The other that looks identical. I'm going to hand it to him when he comes in."

"And this one?"

"Watch me hide it, magically. Somewhere he can't go." Rachel went to the door at the end of the room, opened it, walked through, then almost immediately walked back out. "That'll keep it safe until I can take it to the family. What about the other book?"

"While you were hiding one, I put the other in plain sight. On Frater's desk."

"Good-oh."

"Do you mind if I write up my notes from what I just read while we wait?"

"I can read—heaps of books to choose from. Makes it look natural, too."

And they waited.

And waited.

"Does he come every day?"

"Every day. And he talks to me."

And waited.

"I hate this book," said Rachel, and kept reading.

And waited.

Finally, Frater entered the library softly. He closed the door behind him and started a little when he saw Zelda. He nodded at her and kept walking.

"He didn't see me," Rachel said softly.

"Wait," said Zelda.

Frater reached the place where he'd instructed Zelda to leave the books. He pivoted and came right back, clutching it.

"Where did you get this?"

"The other day. It's a collection of chapbooks, or leaflets. I've finished with it, so I put it back. Is there a problem?"

"Not with that one, no," said Frater.

"That one?"

From behind Frater, Rachel spoke. "We're both dying to know two things. Did you try to break into Zelda's computer? And why do you call yourself 'Frater'? Zelda, help out here, I can't remember the name of the story."

Zelda looked him in the eye as she said, "The story was called 'Frater Diabolus'. It's an odd choice to model a name on in our society."

Frater froze, like an animal in headlights.

"Why?" Rachel asked.

"Because the devilry in his actions depends entirely on a branch of Christian morality that neither I nor Adam aspire to. We talked about it last night. An entertaining evening with a new friend is just that, no more. Not an act of dark against a deity I don't believe in, and not a betrayal of his family."

"That's an interesting comment by Adam," said Rachel. "Mr Frater, did he tell you to go through Melissa's room, or did you do it for yourself?"

"I don't have to tell you anything." Frater's voice was spiteful, but his words and his body language accepted all the claims being thrown at him. "I have family support."

"If family is Adam, you're out of luck. I just rang Uber-Granny, and you don't. Nor does he. I don't care what kind of old spirit you are, or how tricksy you can be, you will be off the property in fifteen minutes."

"My things?"

"Adam can collect them and deliver them to you. Once we've checked them. If any of Melissa's possessions are among them, we will call the police."

Frater was out of the room before Zelda could blink.

"Well, that proves that."

"What?"

Rachel's voice dripped sarcasm and her body quivered with anger. "He played with your desk. He stole something from Melissa. And now he's running scared."

"He's not going to be gone in fifteen minutes. He'll have walked straight to his room to take his belongings."

"I don't think so." Rachel was amused. "Let's see." She stood up and stretched, then led the way to the front door and took a shortcut to the gate. They reached it just ahead of Frater.

"I hate you," he spat on his way out. "You won't be here by next week. I'll come back. To visit. To be friends with the family. As it should be."

He walked out of the driveway and through the gates.

"My eyes must be tired," said Zelda. "He went through the gates. Then he faded."

Rachel looked across at her, considering. "Overwork?"

"Underwork and too much time taken by fools. I'll see if I can make it up today. Is it okay if I get a sarnie from the kitchen now and take it back to the library?"

"You're not the kind who'll damage any books—go for it."

Zelda was in the library until dinnertime. When she joined the others, she had caught up on everything and sat down with a smug smile to the mezze platter. She had already dismissed Frater as irrelevant. After all, he wasn't around anymore. And if Adam was going to have friends like that, well, she didn't need him either. A short but sweet moment in her life, like anyone who simply lacked good sense.

---

After she had finished with Zelda, Rachel had to deal with Melissa's problems.

"Can we do this over a cuppa?" she asked.

"I need one too," Melissa said.

The two took their hot drinks into Rachel's office.

"Let's start with Frater. He was the one who broke into your room."

"He was? But why?"

"For this—we found it in his room once we'd scared him away from the house." Rachel gave Melissa a set of prints. Pictures she had taken. Shadows.

"Well, that changes what I was going to tell you. But how can you be certain he won't come back?"

Rachel looked at her as if she were deciding something important. She gave a brief nod of her head and said, "The whole family knows he's not human. Everyone knows that Adam called a bad spirit in. We won't see either of them again."

"Frater was …"

"Your friend Zelda is a strange one. She's the one who found out who he is. She can research, that woman. He was scared of her too. Then we outed him and got him to go. She saw him fade into nowhere in front of her and she dismissed it. Strange."

"Magic—she can't see magic."

"She can, but doesn't want to."

"Bettina's a bit the same. She sees the portals and comes through them with me, but she hates it."

"That's what you were going to tell me?"

"No. I was going to tell you that the guy at the sea told me to tell him everything and I wanted to check if that was okay. I trust you. And my room being ransacked means I don't trust anyone else."

"It was Frater."

"Dammit. I feel stupid."

"Me too," said Rachel. "I have no idea why he printed these pictures."

"Just those? No others?"

"Yep."

"Interesting. The shadows are really vile just there. They change. That's them being icky but small. They look normal."

"They look as if they're taking over. Gouging out the garden. Diminishing everything. I thought it was your photography."

"Some is. I was aiming for that, which is why I chose that wall—it has the right light and the right shadow. When I went back to take the next series …"

"Can you show me with the printout?"

"They're not here," said Melissa. "Or I took them after. It's all confused right now."

"Double-check."

Melissa did just that. She looked at each and every picture, and mentally recalled when she took them.

"Not here."

"I can see why he wanted them. You got some through a portal, early on." Rachel flicked through them herself. "These pictures are going to make a great exhibition," she commented. "Though probably not the lake bit."

"I hope so. I kinda mucked up my second series. Then the later pictures kinda ruin it."

"Let's see."

Melissa showed Rachel what she'd shown the merman.

Rachel's slenderness reflected all her moods. She shuddered when she reached the pictures of the long shadows; it was all of her that expressed fear. Then her whole body leaned into the camera with fascination as she saw how they shrunk.

"Where did you move to? How did you make them look smaller? And less menacing. That's clever."

"I didn't. I was angrier and more miserable than I've been in ages and I think the shadows ran from me."

"Dammit and dammit and dammit," was Rachel's response.

"Why? Surely it's good they went?"

"Sure. But it means they're not shadows. They're a shadow person."

"Like the sea person and Leafguy?"

"Yes and no. Maybe family. Maybe something like Frater. But not nice."

"Should I stop photographing?"

"No, keep doing it."

"That's good, because you're about to reach today's set."

"Oh! I didn't realise there were more."

"I wanted to tell Seaguy, but I'm a bit shy of him. The shadows are growing again."

"Not good. Look, keep doing what you're doing and keep me or him informed."

"If I run into anything scary?"

"Then run—you're here to take photographs and relax, not to get into danger."

"Danger?"

"I don't think there's danger. I just hate the shadows. But I'm saying ..."

"I get it. And I will walk as quickly as I can away from danger. And get help."

"Good."

"Good."

Melissa didn't feel like facing her friends at lunch again, so she got a sandwich and a drink and found a portal to explore. She'd tried the door earlier, but it had been locked. Today it was ajar.

---

Bettina had been there the day before, tempted by the colour of the door itself, and its texture. It was so very familiar.

She had gone back to her room and found the glass key her mother had left her. Bettina turned it over and over in her hands, looking at the glass from every angle. It was not the same colour as the glass door, but it was the same type of glass. Water from a distant world? She played with the thought as she played with the key. Water turned into glass.

She took the glass key her mother had left her and tried it in the keyhole. What she had seen inside had made her run away, leaving the door unlocked.

---

*This opening a door and finding something strange and wonderful will never grow old,* Melissa thought as she stood next to her newest door. This was one of the glass ones. It felt futuristic and office-like and she couldn't imagine what would be beyond it. That was the lure. The safe and beautiful unimaginable.

It was odd that this door felt exciting and that nice piece of brick wall outside was beginning to scare her. Odd. Like so much else in this amazing house. *I could live here a year and still love it,* Melissa thought. *Except those shadows. I don't love those shadows at all.*

She half opened the door and stopped to smell the air. It was damp, but had a plastic taste on the tongue. Not chemical, but smooth and elastic. This door was going to be very different to the last.

Melissa opened the door fully and walked into another room. One that was long, and wide. Like a big hall. Glass walls and glass ceiling, and through the glass the light rippled peacock colours onto a tiled floor. The tiles would have been black, if the colour of the light had not been so intense. It was overwhelming. Melissa stood on the dark rainbow floor and drank in the colour. She knew she couldn't stay long: this room was too intense.

She walked to the far wall, where there was another door. Her feet were silent on the tiles. She dipped down to touch them and they weren't ceramic or glass or stone. They were faintly warm and slightly soft.

*If I want to see what's behind that door, I might have to hurry.* This place was overwhelming and, now she had felt the floor, it was alien. Like not being on Earth. That was what she had tasted when the door was partly open. It was not the atmosphere she knew.

She put her hand against the wall and … what was flat was also fluid. The wall was made of a soft, glass-like substance. Fluid glass. The colour was not the light that shone through, it was the shade of the water itself. The colour flowed over her hand. It didn't feel the way she expected. It warmed and cosseted her fingers. Her mind kept telling her it was glass. The contradiction in what she thought it was and what it could be shook her mind. She had to find out.

Melissa gently removed her hand from the wet barrier and held her palm upward. In it was a small pool of the water. It was gel-like and very dark. The colours were still those in a peacock's tail, but they were deep and almost black. She brought it to her face and she could smell the suppleness and some sweetness. She closed her palm, and with a *crack* the water shattered. The shards fell to the floor and dissolved into the tiles.

She looked across at the door. She was so close. *This door is not for me. I need to leave.* And she did, gently, softly, inundated with rippling light. She made sure the door was properly closed and heard it lock behind her.

*Tomorrow I'll be braver.*

The next day was a trifle more testing for Melissa. Her body hurt, of course. But it so often did that, which gave her no hints that the rest of the day might not be perfect.

Her troubles began after breakfast. It was another bright day, a day that promised happiness through sunshine. Melissa walked around the house, to her bit of wall, and there were shadows. Each small succulent had a regular shadow. Dark, but the right size for the plant. Reaching away from the wall, they could be made to look dangerous. If they had been the only shadows, this is what Melissa would have done: make them look dangerous.

She snapped her pictures from a new angle. A new distance. She stood left of the bed, in the sunshine, and used her zoom to make it look as if she was standing amongst the dark. From within her screen, the new shadows looked far more dangerous than they did outside the screen. It was as if they knew that she with her camera could scare them and they had woken up with the sunshine and were prepared to eat her.

"This is nonsense," Melissa said aloud. Then she took one step toward the dark. Then another. Then one step into the dark. Then she screamed.

She took a single photograph of them.

Melissa stepped back faster than she ever thought she could. Her mind hurt as much as her body, then it hurt more. One step into the shade was all it had taken. The shadows were eating her soul. She turned off her camera and walked backward until she reached the corner. Round the corner, the shadows weren't visible. She was safe.

Shaken, she went to report to Rachel. On the way, she passed a portal. She opened the door and found another garden. This one had eucalypts and tree ferns and a lyrebird that barked like a dog, and the prettiest stream burbled comfort. She dropped a seashell into that stream.

Rachel wasn't in her office. Melissa left a note and went to get a hot drink. She walked past a hall mirror. She was pale and her eyes were full of shadow.

*Tea,* she thought. *Tea and a biscuit will help.* It wouldn't cure what was wrong. The shadow had left something evil inside her. It wanted to rot her soul and she was not going to let it.

Zelda was making coffee. "Can't stop to talk," she said. Zelda bustled and hurried and was gone in two minutes, without saying any more and without looking Melissa in the face. Maybe the shadow had reached her too? Melissa didn't think so.

This bustle and false bright was something she remembered all too well. It took her back to a moment she'd hidden from herself. To a time she didn't want to remember.

The three girls had been so close that they didn't really have other friends. The only parties they were invited to were the ones that had every class member there. The trio used to puzzle over this and then they'd say, each and every time, "This doesn't matter." For it didn't. They were there for each other. They were there *with* each other.

Early university with its new routines and its higher pressure on the body transformed everything. That was when Melissa's illness changed her everyday life.

Zelda was the one who was not who she had been before. Melissa knew that she would have said, "Melissa is not a good friend." Or, when asked, "Melissa is okay, I guess, but Bettina is my best friend." Zelda's university experience taught her to redefine friends as people who surrounded her, and she pulled Bettina out of a trio that didn't achieve this goal. She pulled Bettina into a friendship that excluded Melissa. Maybe it had done that when they were younger and maybe it hadn't. Melissa had fretted over this for years. She had blamed herself for it too. She was a bad friend. She knew it.

She had known it, but as she waited for the kettle to boil, she wondered. Melissa had crossed a line, Zelda had always said. But maybe it had never been that way. Maybe Zelda had always been all about herself and was the friend who stopped talking because "You never want to do anything with me."

Melissa's two minutes were very long and filled with the darkness from the garden. Zelda had refused to believe that she was not well. That she wasn't doing things with other people and putting them first. Instead, Melissa was experiencing the beginning of the rest of her life, and those times were times when pain was her worst enemy and kept her from doing … anything. Her university life had been very bleak.

The illness was like that shadow. And Zelda had cast her own shadows, exactly like those succulents. Small and could be bad, but never meant to be. She had destroyed a friendship anyhow, without ever admitting it. Zelda didn't remember any of this, of course. Zelda had bustled and refused to look Melissa in the eye ever since those times.

Melissa had to handle this. All of the shadows. She spent her tea and biscuit time wondering how.

---

While Melissa was haunted and Zelda was working furiously and ignoring the world, Bettina was also working furiously and ignoring the world. She would have laughed if told this, but kept on painting. She had found a space just near the tree line and it was visual perfection. She was going to finish this picture today and then she'd have to revisit, for … she didn't let herself think she might be done early, for that would jinx everything. But, if nothing were jinxed, she'd done astonishingly well.

She felt like one of those painters in the Blue Mountains who produced watercolours while tourists were watching, then sold them to the watcher. She wasn't that fast, but she wasn't that far off it, either. This thought was from her tea break, where she walked around for a few minutes, drank from a thermos she had filled with tea at break time, and ached to get back to her painting. It was a good ache, but not a passive ache. In these trees she painted, there might be more pictures too. Different angles leading to different worlds.

Bettina almost purred with satisfaction as she sat down again and let her mind and heart go where they needed. There was a power in her art when she was like this. No one could get in its way.

The women met briefly over lunch. Zelda explained where

she was up to in vast detail and then left to work even more vigorously.

Bettina felt a little left out. “Melissa,” she said. “Can we look at that place you talked about? The door from the other day? The one in the cellar?”

“Sure,” said Melissa. “Or we could try one I’ve never been to and both be surprised.”

“Good idea.”

---

Melissa had never heard a voice sounding less as if it meant what it was saying. She wondered why Bettina wanted to go with her, and if it was just Zelda being Zelda or if she was trying to understand or … *I should stop fretting. I’ll find out in a few minutes. And if Bettina likes what she sees, maybe she’ll stay and look this time and I can get some pictures of the trees. Maybe.*

“You choose the door from the map. I’ve ticked off the ones I’ve been down.”

“This one, then. That dark room with all the black wood panelling should lead to something interesting.”

“It should. Although I’d like … I dunno … a pleasant English garden.”

“I found …” Bettina trailed off, very reluctant to speak. Melissa gave her a moment and she picked up in a new place. “This place is all English garden outside. I want something different.”

“You ache for it.”

“Maybe. I don’t really know what I think. I’m out of my depth.”

“So am I,” said Melissa. “But it’s like a high pain day, you know? Just like chronic illness.” Bettina nodded. “It’s swimming against the tide and the arms are aching and the head is screaming and there is no energy to call on and it’s all in your body so no one can help and you can't … but you have to. Out of one's depth is our everyday, isn't it?"

This silenced Bettina and the silence lasted until they had finished their lunch.

The black-panelled room was a study, off the wood-panelled corridor. Every room of that corridor had wood as a feature, somehow.

"Ebony," said Bettina.

Melissa nodded the nod one gives when one has no idea but it sounds good and one's friend is likely to know.

Bettina walked around the room, looking at the panelling. She felt it. She poked it. She prodded it. Melissa wanted to go straight to the door, but if Bettina wanted to look first—that was her decision.

"Shall I turn on the light?"

"Maybe that's what it is," said Bettina. "If we'd come into this room when we saw the whole house, I'd know where to look, but we didn't. We walked past it."

"Look for what?"

"The door."

"That door?" Melissa pointed. "I thought you were looking for some secret art."

"Just the door. And you can stop joking. There's no door where you're pointing. I just checked there. Not one of these carvings moves and nothing is hollow and … there is no door."

Melissa looked at her friend quietly for a moment, wondering what to do.

Bettina continued, her voice growing grumpier sentence by sentence. "I hate it when you make jokes like this. I really do. I didn't like it when we were eight, and I like it even less now. I'll see you later."

Melissa opened the door that Bettina said wasn't there, went through, and shut the damn door after herself. Bettina could open it again when she'd taken the requisite time to get over her sulk. That was the trouble with old friends. One knew them too well. And tolerated them too much. And this time, Melissa was going to be alone for just a moment.

Ahead of her, everything was beyond black. Melissa walked three ginger steps into it and closed her eyes for a little and when she opened them she could see. It was dark, but the ground had pebbles that glinted a little in the pale light coming from some way ahead. Melissa walked very gently and very slowly, feeling each stop. When she reached the light, she discovered it was the top of a hole. There was a rail around it, so she went right to the hole and looked down.

The light faded into dark, then faded further into something more black than she'd ever seen.

"It's the abyss," a voice murmured next to her. "I'm sorry I couldn't come sooner."

"I'm sorry I jumped. If it wasn't for this rail …"

"I didn't think of that." The merman turned and smiled at her. His scales were silver in the light and she wondered, aloud, if the dark didn't leach colour from everything.

"It's the water at the bottom. It's the heart of this place. The more colour it has the closer it is to the surface is what I always think. I've thought it for two hundred years now."

"I want to make an abyss joke."

"You must have a good reason."

"I thought the peacock room with the coloured walls and those tiles was strange, but this … scares me. I want to make a joke about screaming into the abyss because it'll keep me sane."

Both of them were whispering, although their voices were the only sound in the universe. Melissa's perfume and the merman's scrap of ocean were the only scents. The bar beneath her hands felt tangible, though, and kept her from the abyss.

"If you ever need to, come here and scream. The abyss understands."

"Everything's sentient around here," Melissa half-joked.

"The water is. I don't like the alien water. Earth water with a bit of saline in it and a lot of sea plants and animals is my water."

"Alien water?"

"Not every door leads to Earth."

Melissa was silent for far too long, then admitted, "That's the third time I've gone silent since late morning. I'm having a day of silences."

"I'm sorry. I'm also sorry for what I have to tell you. It's not good. We don't know if there is a way of defeating those shadows. We looked at dawn and they were ... like nothing we've seen. We drove them back, but not as far as you did."

"I saw them this morning and photographed them. Today they scared me."

"Pack your things."

"And go? At once?"

"Not that." His voice smiled a little, although his silver-grey face was still sombre. "Rachel will come and get you and she'll drive both of you to safety."

"What about the others?"

"All they'll see is this house dwindle into something normal. You, I think, are in danger."

"I'll make sure my phone is charged then. I'll be ready."

"I'm sorry." He sounded lost and plaintive.

"Not your fault. Whoever's killing this house—I hate them."

That voice, so full of emotion, became fierce and comforting. "So do I. I'm glad you came here now. I'm glad you chose this door."

"Bettina did. She should've been here by now."

"She chose to unsee magic. I don't know why."

"But she still chose this door."

"That's why your friend was given the fellowship. She has a brilliant gift. We've not seen its like in a long while."

"Then why?"

He shrugged. "I don't know why she doesn't want it, but she's powerful enough to deny it."

"She stopped seeing the doors."

"Yes."

"I just walked through the damn wall."

His voice smiled a little again. "Indeed."

"Can I ask a question?"

"Be my guest." His tone was enticing as the sunlit sea first thing in the morning, the light playing with the waves.

"Where's the best place to go if I can't find Rachel? If the shadows chase me?"

"If the shadows chase you?"

"They started doing that this morning. I wasn't upset the way I was before, and I couldn't scare them. They scared me. It's why I'm accepting everything you say. I'm not normally docile. Well, I think I'm not. Maybe I am."

"The abyss plays with self-perception. She's playing with you now."

"All the water plays?"

"Of course it does. If you have to run and can't leave the house, find the nearest portal. Not the peacock room. Almost any other. You'll be stranded in a strange place when the house is diminished, but you'll be alive. I'll let everyone know I've advised you to do that. We'll come looking for you as soon as we can."

"That's a lot easier than keeping my things packed, you know." Melissa felt acerbic.

"I don't know how long it will take you to get home if you're stranded in the waters. The lands there are not in linear time in quite the same way as our universe."

"They do strange things to people?"

"You have to live a long time there to develop fishlike tendencies." He smiled down at her. She missed Hal. Merman smiles were like his. No wonder she trusted him.

"If I get to a door and throw another shell in more water, will that help you find me?"

"It might. Every so often, throw a shell until the shells run out. The waters will be connected, even if the house is not what they protect."

"Why is the house so important? What does it mean when it is diminished?"

"Now, that I can't tell you. And you'd better go before the abyss calls you."

"And you?"

"Too late." The merman climbed lightly onto the railing, poised for a fraction of a second, then dove beautifully down. Into the abyss.

Melissa shuddered and stepped back, and back, and back, and back. She hit the wall. That was when she turned around and felt for the door handle. She got out as quickly as she could and found Bettina talking to Rachel.

"It was here."

"And here she is," Rachel replied.

"I hate tricks," said Bettina. "I don't want to talk with you."

She left the black-panelled room in a hurry, slamming the door after her.

"I can smell you don't need an explanation," Rachel said with a grin.

"You can smell abyss?"

"Seaguy's been standing near you. You smell of the ocean."

"He said you'd ring me if I had to run."

"We can set up a special tone, if you like."

"One for running and one for finding the nearest portal. He also says my friends will be safe."

Rachel looked sad. "I'd rather keep the magic than be safe."

"What I want right now is a giant magic torch to frighten the shadows away."

"That's where they've been too clever. This place is protected by water."

"Not light. And the shadows chose the driest spot in the garden to enter."

---

While Melissa was dealing with the present, Bettina had thrown herself into her past. She couldn't be Melissa. She didn't want to be Melissa. She didn't want to see special things or open strange doors. Seeing Melissa opening a pretend door and walking through the wall had told her what she already knew: she still wanted to be like Zelda.

"I thought I was past this," she told herself, spending her anger safely in her room where there were no portals and no old friends. The soundtrack in her mind was her personal history. "I was so like Zelda. So accomplished. So able to do things. What happened? How did I fuck everything up?"

It wasn't the art. That was her life raft, and it got her through everything. Her first show had given her dignity when she had left that city job. That city job was nothing but a can of worms that she should never have opened. It was when she developed the mental health issues she hid from everyone except those who had to know, and they were all in medicine and psychology, not in her groups of friends. And she handled it well. So well. Her people said so.

How the fuck had she come to seeing things? How had she returned to envying Zelda? She'd walked out of that second university job once she had enough money. She took her package and said, "I'm not Zelda. I don't need to be Zelda." She'd found a way of handling the fucked-up family and made her own life. An unusual life, but her own.

Bettina was determined that it would not all fall apart. She had to keep in mind that dream. The one that started it all. Not this new magic that had come on her and made her unhappy and then had just … gone. It was a dream. Not the real type of dream that was the epical part of her life, but Melissa's special imaginary time.

Melissa took over realities. She had made up games when they were children and she was making her imagination come alive now. Bettina would return to the real dreams. Like her mother's. The only thing she ever wanted from that mother of hers.

Not Bettina's first dream, but the first time she realised that her dreams meant something. Could do things.

This was when she was in her twenties and had no idea just how complicated it all was and that she'd never get a handle on it. In her thirties, she'd watched every TV series and read every book on magic schools, yearning with a desperate solitude for some sort of training or even for a society where she could talk about this with someone. Understanding it was always beyond her. When she was twenty-three, however, she hadn't thought this. There had been that moment of revelatory horror.

It was Saturday night and Bettina had been beyond exhausted. Summer heat and too many extra shifts. Being an artist was a dreadful dream most years back then. Whatever she could get work at (supermarkets and even factories) kept her going. She hated writers for ten years, because they could get other types of jobs. Then she discovered that other artists could be teachers or public servants, and she hated them too.

Bettina stuck with it and gradually built up everything that had to be built up, but that one summer was almost impossible. That Saturday, the only thing keeping her going when she finally set out for home was the fact that she could sleep in on Sunday.

She was hot and exhausted and should've had a shower when she got home, or eaten a late dinner, but instead she gulped water, took painkillers, and went straight to bed. It took two hours of lying there, tossing and turning and feeling hot and burdened, before the stress seeped out and she was able to sleep. No dreams. Too tired for dreams. That was something, she told herself, in the morning. She lay there, wondering why she was awake when it was barely dawn. She could see light through her blinds, but it wasn't much light. She checked the time. Six o'clock. What was she even doing checking the time? Then she heard it. Neighbours talking and Bettina's open window trapping the sound. Bettina tried to go back to sleep, but whenever she was almost there, the sound of a heartfelt conversation crossed into her bedroom. *If only I could dream no-voice at someone.*

That night she dreamed precisely that. She was in a world of someone else's making. A novel. Walking through someone's invented streets, admiring the infamous magician's house. She knocked on the door.

"What do you want?" The magician was infamously a grump.

"I need my neighbours to both lose their voices until I get enough sleep," Bettina said.

"I will do that to them if you go away. I'm tired of being bothered by people like you." Bettina was impressed at how much her dream reflected the novel. It really was a good dream. And her inner self was awake during it, so she could enjoy it. She walked through the streets and noted all her favourite spots from the story, but was rather glad nothing was actually happening.

The next morning, she woke up to blessed quiet.

Coincidences are the nicest thing sometimes, she thought as she prepared for work.

On her way home that night, she walked through a bundle of other neighbours on the street. They hailed her and asked if she knew how infectious the virus was.

"Virus?"

"Number 54 has laryngitis," said Number 45.

"Not laryngitis," said 34. "No voices."

"I'm next to them and I can speak," offered Bettina. "I hope they're not in any pain."

"Not at all. They just can't talk. They write me notes to get help with things."

"They could've asked me," said Bettina.

"They felt guilty," said Number 45.

"Guilty?"

"You slammed a window on Sunday morning."

"It was 6 am and I'd been working late. All I was trying to do was get some sleep."

"Fair enough. But they didn't want to bother you."

"Fair enough."

What wasn't at all fair enough was the lack of explanation of how she'd done it. It looked simple, but other dreams didn't have straightforward outcomes. This was her danger-dream, the one that kept her from trying to do anything too drastic. Imagine if she'd gone to the other magician in the story-book world. One magician was grumpy. The second magician was cheerful and charming and murderous.

She had made her choice then and she made it again now. She would accept some of her dreams. The rest of her was her art and her adopted family. Zelda would get a phone call from time to time as she always had. Less regularly, but still there. Bettina didn't need to be Zelda and to succeed in the academic world that Zelda loved so much. She would follow her art dream and her other dreams, and all her childhood with its vast abysses of suckitude could be buried. Would be buried.

She needed to talk to Rachel.

---

In the hours it took Bettina to formulate herself and her future, Melissa had, unfortunately, run into Zelda. Zelda did what she always did when life was strained and started to tell Melissa what she should be doing. What sort of person she was.

"You know, Zelda, this was great when we were both young. It gave me something to hang onto."

"What do you mean?"

"You're telling me what I am. It's very informative, but I'm not that person."

"You know I care about you."

"What I don't know is why caring about me means informing me about my personality."

"That Frater—he tricked me."

"This is terrible!"

"I don't like it and I don't like him, but it's not relevant."

"Why did you tell me … Oh, I get it. You want the world to knuckle down and behave. Like when we were kids. Tell us who we are and we're to behave like that."

"Just stop this at once. This is not about me. It's about you."

"Okay, tell me." Melissa was tired of everything at that moment and didn't care about the climax that was going to come or the effects. She just wanted Zelda to be clear and to hit a wall and then she wanted to move on. She wasn't listening out of courtesy. For her, this was a moment of completion. Zelda scolded her and Melissa's inner running commentary kept it from hurting. *It's a pity Zelda can't see this. She's going to lose a friend and she can't see it. Do I care? That's the question.*

Finally, Zelda said, "I cannot live in a world where I am not defined. Stop doing this to me. I need my space to live. You've been brought up badly and have no sense of other people."

"Then it's better if we don't spend too much time together," said Melissa, calm but pale. She was very proud of herself for saying this and not trying to find out what she'd done. Too often. She'd seen it too often. People who saw their own hurt as the only thing in a big world. She wondered how Bettina dealt, then realised that Zelda probably gave her a free pass. Special people were given free passes.

Melissa wanted to throw up at this. Not special. Not important. All Zelda wanted was for her to change who she was in order for Zelda to be the sort of person she was.

She wished Hal were there to talk to. She could ring him, but ... this was something she had to sort through by herself. Because something had changed inside her. Thanks to Hal. Thanks to the magic. She was not the person who would accept a rubbing out. She allowed herself to exit the friendship gracefully.

Melissa ignored Zelda's pontificating and shook her head at herself, partly at the way she'd used to treat herself. Being ill meant she'd given space to everyone. Room because she was hard work. Allowed them to be as big as they liked and shrunk herself to fit. This is how society trained people like her to act. She thought back and realised that Bettina had done much better than she had, but still contained a bit. Zelda's opinions ruled their relationship.

"Are you even listening?" Zelda demanded.

"Sorry," answered Melissa. "I was thinking through everything you said. You don't think I'm as nice a person as I was and I don't think you're as nice a person as you were. We're not destined to be BFFs." Zelda's face was aghast and her mouth agape. *Mouth open, mind blank,* thought Melissa. *If I'm going to go this far, I might as well go the whole distance.* "This reminds me of a film. A scene in a film, rather. People weren't listening to each other. It was a Russian film. I should say things in order. Anyway, the bit I remember had eight bodies littering a forest in winter. Just lying there. And it was because of a situation exactly like this one, except no one walked away. Everyone was determined to get their point of view across to the others. I've decided I can't do that, and I accept that you don't like me anymore, and that we should walk away from each other. Or rather, I should walk away from the two of you before anyone gets more hurt. And that's the longest speech I've made in twenty years."

---

"Eight corpses in a Russian forest," echoed Bettina, who'd entered the kitchen just in time to hear about those bodies in that forest.

"You know the film? Because I forget the name."

"No," Bettina admitted. "I had a dream about it."

"No dreams. No drama. And Melissa, I have lost all respect for you. That was very rude, what you said."

"And in the corpse scenario, I'd remind you that what you said was just as rude and we'd each keep pointing out the wrongs of each other and get louder and angrier and it would be a waste. I might go and rest before dinner. I don't need to finish my coffee."

"You've rested twice today," said Bettina.

"High pain day," said Melissa. "When prescription-strength painkillers at their fullest don't quite do the trick." They didn't need to know the rest of it. They, after all, were safe.

"High pain day," echoed Bettina, her voice amazed. Bettina looked at Melissa's face and realised that something had changed. She'd seen her old friend as the pastel one of the three and their conversations had reinforced this. Melissa was funny, but just not part of serious conversations and was ... pastel. Now she was the swirling peacock glass in that key. Bettina looked at Melissa and saw no story in her face. She saw the key her mother had left her.

"Commonly known as everyday life," Melissa continued, ungently and frank. "Just like yours, I expect. I would rather you didn't hurt, you know. I was so sad when I found out you were also sick. You didn't deserve it. We may not be as close friends as I wanted, but that doesn't mean you deserve any of the foul things." She was fierce in her defence of Bettina's health.

Bettina saw the grace and recognised the gift in the smile. It was as if a shadow overhanging Melissa had been rubbed away. She wished for a friendship that had never been. It was too late. She was too late.

Zelda excused herself from the conversation. Bettina realised that Zelda saw nothing and Melissa saw everything. Wrong friend, and wrong time to make this discovery.

There was something she could do. A gift she could give that would show that she saw the farewell and appreciated its gentleness. Bettina excused herself too. She had something to do.

---

*Just as well I didn't show Bettina anything other than portals,* thought Melissa. *What would Bettina think if she saw me walk through closed doors and then saw me magic up things with my photos and book covers?*

And without any other words, even to herself, she went to her room and lay down. As she rested, she thought that she'd done something very wrong, but that it felt … like a relief. Zelda was going to do something worse than leave her to walk beyond her physical capacity, and she was going to do it with the best intentions, and everyone was going to hurt. This was better.

When the pain had lowered itself to a more tolerable level, she went to find Rachel. "I can't explain why," she said, "but Zelda and I had a falling out. This is probably a good thing, under the circumstances."

"I saw that coming," Rachel said gloomily. "Zelda's a strong blind bitch. I shouldn't've said that. Big Sis is teaching me."

"I'm glad you did. It means I feel less guilty asking you what we can do about everything."

"Dinner with me? And with Big Sis when she gets back? We can complain about tablets like junkies. We can do that every night."

Melissa liked the pretence that everything wasn't going to end in tragedy. It gave life a hint of hope. That's all life needed some days.

"I like the pretty colours," Melissa said in her stupid voice.

"I used to make patterns with them," said Rachel. "Then I made it so's no one saw I was taking them. I hate being talked down at."

"That's ..."

"Yep," said Rachel. "Your ancient school friend doesn't even know I'm one of them. Neither of them do." She stopped for a moment. "Maybe Bettina does, in her strange way. But never Zelda. Which reminds me." Rachel stopped to rummage for something in a desk drawer.

"How can they miss it?" Melissa kept talking.

"Yeah," said Rachel. "That's the thing. You saw it. We saw each other."

"Sub-culture," Melissa said. "We have a sub-culture."

"Secrets ..." Rachel's voice drew out the word and made it captivating. "I gotta do ick paperwork, but come here for dinner. Here—this is yours. Snack bars."

"Thanks," Melissa said as she took the package. "Can I get those boxed lunches you said were possible? I've been kinda improvising with your snack bars till now."

"Cool. What'll you do with them?"

"Take them into the garden and explore. I thought I could just come back to the house, but there are ..."

"Some days? Let's not talk about that."

"There's that thing we won't talk about and ..." Melissa wasn't certain she should mention it and then the words rushed out in a moment of bravado. "Old friends who aren't old friends anymore. And ... I don't need new doors yet. Not right now.

Mostly I don't want Zelda to also see me going in and coming out. I think it's one of the things that made us uncomfortable."

"So, she thinks you're a liar as well?"

"Yep. And she tried to put me in my place the way she always did. Told me who I was. Only I'm not the person she thinks I am."

"Explore then. Stay within sight of the door. Doors don't disappear within a line of sight. Those doors are the safest place here right now, for you."

Melissa looked at Rachel in silence. Unexpected. Scary. And very, very exciting.

"Can I experiment?"

"What with?"

"I've just remembered a thing that was happening at home. I don't have my equipment here, but … there's water behind all the doors and I want to experiment. If I may."

"Can I help?"

"I need paper. And on that paper, I need prints of all the pictures that have shadows. I don't know what this will do. It could make things much worse. Forget it."

"Tell me. Tell me! Did you do any magic with water before you came here?"

"Yes."

"Tell!"

And Melissa told.

"Can I tell Uber-Granny?"

"As long as you ask her if I can do this thing."

"That's why I want to ask. Because. It's new. It fits. And no one knows. And and and …"

"I frightened the shadows. Go ask. And here," Melissa took a back-up out of her handbag, "here's all the pictures. If Uber-Granny says yes, then print them for me?"

"Damn right I will. Pronto."

"I won't tell anyone," said Melissa. "Not even Seaguy."

"No one's going to believe it anyhow."

"They don't have to believe it," said Melissa. "All they have to do is see the end result. It could be pretty watercolours from fantasy lands. It could be wet photographs."

"I have no idea what this is going to do."

"I have an idea. It's only an idea though. Seaguy said that shadows got in through the dry. I think that's the critical clue."

"Shadows? I don't get it."

"Colour versus dark, you know. Wait, let me show you." She whipped out her trusty but small camera and took a picture of the overhang from the wall. She pressed the buttons and showed it back. Dark on the light background. Bold, not threatening. Rather nice, in fact.

"I'm going to take pictures like this all over the house and garden. And then they can be printed with the evil ones. And I'm going to show the house what it looks like."

"How?"

"I don't know if this will work, so I'd rather not say. But if you could ask Uber-Granny?"

"Why don't I just print the damn things and we can start sooner?"

"We?"

"Someone has to keep an eye on this side while you're behind those damn doors."

"You don't like the doors?"

"I love six. Only six. My Big Sis loves ten. She's greedy. The rest can go hang themselves."

"Which door scares you the most? The one in the black room?"

"Oh, yes." Rachel's voice became very soft. "I never go there."

"Can you do me two copies of each picture? I always do two of everything. Damn, you won't have enough paper."

"We keep stores of it. Living in the country means we keep stores of everything. Two in two piles?"

"Please?"

"Only, I'll ask Uber-Granny. Just to be safe."

"How long will that take?"

"This is urgent. Wait." She pressed autodial on her phone and said into it, "Big, big problems here. Scary. You should come. Also, the photo fellow has an idea. You want me to explain it … Okay then, I'll tell her." Rachel hung up her phone and announced, "Anything. She says you can do anything. She says the house trusts you."

"The house trusts me." Melissa was bewildered.

"Go figure."

---

Zelda was uncomfortable with what she'd said to Melissa. That discomfort sent her wandering the house, thinking. She didn't want to see anyone. She just wanted to wander.

She passed the office and heard the printer. Maybe she could ask Rachel for a printout of her work so far, and she could take the copy to the garden when she needed a break from the library. Editing on paper was always better.

The printer was spewing out pictures. Slowly. A lot of them. There would be no printout for her here. Still, Zelda was curious. She flicked through and then put them back, feeling somewhat dirty. These were Melissa's pictures. And Melissa was no fill-in for someone else. She was a photographer.

Zelda wanted to go into compensation mode. Normally, this is what she'd do. But … if Melissa could take photographs like this, maybe she wasn't exaggerating about her health. Maybe her life had been … *I'm not going there. Melissa imagines so many things. She always has. I've done the right thing.*

The most she decided was to keep her head down, as she had promised, and finish her work. *Then I'll pick my daughter up and go home and all this sordid time will be past. No more uncertainty.*

If it wasn't for the library, she'd go at once. She still had to work through the library and finish her book. If she dumped the social stuff, she could work long hours and she could finish everything. Without having to look at those pictures and think about that night and that moon. And without this nagging feeling that, somehow, she had taken a wrong turn. Because she hadn't. Zelda knew her work and knew how much effort it took and she was proud of her choices and of her life. Simple.

On that thought, she went back to the library.

On her desk was a note from Frater. "I'm finished. Can't do any more. Leaving the work to stronger souls than I am. The library's yours."

She wrote a little note to go with it and left both on Rachel's desk when she finished writing for the day, much later. She went to bed and slept the sleep of one who has accomplished much good work.

---

That night, Bettina had one of her dreams.

It was a memory-dream. It felt real. So very real. She was lucid throughout so she knew she was asleep and could even feel the bed. This disturbed her, even during the dream. It disturbed her even more when she woke up the next morning, still feeling the bed around her and knowing that the dream was in her. Like all her other lucid dreams, it would never go away.

In the dream, a cat was run over and Bettina and Zelda saw it on the road. It was Bettina's cat. The end of their small universe was seeing it there, laid out like splatter. They buried it. Bettina and Zelda were children and they did the burial thing properly. Bettina remembered this with agony.

That night, in the dream, her cat jumped into her room using the window, as it always did, and climbed down to the bed without so much as a by-your-leave. This was what her cat always did. But her cat was dead. The window was open. The full moon shone down. And the cat on the bed looked perfectly alive and imperiously demanded attention.

Bettina looked at the cat, the cat looked at her. Bettina wanted to shut herself in her room and cry but there was her cat, very much alive. It was too much. Even for waking Bettina it was too much.

Batchette was standing on her pillow looking down on her. That kitten had the same soft blackness of her childhood cat. And they had indeed buried a cat when they were children, except that it had turned out to be a stray that looked like Bettina's cat. The full moon and the cat on the bed—these were inventions. They were more real than reality. Cruel inventions. One of the cruel inventions jumped to the floor and sauntered out of the room as if she had made a point.

Bettina didn't want to be in this strange house anymore, having nightmares from her childhood. She wanted to go home.

It was morning. Rachel would be in her office soon. She would see what could be done.

---

Melissa took her shadow pictures and escaped from the garden as quickly as possible. Those shadows were deep and drear and engorged the earth.

She spent the rest of the morning walking softly to banish pain. While she walked, she thought about those papers waiting for her. Rachel had left them outside her door that morning and she couldn't wait to try something, but first she had to walk and to think. There had to be a link between those book covers from home and the way the shadows had cringed from her that one time. Rachel had left her a prepared lunch with the papers, and she took that outside and would have sat in the sun, but there were no safe places outside the house.

Melissa finally ended up picnicking in her own room, looking at one of the two piles of pictures. She was tired and clumsy and doing too many things. *I shouldn't do this,* she scolded herself as she looked at her hand. The water had splashed her hand first and then dripped onto the first of the pictures. A wet hand and a wet picture. It could've been worse.

Then Melissa looked at the picture more closely. The ink had run. Had Rachel used an inkjet? Even then, something was wrong. Or rather, something was right.

That black abyss was still full of water. She knew it. Her merman had dived into it. It was black water because black was all colours, just as the alien water had been peacock and the seawater had been different colours in different lights. That was the protection this house had. All the colours. All the water. The shadows were using the dry outside to eat the land. But shadows were full of colour, too.

"If I have one magic ability," Melissa said to herself, "it's to do with liquid mixed with colour. I don't know how the results happen, but I know something in me makes them happen. Also, I can talk to the water. And the water is supposed to protect this house."

She played with her water bottle and pictures for a little, and watched the patterns and saw what she could do. Her hand dripped water over the picture and then she used her fingers and drew rough shapes. She could change the picture. Instead of being full of shadows, the pictures were full of flowers, like Monet. So like Monet. The strongest colours were water colours.

It was tiring. It was beyond tiring. Melissa sat on her bed and thought. *Just a few minutes lying down and I'll take the water and the pictures outside and I'll fight that damn shadow directly.*

---

While Melissa thought, Bettina had reached endgame.

She went to see Rachel.

"Did you give my present to Melissa?"

"Not yet. Too busy. Want it back?" Rachel looked even more tired than before.

"You may want it yourself. I don't know. I don't really care. It was my mother's. I travelled to Eden to collect it and she never said why."

"Ask her?"

"She left it to me in her will." There was an uncomfortable silence. "Anyhow, it's a key to a door here. In this house. I've not been fair to her as a friend and I wanted to make it up and I thought …"

"Do you know why your mother had a key for this house?"

"I know. Well, I half-know. She did some strange things. She had a friend. Mum used to say the friend was water and the key reminded her of that friend. I was freaked out by that side of Mum. I tried to forget. Every time I dreamed and my dreams were real, I hated Mum more. Now I just want to go home. I want to put those dreams behind me. Move on."

"You don't want magic in your life," Rachel said softly.

"I never wanted magic," said Bettina. "I know what shape my life is without the magic, and it's enough for me. I could reach it, if I tried, but seeing it here … I knew I didn't want to try."

"The key? Why Melissa?"

"I had a dream of something my mother did. Melissa thought it was a movie. She's linked into stuff. I just want none of it."

"You want your life back."

"This fellowship wasn't given to me because of my art. It was given to me because I'm the person the committee wanted to recruit."

"Without your art, you'd never have got it," said Rachel.

"Seriously. But yes, Big Sis said that all of you had other qualities and she was staying out of it."

"All of us?"

"They wanted Zelda for her learning, but she doesn't share, does she?"

"She builds a fortress around herself. I'm very lucky to be inside that fortress. She's special."

"But she doesn't share."

"Not with most people."

"The interview panel shoulda got that. They didn't want what we needed."

"And Melissa is magic?"

"If I tell you this, promise you won't tell anyone else? Promise?" Rachel so looked distressed that Bettina agreed at once.

"Why are you willing to tell me?" This was what she needed to know.

"You want to give her the key. You see it too."

"She nearly didn't get a fellowship. They only found her at the last minute, and Adam avoided her."

"Oh, big time. He avoided her because of her husband."

"Her husband?"

"Melissa thinks he's moving his mother into a nursing home. Instead, he's moving her somewhere you don't want to know."

"What?"

"He's family. He wanted to bring her months ago, but I don't know why. Then she applied for the fellowship. No one knows how she got the form. They're targeted."

"I sent her one."

"You're always going to be magic, you know." Rachel said this with nonchalance, and sat on the corner of her desk.

"I'll keep it small, then. I'm fine with happy coincidences. I never want to open one of those doors again."

"That's why you don't want to know where Hal's moving his mum."

"But Melissa went to the nursing home. She told us about it."

"Sure. And Auntie will 'die' soon. And Melissa is supposed to go to the funeral and everything. Now she'll probably come here and say hi."

"I didn't want to know that."

"The other side of the doors are different. I don't go to most of them. I don't want to change."

"Melissa does. I mean, she likes the doors."

"She married family before she even knew the family existed."

"Okay, that makes sense."

"Of course, it makes sense. Only, what do you want to do? Give the key to Melissa and …?"

"I want my own life, not my mother's."

"Fair enough," said Rachel. "The fellowship?"

"I'm stuck with it. Zelda needs my car," Bettina explained. "I don't want it. I'll never know how much was me and how much was my mother."

"I'll take care of that. You take the train and go home."

"I thought the station was moribund."

"Tourist train once a week. Today's Thursday, so it's this arvo. I'll get you on it, if you want."

"I want," Bettina said fervently. "I can't carry everything."

"I can take care of that, too. Paintings and equipment to your place in a week. Sound good?"

"I'll pack now," said Bettina. "Excuse me."

And she left. Just like that. The very moment she caught the tourist train from Robertson, a car was on the road, carrying her stuff. Leafguy was the driver, making sure the paintings were out of the house before anything else happened. That was Rachel's response to the shadows. Making sure that one person and one person's possessions were entirely safe. What she'd said to Melissa about Bettina and Zelda was not true at all for Bettina. Even without the key, Bettina was special.

"She'll find out elsewhere," Rachel reported to Uber-Granny. "She needs time. Maybe she needs to be dragged out of her cocoon too. Should I give the key to Melissa?"

Cockatoo Run was the special train. It left Robertson for Sydney at 3.24 pm and it took Bettina to Sydney just in time for dinner and in time to catch the sleeper-train to Melbourne. She took her most important paintings with her, and nearly regretted it when she was dining on magnificent junk food at Central. She was begged at three times and her paintings were almost stolen twice. Bettina felt very odd in a sleeper, but the train thump-thumped her to sleep and it was fine. Her last thought before she slept was, "I never did let Sheila know what happened." She dreamed about toasties at a truck stop.

---

That few minutes turned into hours. Melissa woke up to Rachel's knock on the door.

"I saved dinner for you," Rachel said apologetically.

"Were the shadows bad? How are the others?"

"Zelda's fine. Doesn't see a thing. Quick meal, then back to work. Bettina's gone."

"Gone?"

"Took the train back. Finished her work."

"I'm glad. I didn't like to think of her outside." Melissa unmuddled her brain a bit more with each answer. She was still standing in the doorway, the door half open. *Only half awake,* she noted about herself.

"Me neither."

"I didn't know there were trains."

"Not many. Tourist trains. Today and Sunday."

"That's why she left without saying anything." Melissa felt relieved. She had been worried for Bettina.

"That's right. No time. She told me she wanted to go and

packed and went."

"You didn't want to encourage her to stay." Melissa was proud of her perceptiveness.

"I wish neither of you were here."

"Don't stand there—I'm not really hungry and I have something to show you."

Rachel came into the room and saw the mess Melissa had made.

"I dripped water on the pictures. Look at them."

"Impressionist. Flower gardens."

"This is one of the sets of pictures you printed."

Rachel's face was everything Melissa hoped it would be. Her voice was sharp. "When did you do this?"

"This morning."

"Damn. It didn't get rid of the shadows. I thought …"

"It shows us stuff." Melissa made her voice show her determination and resolve.

"But?"

"No 'but'—this is the beginning."

"We're out of time. I talked to Uber-Granny. I was going to feed you dinner and drive you and Zelda to Wollongong. You can catch trains from there in the morning."

"It's that bad?"

No wonder Rachel looked as if a light breeze would send her toppling. While Melissa had been asleep, Rachel had been fighting shadows. And talking to Uber-Granny.

*I still can't get a mental image of Uber-Granny. Maybe I don't want to have one?*

"It's horrible. Uber-Granny will be in the house itself tomorrow, but it will be too late."

"Then how do we get to your car?"

"It's in the garage. We're going to drive through those damn shadows with the headlights on and the stereo blasting."

"Zelda will think we're mad."

"Already does."

"Also, she won't want to go till she's finished. That's who she is."

"Got any better ideas?" Rachel sounded fully sarcastic. This lightened Melissa's burden a little. The end was not yet here if Rachel could be sarcastic.

"Can we try something first?"

"Can't talk to anyone else. Leafguy chased Adam away and Seaguy has gone. Dunno where."

"I know where. He dove into the abyss."

"And he hasn't brought back help. That's bad. Very bad." Rachel sat down on the edge of the bed. Her whole body looked damaged.

"If you can keep Zelda busy—talk to her in the library—I can try something. If it doesn't work, I'll come get you and Zelda and we'll all run away. Instantly."

"Scream at us 'The house is on fire'—that'll do it."

"More effectively than the truth. Isn't that tragic?"

"I'll be in the library with her ignorant majesty, then. And the car keys."

"I don't want this to be happening," Melissa said softly.

"Solve it for us, then."

"You don't have magic?"

"I see magic. Others dream it into being. That's all we thought anyone could do who wasn't family. Go, do something with these pictures." Rachel held out the water-stained garden she was holding.

"Not that set. The other set you did me."

"You knew you needed two?"

"I'm so good at mucking things up on bad days that I get two of everything in case."

"Good. Go!" Then, almost instantly, "No! Wait! This is yours. From Bettina. With her apologies or something." Rachel thrust the key at her and Melissa looked at it, puzzled.

"What do I do with this?"

"How do I know?"

Melissa shrugged her shoulders and put it in her handbag. She could worry about it later. She added her near-empty water bottle, put her bag on her shoulder, then put the stack of pictures in her other arm.

Rachel moved to open the door for her, but Melissa beat her to it. That was the thing about hurting. One got used to doing things cleverly.

Melissa needed water. She had so very many choices. Her best bet, she thought, was that gentle misting waterfall. The trouble was, she couldn't remember which door she'd gone through for it. A cellar door, perhaps?

She walked slowly downstairs, the pile of paper reminding her every step how much of a burden it was. Downstairs, then on and on and on through the cellar. This couldn't be right. But the house shifted. She had to reach the door to find out.

She finally reached the door and it looked familiar. *This would've been a lot easier if I had marked up my map,* she thought, and not relied on memory. Still, it looked familiar. Melissa opened the door.

When she opened it, there was a tunnel. Nothing green. But still, maybe the tunnel was the same tunnel she'd been in before. It was a long walk back across the cellar and the stairs would hurt more going up. *Best check.*

Melissa took her time. It was easier on this side of the door, but the atmosphere was very tunnel-like. A little damp. A little dank. It was conducive to pain and not at all conducive to confidence. She nearly gave up three separate times, but her slow, determined plod kept pushing her through the tunnel even when she wanted to turn back. Eventually, she saw a light at the end. She didn't speed up. She kept walking and kept walking, and finally, she reached a waterfall.

This waterfall was too heavy to use. It was more like a

vertical stream than a waterfall. Very beautiful, but what would it do to paper? She needed the door that she'd mistaken this one for. Or … maybe she hadn't mistaken this one. Maybe the tunnel and the vertical stream was the house defending itself against her. That was a worry. A big worry. Melissa turned back. She had to talk to Rachel again.

She'd only walked three paces when she heard a gurgling "Help!" from the stream. Melissa turned around and there, being driven back from the tunnel by the sheer force of the water, was Frater.

"Give me your hand," he cried. "Pull me out of here."

Melissa gave a sigh of relief. This was the door she'd looked for. Only she wasn't the first one there. She said, "I don't think this is as dry as you intended."

"I got here. It'll be dry soon enough. Just get me out." His words were shaped as if it were a normal conversation, but every one of them was gasped or yelped or shouted as the running water pushed at Frater.

Melissa had no such impediment.

She looked through the water at Frater and assessed him. "I don't think you and I get on. This isn't where I want to be anyhow. I'll just leave you."

"I can't get out."

"Ring Adam. I'm sure he'll help."

As she went back up the stairs, she texted Rachel to let her know that Frater was not only where he shouldn't be, but was stuck.

A text came back soon saying, "We're on it. How are you going?"

"Don't know yet. Too much water here. Need somewhere without Frater. I was thinking the sea and the green light."

"Don't go to the sea. No one to protect you when Seaguy is busy. Try somewhere else."

"Let me know when the sea guy's free." Melissa understood

why she had no name for the man with the scales: he hadn't given her one. Rachel was different—why did Rachel keep calling him "Seaguy"? One day there would be answers. Today there were only questions and attempts to save this house.

"Can't. Everything happening. The garden. All scary."

Melissa thought of the shadows that day when they had threatened to overwhelm her and she winced. "Damn. I'll try something else then. Thanks."

It took some time, but eventually Melissa's near-blue eyes echoed in the faded sky beyond another door. This was a new one. The water was not on show here. Or the shadows had made it run. Or it was all fighting Frater. Either way, she'd look for it.

She liked this space. Melissa felt that pale eyes in a dark skin made her look ill, but she could recognise her own faint hazel tinge in the sky and felt as if she were coming home in her own way. She turned to Hal to make a joke about the sky having recessive genes, but Hal wasn't there. She missed him with a fierce ache. Until that moment she could have sworn that she was not fierce in any way.

There was no water in this place. If she didn't do something, the house would be dead soon. She patted a rock protectively and left, determined to find the next door and the next until she had a solution. As she opened the door to go back into the house, Melissa realised, *Solution. That's what I'm missing. I know what to do. I so know what to do.*

---

Zelda wasn't sure her writing this last hour would stick. She'd spent too long walking around the house and wasn't in tune with her research yet. Still, it was interesting. She'd hang onto it in case it was related to something.

That happened all the time with her. She would write something and it would become her next paper or her next project. Clever little backbrain. She found herself thinking that she had no idea what her clever little backbrain was doing as she read this draft. It was notes, thankfully. She'd leave the notes and when it fitted somewhere then she'd turn it into writing.

Water was one of the Celtic aspects of the world she was interested in, but she wasn't arguing anything solid here; she was just dreaming. She dreamed of Bernard de Cluny, who linked tides and fortuna. He was no use to her, being unCeltic, but the idea of fortuna and tides were close to her thoughts on the full moon, so she made a note for that other project. The idea that women were linked to tides and the moon and to magic was a whole chapter in her work already. It was odd writing this in the middle of the dry Australian countryside. Although there was a waterfall nearby.

In honour of that waterfall, she wrote notes.

> * Water is both predictable and inconstant. Tides, waves, submersion, life-giving—secret place is (in its way) surrounded by water. Take this location. Robertson and the mountains are the real surrounds—only the apparent. This house is within that. Life within the house makes the house change. At the same time, it protects and gives life. Effectively Celtic. But is change a part of the Celtic world view or am I taking this idea from somewhere else? Need evidence.
>
> * Water contains emotions: anger, peace—i.e. it's not a neutral confinement. Dealing with each emotion leads to self-governance. Governing oneself gives power. Sea change again, in its different aspects. Note: had reference for this. Find it!
>
> * Some modern Celticist narratives are question narratives. Protagonists start off exploring, but cannot be given secrets until they're experienced and the experience is not only

discouraged, but almost illegal. Good little girls do not deserve fruit.

That was where her notes stopped. Her research had turned up a link to Isidore of Seville on the primordial abyss as the place where navigation fails and she wanted to find evidence that this near-sentient depth with all the water was linked to the Celtic world. She had notes of sources, but those sources were not here. That chapter would have to be finished back at the university. Her title for it was "Head and heart and the world waters".

This was for a section on numinous places. Water was one, but there were others and it didn't matter how many times Zelda read her notes, she couldn't make them fit. There was not enough evidence.

*I'll get back to that one. No, I'll chuck it in my "sorry, you're gone" file.*

---

Bettina was asleep on the train. She frowned at herself in her dream. She didn't like this one. She was picking her way through the corpses in a Russian forest. She tried to wake herself up, but that didn't work. She could feel the crackle of old leaf underneath and smell the trees that surrounded her. There was no scent of rotting meat.

She tried to walk past the corpses and leave the glade behind, but this didn't work either. When she reached a point, her body took itself back to the beginning of the dream and she started again.

Bettina felt a slight warmth on her bare arm. Sunshine. Gradually the forest warmed.

When the sunshine had reached all the bodies, they also

started warming up. Then they moved. Bettina wanted to scream, but it was her dream and she couldn't.

One of the corpses looked her in the eye.

Awake now, and thoroughly rattled, she wondered if she could ever escape that damn dream. She very much wanted to. That first body's eyes had been the sun-warmed brown of Melissa's. Maybe she'd made a big mistake. Maybe she hadn't given up the magic from her life to Melissa. Maybe she'd given up the key to understanding it. Literally.

---

Melissa checked outside quickly. She wanted to know what had terrified Rachel so. She saw shadows upon shadows. Angry shadows. Hungry shadows. Shadows eating the light and drinking the moisture. The air was dense and dreadful.

*Alien room first. And damn the pain, I'm going to hurry.*

This time she found the right door. It was locked. A part of her said, "This room cares about you—it's okay that you can't get in." Another part knew that the shadows would probably leave that crystalline water until last.

"A key, a key, my kingdom ..." Her voice addressed the keyhole as if a command would open it. Then she remembered that Bettina had given her a key. A bloody glass key, too. Bettina did stuff, then denied she was special. Melissa decided it was time to give up trying to understand Bettina. But she'd try that key.

She slipped the glass into the lock and it turned gently. The door unlocked as if it was douce and gentle.

Melissa went straight into the room, thinking, *What happens if this is the room I get stuck in?* She drank her last bit of water and dipped the bottle into the alien goo. Then she got straight out, locking the door behind her.

Her next stop was the closest portal to this. She couldn't get samples from everywhere. She couldn't go to that sea safely, for instance. All she could do was choose colours the way she did for her work. One colour, then another, then combine them in the tray, carefully and gently. Then apply to paper in the tray. Carefully and gently. Result: mottled and dappled and patterned paper.

Except she was mixing everything in a bottle because that was the only thing she had to hold liquid in because she was making this up as she went. And the pictures were going to be diluted, not created from scratch. And she had no idea if this would work. Except for all that, she was working the way she'd have worked at home.

Thinking got her past the pain and to the next portal. She found a stream that had dried to a trickle and she added water from it to her bottle. Each time she found a portal on the way to her ultimate destination she added a bit of wet stuff. Any kind of wet stuff. There was less and less of it as she made her pilgrimage. Finally, she gave up and went straight for the other room with the glass door. The dark room. The room with the abyss. Melissa scared herself into walking through the room to the handrail.

She stood by the abyss, then piled her pictures on the floor. She picked up a picture of shadows, dribbled some of her shook-up mixture on it, waited until the picture started to change, then flung it into the depths.

*I have no idea if this is working,* she realised, but kept creating magic art and sending it to the depths. It was all she could do.

The pile of papers took time to work through and Melissa felt tired. So tired. She understood Rachel's concern for her, but Melissa kept going.

The door thumped shut behind her. Melissa turned to see who had entered the room.

"What the fuck are you doing?" shouted Adam.

"Banishing shadows," Melissa said calmly.

"They are my shadows and this is my house. You're ruining everything." His metro nature had changed from elegant soiree to ugly traffic jam. His voice was a thousand horns, blaring. He strode toward Melissa, leaning and ready.

"Don't push me in," she said, voice still steady.

"Do you think I care a fuck about you? I will push and it will kill you!"

As his right arm reached out to shove her into the abyss, it was grabbed and held.

"Don't," said the merman to Adam. "Keep on doing what you're doing, Melissa," he said to her, "for it's working. The waters are rising again. We're fighting back."

The cousins fought silently. Melissa saw it out of the corner of her eye. And she felt it as she was nudged and kicked and hit because she was too close to the fighting. Twice she saved the pile of papers from being kicked down the hole, three times she saved herself, and once she saved her drink bottle.

Still, she created. One page at a time.

The two men fought. And struggled. And acted as only close kin can when beyond love. Melissa had to move toward the wall. It was too dangerous where she was. She hoped she'd done enough. It would be safer by the wall.

The men still struggled in silence. Melissa noticed so many things. That the merman moved like Hal. That she had left the water bottle on the pile of papers and had forgotten to put the lid on. That Adam's face was ugly when he was furious. That if she paid attention to trivia, she wouldn't notice how sick this fight was making her.

The fight ended abruptly when Adam tripped over the pile of papers. He tumbled into the abyss, papers and water falling with him. They fluttered down together in a strange jumble.

"Get me out," she heard Adam cry.

"He's family. He won't die down there," the merman said by her ear.

"Where have you been? We were looking for you."

"Fighting the damn shadows," he said. He said it in a normal voice. Until now he had merely murmured. "Nothing worked. Magic didn't work and water didn't work and then my grandmother called me to her room." This voice was more than familiar. The words were more important right now. She needed to know.

"If Adam's suffering, that's okay. If he's dying, that's not okay. Did we kill him?"

"He's not even suffering badly. He's probably being disciplined by Grandmother."

"Uber-Granny is the water."

"And the abyss is her home and her grandson has just tried to kill her. Everything he gets down there, he deserves."

"I hate this," Melissa said confidentially, "but I hate the shadows more."

"Let's go then." He took her arm and supported her as if she was aching all over (which she was) and led her out to the lawn and there they both stood, staring. And the man next to her was not in a strange world and she knew precisely who he was and wondered how she ever could have missed this.

Melissa didn't want to ask how Hal had got there. "Last time I looked, it was all angry shadow."

"It was."

"Now it's a placid shallow pool."

"The water treatment you gave worked."

"Nothing worked at all until a few minutes ago," Rachel said, joining them.

"We won."

"Not us." Rachel shook her head determinedly. "This happened with rainbows and colours and …"

"What kind of colours? Like the alien place?"

"Very much."

"I used some of the water from the alien place and some water from other places and I did my thing with the pictures."

"When?"

"I started doing it a little while ago. Then Adam came in."

"I meant how did you combine them?"

"I threw them down the abyss. You could see the colours mixing as they went down. Clouds of them."

"I might ask if we could get those pictures back for you," said the merman who was her husband. Adam probably hadn't wanted her to have a fellowship at all, given that Melissa was family. "We might have to keep them with the books."

Rachel looked from one to the other. "You two just met. This week."

"We two," confided Hal, "are married."

"I knew you were married to family, Melissa!" Rachel defended herself. "I thought it was a cousin."

Hal laughed. "You would've found out in a few months, when Mum gets here."

"I have a note in my handbag that precisely fits this moment," declared Melissa, feeling suddenly exuberant. "It's for you, Hal. And for me. Let me quote me at you and you at me. To round off our adventure."

Hal was puzzled, but not without enthusiasm. Rachel was merely puzzled.

"I got lost. I found my way back because you were my guiding light. I need to take up this offer to consolidate, and to do the world's best photo exhibition, and dedicate it to you. And it has to include a joke for every year of our marriage, for we are the funniest couple in the universe."

"And?" Hal's voice rumbled his emotion.

"We need to invite Rachel. D'you know she's walked in other worlds and never ever seen a photograph exhibition?"

The three of them stood staring at the puddle that was once lawn until Rachel said, "I'm making coffee. Who wants one?"

# ACKNOWLEDGMENTS

So many people helped with this book. Most did so quite privately, so I can't share their names. I was given stories of personal lives affected by chronic illness and I built Melissa's life from those stories. I tried to be true to my sources. I hope I succeeded. Most people who gave me stories of their lives thanked me for writing the novel, so I am very worried about whether I wrote it well enough. The stories I was given added to so much more than I could tell from my own knowledge. For some people, chronic illness is pain and occasional battles; for others, it is frequent pain and continuing battles; and for others, it is every minute of every day.

Thank you for your stories.

I emerged from writing this novel with a tremendous respect for all people who handle ongoing physical problems. I have some myself, but I didn't realise the magnitude of everyday life and the problems it spawns until I wrote this.

Thank you to my Patreon supporters for making this happen. I didn't have the income to write and they said, "We'll get you through summer. We need to read this novel." Well, here it is, thanks to Odyssey and especially to Michelle Lovi.

Thank you to Grahame Cheers and Jane Virgo for taking me to Moss Vale and Robertson, and to Lesley and Griff Rose for showing me part of the route. Special thanks to Conor Bendle for helping me find the right sort of books for Melissa's art.

Mindy Klasky published the precursor to this novel in *Nevertheless, She Persisted,* and without her, my friends at Book View Café and in the Treehouse, and without the support of Jean Weber, both the short story and the novel would have been a lot more difficult to write.

# ABOUT THE AUTHOR

Gillian Polack writes fiction that others have trouble defining. Most (but not all) of them are set in Australia. Most (but not all) of them are contemporary fantasy, although some are science fiction and quite a few use her background as an historian to mess with readers' minds. She believes her PhDs should be useful and shares her Medieval and her food history background with other writers, but only plays with readers' minds by putting this part of her life into her fiction when she feels like it. Gillian admits to a sad addiction to books of many kinds and also to cooking. Some of her photographs have been published, but they are mainly taken to fuel her writing and research.

You can find Gillian online in places such as Patreon and Twitter, as well as on a number of websites including the History Girls blog.

gillianpolack.com

www.ingramcontent.com/pod-product-compliance
Ingram Content Group UK Ltd.
Pitfield, Milton Keynes, MK11 3LW, UK
UKHW041842190726
13854UKWH00002B/683